THE PAINTED MAN

Recent Titles by Graham Masterton available from Severn House

The Sissy Sawyer Series

TOUCHY AND FEELY
THE PAINTED MAN

The Jim Rook Series

ROOK
THE TERROR
TOOTH AND CLAW
SNOWMAN
SWIMMER
DARKROOM

Anthologies

FACES OF FEAR
FEELINGS OF FEAR
FORTNIGHT OF FEAR
FLIGHTS OF FEAR

Novels

CHAOS THEORY
DESCENDANT
DOORKEEPERS
EDGEWISE
GENIUS
HIDDEN WORLD
HOLY TERROR
MANITOU BLOOD
UNSPEAKABLE

THE PAINTED MAN

Graham Masterton

This first world edition published in Great Britain 2008 by
SEVERN HOUSE PUBLISHERS LTD of
9–15 High Street, Sutton, Surrey SM1 1DF.
This first world edition published in the USA 2008 by
SEVERN HOUSE PUBLISHERS INC of
595 Madison Avenue, New York, N.Y. 10022.

British Library Cataloguing in Publication Data

Masterton, Graham
The painted man
1. Fortune-tellers - Fiction 2. Police artists - Fiction
3. Murder - Ohio - Cincinnati - Fiction 4. Horror tales
I. Title
823.9'14[F]

ISBN-13: 978-0-7278-6596-0 (cased)
ISBN-13: 978-1-84751-047-1 (trade paper)

All Severn House titles are printed on acid-free paper.

Typeset by Palimpsest Book Production Ltd.,
Grangemouth, Stirlingshire, Scotland.
Printed and bound in Great Britain by
MPG Books Ltd., Bodmin, Cornwall.

For Wiescka,
with all my love, always,
and for Edwin Buckhalter,
with thanks.

The Miracle of the Rose

The miracle happened early on Tuesday afternoon. It was the tiniest of miracles, and it appeared to be a happy one. But it was only the first of many more miracles – miracles that grew darker and more frightening by the day, like statues that turn their heads around and baths that fill up with blood and dead people seen walking through the streets.

Three Warnings

It was the second week in May. Molly was painting a scarlet rose with a yellow ladybug crawling up its stem. Sissy came into her studio and stood watching her for a few minutes. Molly was sitting next to the open window, so that a warm breeze blew in from the yard, and the sunshine fell across the gardening book that she was using for reference.

An oval mirror stood on the opposite side of her desk, and Molly's painting was reflected in it, as well as her hand, busily washing in the petals with a fine sable brush. She wore silver rings on every finger, including her thumb; and her fingernails were polished in metallic blue.

She was also wearing a spectacular antique necklace, more like a charm bracelet than a necklace, hung with bells and mascots and stars set with semi-precious stones. It flashed and sparkled and jingled as she painted.

'How about some more wine?' asked Sissy.

'Just half a glass. I always zizz off if I drink too much.'

Sissy came back with a frosty glass of Zinfandel, and set it down on the windowsill. 'That's beautiful,' she said, nodding at the rose.

Molly tinkled her brush in a jelly jar full of cloudy water. '"Mr Lincoln", they call it. It has a wonderful smell. I just wish I had a green thumb, and I could grow some in the yard. But everything I try to grow dies of some kind of horrible blight, or gets eaten by caterpillars.'

'Being a gardener, you know, it's like being a nurse,' Sissy told her. 'Your plants are your patients – they need constant fussing over if you want to keep them happy. Me – I always sing to my flowers.'

'You *sing* to them?'

'Why not? My climbing roses love *Stairway to Heaven*. Trouble is, I'm always gasping for breath by the time I get to the last verse.'

'You shouldn't smoke so much.'

Mr Boots, Sissy's black Labrador, came trotting into the study with his pink tongue lolling out of the side of his mouth.

'Hey, Mr, I suppose you're pining for a walk,' said Sissy, ruffling his ears. 'Well, it's too hot right now, but let's go sit outside in the shade.'

Molly said, 'I'll come join you, soon as I've finished this. My deadline's next Friday. *Fairy Fifi in Flowerland,* this one's called. You should read the text. Or rather you shouldn't, unless you have a strong desire to barf. "*Fairy Fifi skipped and danced, all around the roses. She had bellses on her fingerses . . . and bellses on her toeses.*"'

'Saints preserve us!'

From the day that Trevor had first brought Molly home to meet Sissy, they had become the most comfortable of friends. There might have been thirty years between them, but they were both spectacularly untidy, and they both dressed like gypsies, and they both liked wine and fortune-telling and jingly-jangly 1960s hippie music. '*Hey, Mr Tambourine Man!*' they would sing in chorus, arm in arm.

Such was the warmth that had developed between them that they could sit for hours together saying nothing at all, but occasionally smiling at each other, as if they shared a secret which they would never disclose to anybody else, not even Trevor.

Ever since he was in grade school Trevor had complained to Sissy that she looked and behaved like a fortune-teller from a traveling carnival, with her wild gray hair and her dangling earrings and her black flowery-printed dresses; but Molly was a free spirit, too, and Sissy believed that Trevor adored her all the more because she was just as unconventional as his mother.

Molly reminded Sissy of a young Mia Farrow, from *Rosemary's Baby* days, with hair like little brown flames and a heart-shaped face and enormous brown eyes, and a coltish, apple-breasted, skinny-legged figure that always made Sissy think to herself that *she* used to look like that once – but that was when The Platters had just released *Only You* and her father used to collect her from high school in his new powder-blue Fairlane.

Sissy went outside, into the small backyard, with its red brick paving and its terracotta plant pots. The sky was hazy but cloudless, and the humidity was well over eighty percent. She sat in the shadow of the vine trellis at the far end of the yard, in front of a small green cast-iron table, and took out her Marlboro cigarettes and her DeVane cards. Mr Boots flopped down at her feet, and panted.

Through the open window, she could see Molly's reflection in the oval mirror, and she waved with her cigarette hand. Smoke drifted up through the vines.

Sissy began to lay out the DeVane cards. They were huge, much larger than tarot cards, worn at the edges but still brightly-colored. They had been printed in France in the eighteenth century, and even though they were called The Cards of Love they were also crowded with mysterious signs and veiled innuendoes, and omens of impending bad luck.

The DeVane cards might well predict that a young girl was going to meet a tall, handsome stranger and plan to get married before the end of the year, but they might also predict that her wedding car would overturn on the way to the church and that she would be seriously disfigured by third-degree burns.

This afternoon, Sissy wanted to ask the cards if it was time for her to return to Connecticut. After all, she had been staying in Cincinnati for almost seven weeks now, and she was beginning to suspect that Trevor was growing more than a little irked by her being here so long.

She laid out the cards in the traditional Cross-of-Lorraine pattern. Then she laid the Predictor card, which represented herself, across the center. Her card was *La Sibylle des Salons*, the Parlor Fortune-Teller, depicted as an old woman in a red cloak and gold-rimmed spectacles. Sissy had been able to tell fortunes since she was eleven years old, and she could interpret everything from tea leaves to crystal balls. She had never asked herself *how* she could do it. To her, seeing how tomorrow morning was going to pan out seemed as natural as remembering what had happened yesterday afternoon.

The first card that came up was *Les Amis de la Table*, which showed four people sitting at a dinner table laden with roasted pheasants and joints of beef and whole salmon decorated with piped mayonnaise and slices of cucumber. Every place at the table was set with seven pieces of cutlery, and this was a clear indication that Sissy would be welcome for at least another week.

The pretty young woman at the head of the table was holding up a pomegranate and laughing, and the young man sitting next to her was laughing, too. Pomegranates were a symbol of purity and love, because they were the only fruit incorruptible by worms, but they were also a symbol of blood, because of the color of their juice.

Although the young woman and the young man appeared to be so carefree, there was an older woman sitting close beside them, and the older woman's expression was deeply troubled. She had her left hand pressed to her bosom, and she was frowning at the fourth dinner guest as if he frightened her. However, it was impossible to see his face, because he was wearing a gray hooded cloak, like a monk's habit, which concealed everything except the tip of his nose.

On the table in front of him there was a shiny metal dish-cover, and his face was reflected in that, but the reflection was so distorted that Sissy was unable to make out what he looked like.

So here were four companions eating their evening meal – but one of them was a mystery guest, and his presence was clearly disturbing one of the others. There was another strange element in the picture, too: a red rose was hanging upside down from the candelabrum just above the center of the table.

Sissy turned up the next card. *La Blanchisseuse*, the Laundress. It showed a young woman in a mob cap lifting a white dress or a nightshirt out of a wooden tub. The young woman's eyes were closed. Either she was very tired, or she was daydreaming, or else she didn't want to look at the horror of what she was doing, because the wooden tub was filled to the brim with blood, and the nightshirt was soaked in blood, too.

A small side window in the laundry was open, very high up, and a man was looking in. Presumably he was standing on a ladder. He had staring eyes and a ruddy face, almost as red as the blood in the wooden tub. All around the window frame, red roses were growing.

Sissy stared at the card for a long time. Mr Boots realized that she was unsettled, because he lifted his head and made that mewling sound in the back of his throat.

'What do you make of this, Mr Boots?' Sissy asked him, showing him the card. 'It looks to me like somebody's going to get badly hurt, and somebody else is going to try to wash away the evidence.'

Mr Boots barked, just once. Sissy slowly put down the laundry card and picked up the next one. This was even stranger, *Le Sculpteur* – showing a young sculptor in his studio. The sculptor was slim, with long hair, and strangely androgynous, so that he could have been a girl in boy's clothing.

He was chiseling the naked figure of a man out of a block of white marble. The figure was holding up both hands, as if it were surrendering, or appealing for understanding, and both of its hands were bright red, as if they been dipped in blood.

All around the studio ceiling, there were stone carvings of roses.

'Somebody is going to get badly hurt, and then somebody is going to wash away the evidence. But it looks to me as if a third person is going to create an image that shows who really did it. Now – who do we know who can do *that*, Mr Boots?'

Sissy picked up the cards and was about to take them inside to show Molly when she saw something bright and red and blurry out of the corner of her eye. She turned, and there it was, in one of the terracotta pots. A tall scarlet rose, its petals almost tulip-shaped.

She approached it very slowly, took off her spectacles and peered at it. She hadn't seen it on her way out. In fact, she was absolutely sure that she had never seen it before, ever.

She sniffed it, but it had no fragrance at all.

'Molly!' she called, too softly the first time for Molly to hear her. Then, '*Molly!*'

'I'm in the kitchen,' Molly called back. 'I'm just getting myself some clean paint water.'

'Forget the darn paint water. Come out here.'

Molly appeared on the back porch. 'What is it? I really have to finish this illustration.'

'I thought you couldn't grow roses,' said Sissy.

'I can't. I told you, I'm the Angel of Death when it comes to gardening. Even my fat hen curls up and dies.'

'So what's this?'

Molly came barefoot into the yard. She stared at the rose in disbelief. Then she laughed and said, 'Oh, you're nuts! You stuck it in there yourself, just to fool me!'

Sissy shook her head. 'Look at it, Molly. It's the exact same rose you've just been drawing. Right down to the yellow ladybug.'

Molly took hold of the rose by the stem and gently tugged it. 'You're right,' she said, and her wide eyes widened even more. 'It's rooted. And it *is* exactly the same. *Exactly*. Look – this is *insane*! – it even has brush marks on the petals.'

'It's not possible,' said Sissy. She sniffed the rose again. 'But it must be possible. It doesn't smell. I can *see* it, and I can *feel* it.'

'We should show somebody else,' Molly suggested. 'Maybe there was something in the salad.'

'Something in the salad like what?'

'I don't know. Jimson weed or something. Maybe we're, like, hallucinating.'

'How could jimson weed have gotten into your salad? I watched you make it. It was nothing but rocket and scallions and sliced beets and hard-cooked eggs.'

'But how can this rose possibly be real? I didn't grow it, I *painted* it!'

'Maybe it's a miracle,' said Sissy.

'You don't really believe that, do you?'

'If it's not a miracle, what else could it be? Maybe it's a sign from God.'

'Why would God send us a sign like this? I mean, even if He did, what's He trying to tell us? We don't have to grow roses from cuttings? All we have to do is paint them?'

Sissy said, 'Maybe it's more than a miracle. Maybe it's a warning.' She held up the DeVane cards. 'I was just reading my immediate future. Look at this – four people sitting at a table, but one of them looks as if he's some kind of threat to the other three. Then there's this – a washerwoman rinsing blood out of somebody's clothing. And this – a sculptor carving the likeness of a living man, but the man has blood on his hands.'

'I don't understand. What does it mean?'

'I think it's something that's going to happen to us – or something that we're going to find ourselves involved in. Somebody's going to get hurt, maybe killed even.'

'Not one of us?'

'I surely hope not. But this sculptor – I think he might represent you. Whoever's responsible for this wounding or this killing, the police are going to ask *you* to sketch his likeness.'

Molly shook her head. 'Come on, Sissy – I haven't been asked to do any police sketches for *months*. February, I think, was the last one, when that teacher got raped at Summit Country Day School. The CIS prefer computers these days.'

'It's here in the cards, Molly. The cards don't have any reason to lie to me.'

'Well, maybe you should read my tea leaves, too, just to make sure. The cards may not be lying but they could have made a mistake, couldn't they?'

'Molly – there are *roses* in all of these cards, and *they* mean something, too, although I don't know what. And what do we have here, blooming right in front of us?'

Molly looked confused and unhappy. 'Look,' she said, 'I don't know what to think of this. I'd best get back inside and finish my painting. Why don't you try the cards again? Could be they'll tell you something totally different this time. Something less – you know, *brrrrr*!'

Sissy shrugged. 'OK, I can have a go. But I promise you, they'll come out the same, or the same message told with different cards. They always do, like the night follows the day.'

Molly reached out toward the Mr Lincoln rose, and for a moment Sissy thought that she was going to pick it, but then she hesitated and drew her hand back, as if picking it would somehow make it more real. 'Might as well leave it,' she said. 'Probably the only rose I'll ever manage to grow.'

She gave Sissy a quick, unconvincing smile and went back into the house. Sissy turned back toward the vine trellis.

'Come on, Mr, let's see if we can make the future look a little more rosy. Or a little *less* rosy, I should say.'

She had just hitched up her dress to sit down when Molly appeared at the back door again. '*Sissy?*' Her voice was as colorless as cold water.

'What is it, Molly?'

'Come see for yourself.'

Sissy followed her into her study. On her desk lay the gardening book, still open at the photograph of the Mr Lincoln rose. The oval mirror was still there, too, and so was Molly's box of watercolors. But the sheet of cartridge paper on which she had been painting was completely blank.

Sissy turned toward the window. Outside, in the bright unfocused sunshine, the scarlet rose nodded and nodded, and the yellow ladybug slowly crawled up its stem.

She turned back to Molly. 'Paint something else,' she told her. 'Another rose. A bird, maybe. Anything.'

The Red Elevator

Jimmy jabbed the elevator button yet again, and said, 'What the hell are they doing up there? My slider's going cold.'

'Some doofus has probably jammed the doors open,' said

Newton. 'They're always doing that when they're moving their furniture from floor to floor. Tough shit if anybody else wants to get back to their office.'

Jimmy pressed his finger on the button and kept it there, but the elevator's indicator remained stuck at fifteen. Six or seven other office workers had gathered around the elevator now, carrying box-lunches and Styrofoam cups of coffee, as well as a delivery boy from Skyline with a persistent sniff and a large bag that smelled strongly of cinnamon chili.

'This is goddamned intolerable,' grumbled a shirtsleeved accountant who was trying to balance three La Rosa's pizzas and three cups of soup on top of his briefcase. 'Any volunteers to run upstairs and check out what's wrong?'

Jimmy pressed his hand against his chest and wheezed. 'Sorry, dude. It's my asthma. Fifteen floors, that'd kill me. Newton, how about you, man? I'll hold your cheeseburger for you.'

Three more office workers arrived, all of them carrying take-out lunches.

'Goddamned elevator's jammed again,' explained the shirt-sleeved accountant, as if it wasn't obvious.

There were three elevators in the Giley Building in downtown Cincinnati, but most of the time only one of them was working, and even when it did, its doors shuddered so violently whenever they were closing that Jimmy was always worried that they would refuse to open again, and he would be trapped inside.

The Giley Building had been built in less than eleven months during the Depression, by hundreds of hands eager for the work. It had been scheduled for demolition more than three years ago, but local conservationists had fought to preserve its brown-brick Italianate façade, as well as its gloomy brown marble lobby, with murals of Cincinnati's history, like the arrival of the first riverboat, and the building of the first suspension bridge over the Ohio River, and the opening of the Procter & Gamble soap factory.

Today, the building was less than two-thirds occupied, and many of the floors were deserted, with echoing corridors and tipped-over chairs and noticeboards that were still covered with yellowing sales charts.

Newton said, 'Oh, *man*,' but handed Jimmy his White Castle burger box all the same. He crossed over to the staircase, and he had already opened the door when there was a *bing*! and the elevator's indicator light went from fifteen to fourteen and then to twelve.

'Hallelujah!' said the shirtsleeved accountant, and the rest of the office workers gave a cynical cheer.

Newton came back and reclaimed his cheeseburger. 'I'm going to change my job, man. I'm going to work in a building with elevators that actually go up and down, and the fricking air conditioning actually conditions the fricking air, and half of the offices ain't populated by ghosts.'

Newton thought that he had heard people walking around the empty floors late in the evening, and echoing voices, and telephones ringing that nobody answered.

'You're crazy, dude,' Jimmy told him. 'You know there's no such thing as ghosts.'

'Oh, yeah? And where do you think that dead people go when they die?'

'They don't go nowhere. When you die it's like someone switches the lights off, that's all, and doesn't never switch them back on again. And even if dead people *did* go somewhere, they sure as hell wouldn't go to the office.'

'I know I darn well wouldn't,' put in the shirtsleeved accountant. 'When I die, I'm going to Vegas.'

The elevator's indicator continued to *bing*! its way from twelve to eleven and ten and nine, and eventually it reached the lobby. The office workers crowded around it, waiting for the doors to shudder open.

At last, they did, *chug-chug-chug*, and everybody took a step forward. But as they did so, a figure inside the elevator toppled to the floor, and they immediately took a step back.

'Jesus,' said Jimmy.

'Oh my good God!' said a woman, right behind him.

A young woman was crouched face down in the middle of the elevator floor, where she had just fallen, and underneath her a middle-aged man was lying on his side, with his back to them. The young woman was dressed in a cream-colored pants suit and the middle-aged man was wearing a pale blue sport coat, but both of them were covered in blood. The elevator was plastered in blood, too, all the way up to the ceiling. There were sprays and runs and dozens of bloody handprints all over the mirrors.

Most horrific of all, a large kitchen knife was still sticking out of the young woman's right shoulder.

Without any hesitation, the shirtsleeved accountant tossed his cups of soup and his pizzas and his briefcase on to the lobby floor. 'Call nine-one-one!' he shouted. He stepped into the elevator and placed two fingertips against the young woman's neck. 'She's still alive! Help me!'

Jimmy pushed his box-lunch into Newton's hands and stepped into the elevator, too. The floor was so slippery with blood that he skidded and almost lost his balance.

'What do you want me to do, dude?' he asked the shirtsleeved accountant.

'Let's lift her out of here – gently. Lie her on her side on the floor. Has anybody called nine-one-one? We need coats, blankets – something to keep her warm. And we need to find out where she's been stabbed – keep some pressure on any arterial wounds.'

Jimmy said, 'Shouldn't we take out the knife?'

'No – leave it there. The paramedics can do that. A lot of stab victims die like that, taking the knife out.'

Between them, he and Jimmy dragged the young woman out of the elevator and laid her on the floor. A matronly secretary knelt down beside her and unbuttoned her coat and her blouse, trying to locate her wounds.

The shirtsleeved accountant went back into the elevator and checked the pulse of the middle-aged man.

'How about him?' asked Jimmy, but the shirtsleeved accountant looked up and shook his head.

'Looks like he was stabbed straight in the heart. Couple of times in the lungs, too.'

'Unbelievable,' said Newton. 'Fricking unbelievable.'

The matronly secretary said, 'This young lady's been lucky, I think. I can only find cuts on her hands and her arms. She must have been fighting for her life.'

Jimmy hunkered down beside her. The young woman's hazel-colored eyes were open, although she appeared to be staring at nothing at all. She was in her mid-twenties, with light brown hair that was cut in a long bob, but which was now stuck together with drying blood. There were bloody fingerprints all over her forehead and her right cheek.

'Are you OK?' Jimmy asked her. The young woman didn't answer, but she was still breathing, and he could see her lips move slightly.

'You're going to be fine,' Jimmy told her. 'I promise you, you're going to be fine.'

They heard sirens outside as paramedics and police arrived, and the lobby was filled by the kaleidoscopic reflections of red and blue lights.

Jimmy stood up. The shirtsleeved accountant came up to him and laid a hand on his shoulder. 'You did good, son. Thanks.'

'Hey, I didn't do nothing. You a first-aider?'

'Ex-Marine. Served in Iraq. You get plenty of practice out there, I can tell you, patching up people with various kinds of holes in them.'

'Shit!' said Newton. 'Whoever did this, he's still in the building, right? He didn't come down the stairs, did he? So there's no way he could have gotten out.'

'Not unless he jumped from the fifteenth floor,' said the shirt-sleeved accountant, grimly.

The Garden of the Inexplicable

It was evening by the time Detective Kunzel rang the door chimes, and most of the garden was in shadow. But Sissy and Molly were still sitting under the vine trellis, drinking wine and looking at the terracotta pots with a mixture of awe and disbelief, but with delight, too, because what had happened was so magical.

During the afternoon, Molly had painted five more roses, of varying colors, from buttery yellow to darkest crimson. She had also painted a purple hollyhock and a sunflower and a ragged white Shasta daisy. And here they were, nodding in the breeze, as real as if she had grown them from cuttings and seeds.

'How do you think it happens?' asked Molly. 'Do you think it's some kind of *mirage*? You know, like an optical illusion, except that you can touch it, too?'

Sissy blew out smoke. 'If you ask me, sweetheart, it's more important to find out *why* it happens, rather than *how*. Nothing like this ever happens for no reason. Never did in *my* lengthy experience, anyhow.'

They had witnessed the miracle as it happened, right in front of their eyes. After Molly had painted a rose, they had stood back and seen it gradually fade from her sketchbook, as if the paper had been bleached by the sunlight. At the same time, they had looked out of the window and seen the same rose materialize in one of the pots – only the ghost of a rose to begin with, a faint red blur, but then more and more solid, until it was real enough to be picked, and its thorns actually pricked their fingers, and drew blood.

They had watched it happen with every flower, and a Japanese beetle, too. Molly had been reluctant to paint a bird, though, in case it wasn't anatomically correct, and it couldn't fly.

Sissy had dealt out the DeVane cards yet again, and asked them to explain the miracle in more detail. This time, however, the cards were unusually obscure, and difficult to interpret. When they behaved like this, Sissy always complained that they were *muttering*.

The last card was *Le Sourd-Muet*, the Deaf Mute. It showed a young woman wearing nothing but a garland of pink roses around her hips. She had one finger raised to her lips, and one hand cupped to her right ear, as if she were straining to hear. She was standing close to a dark lake, on which three mute swans were swimming. On the far side of the lake, there was a grove of trees, in which a naked man was hiding. His skin was very white, as if he were made of marble, but both of his hands were scarlet.

'What on God's earth does *this* mean?' Molly had asked her.

'I don't know. Maybe it means that we shouldn't ask too many questions. Not yet awhile, anyhow. Swans are a symbol of patience, but they're a symbol of tragic death, too. And – look – there's that figure again – like that statue in the sculptor's studio. And *more* roses. This is all very odd.'

'I thought the cards were supposed to *explain* things, not make them even more confusing than they are already.'

'Not always,' said Sissy. 'Now and then they simply tell you that they can't tell you anything. That usually means that you have six or seven possible futures waiting for you, and the cards can't decide which one of those futures is actually going to happen.'

'But I thought my life was all mapped out, every second, right from the moment I was born? You know, like *karma*.'

'Oh, *no*, not at all! You always have choices! But there are certain critical moments in your life when your entire future can be altered by a single random event – like whether you overslept and missed that bus, or whether it was raining and your shopping bag broke and some really attractive stranger helped you to pick up your shopping. Look at the way you met Trevor, at the Chidlaw Gallery. He was only going there to give them a quote on their insurance.'

Molly nodded, and smiled. 'The first time I talked to him, I thought, What a good-looking guy – but what a stuffed shirt. But then he looked at my painting and said, "That's amazing . . . that really comes alive." And he didn't even know it was mine.'

'Exactly,' said Sissy. 'At moments like that, the cards seem to be waiting for one more piece of the jigsaw to fall into place before they're ready to tell you what's going to happen to you next.'

She finished her glass of wine, and said, 'The DeVane cards are not just for fortune-telling, though. They're like a key to all of the inexplicable things that happen in life. Why are we born? What are we here for? That red-haired woman I saw in Fountain Square last week – why was she crying? Why did Frank die so young and leave me widowed for so long?'

'How come I can paint roses and they appear for real in my garden?'

Sissy picked up her glass but it was empty. 'Ha! I wish I could tell you. But maybe you could paint us another bottle of Zinfandel.'

The door chimes rang. 'You're not expecting anybody, are you?' asked Sissy.

'It's probably Sheila, bringing my cake ring back. I don't know why she doesn't keep it. I'm worse than you when it comes to baking.'

'My dear – *nobody* is worse than me when it comes to baking. Whenever I used to bake, I got answering smoke signals from the Comanche.'

Molly went inside. Sissy took out another cigarette but Mr Boots tilted his head on one side in disapproval, and so she tucked it back into the pack.

'You don't have the spirit of Frank hiding inside of you, do you?' she asked him. She leaned forward so that her nose was only an inch away from his, and said, 'If you're in there, Frank, I promise to cut down. I'll even try the nicotine gum.'

Molly came back out into the yard, accompanied by two men. One of them was broad-shouldered and bulky, with brush-cut salt-and-pepper hair, and eyes as deep-set as currants in Pillsbury's dough. He wore a tan-colored suit that was far too tight for him under the arms, and a green shirt that looked as if it was buttoned up wrong, and his belly bulged over his belt.

Behind him came a thin, snappy-looking individual with deliberately mussed-up hair and the face of a handsome rodent. He wore a black designer shirt and he had a pair of D&G sunglasses hooked into his breast pocket.

Molly led the two men down to the arbor. 'Sissy . . . this is Detective Mike Kunzel and this is Detective – what did you say your name was?'

'Bellman, Freddie Bellman.'

'You caught me talking to my late husband,' said Sissy. 'You must think I'm going doolally.'

Detective Kunzel looked down at Mr Boots and said, 'Not at all, ma'am. I used to have the worst-tempered Labrador bitch you ever met, and I was one hundred percent sure that she was possessed by the spirit of my late mother-in-law, may she rest in peace.'

Molly said, 'How have you been, Mike? How's Betty? Still singing for the Footlighters?'

'Betty's great, thanks for asking. They just gave her the part of Milly in *Seven Brides for Seven Brothers*. I've had *Goin' Courtin'* stuck on my brain for weeks.'

'Jesus – you and me both,' said Detective Bellman, but then gave a quick, sly grin to show that he meant no offense.

'So what can I do for you, Mike?' asked Molly. 'How about some refreshment? Limeade? Cranberry juice? Ale-8-One?'

'If I wasn't on duty, Crayola, I could do righteous justice to an ice-cold Hud. But I'm good, thanks. I came to ask you if you could come over to the University Hospital and do your forensic artist stuff.'

Molly looked across at Sissy and the expression on her face said, *My God, your Sculptor card predicted this, only hours ago*. But she turned back to Detective Kunzel and said, 'Thought you were all computerized these days.'

'Well, pretty much. But Lieutenant Booker thought you were the right person for this particular job, on account of your interview technique. We have a young woman in the Trauma Center who was attacked in the Giley Building round about lunchtime today. Some knife-wielding crazy trapped her in an elevator and stabbed her three times in the back. She survived, but there was another guy in the elevator with her who wasn't so lucky.

'She's very shocked, very distressed, but the elevators in the Giley Building don't have CCTV and obviously we need a composite of the perpetrator as quick as we can get it. That's why Lieutenant Booker wanted somebody with real sensitivity when it comes to asking questions, and there isn't nobody with more real sensitivity than you.'

'Nice of you to say so. I'd be glad to do it. Do you want me to go over there right now?'

'Give you a ride if you like. I can give you all the grisly details on the way.'

Sissy said, 'Did anybody else see the killer?'

'No, ma'am. The young woman who was stabbed was the only eyewitness. We searched that building top to bottom, all twenty-three floors, and we're still not sure how the perpetrator managed to escape. But over seven hundred and seventy-five people still work there, and so it couldn't have been too difficult for him to mingle with the crowds.'

'Or *her*,' Sissy corrected him.

'Well, sure. But this is not the type of attack that I would normally associate with a female perpetrator.'

'Not unless the young woman and the dead man were having an affair, and she was a jealous wife.'

'You sure have some imagination, ma'am,' said Detective Kunzel. 'But right now I think we'd better stick to the empirical facts.'

'Sometimes the facts can be very deceptive,' Sissy countered him. 'It's *insight*, that's what you need.'

'My mother-in-law tells fortunes,' Molly explained. 'She's very good . . . she can practically tell you what you're going to choose for dessert tomorrow.'

Detective Kunzel tried to look impressed. 'Wow. We could use a talent like that. Maybe I can call on you, ma'am, if this cases reaches any kind of an impasse. Or if I need to find out a sure-fire winner for the Kentucky Derby.'

'You're being sarcastic, Detective. But don't worry, I'm used to it. My late husband was a detective in the Connecticut State Police, and he was a skeptic, too, when it came to fortune-telling. But I would be more than happy to help if you want me to. So long as you say "please."'

'Please?'

Sissy was quite aware that 'please?' was the distinctively

Cincinnati way of saying 'pardon?' or 'excuse me?' but she pretended that she didn't. 'There,' she said, 'you've managed to choke it out already.'

At that moment, Trevor came out into the yard, holding Victoria by the hand. Sissy's first and only granddaughter was nine years old now, very skinny, with huge brown eyes like her mother, and long dark hair that was braided into plaits. She wore a pink sleeveless top, and white shorts, and sparkly pink trainers.

Trevor was so much like his late father, with a wave of black hair and clear blue eyes, although his face was rounder and not so sharply-chiseled as Frank's had been, and he hadn't inherited Frank's quick and infectious grin. He had shown no inclination to join the police force, either, like his father. He was much more introspective, and cautious, and he believed in calculating risks, rather than taking them. He was wearing a blue checkered Timberland shirt and sharply-pressed khakis.

'Hey, Mike!' he said. 'What are you doing here, feller?'

Detective Kunzel clapped him on the shoulder. 'Hi, Trevor. Sorry about this, but we've come to borrow your talented young wife for an hour or two.'

'What is it? Missing person?'

'Homicide. We had a stabbing this afternoon, down at the Giley Building. One dead, one serious.'

'I heard about it while I was going to bring Victoria home from her party. Jeez.'

Sissy said, 'Why don't I take Victoria inside and give her a drink? How was your dance class, Victoria?'

'I was *terrible*. I kept do-si-doing round the wrong way.'

Sissy took her hand and led her into the kitchen. 'I used to dance like that, too. Always do-si-doing round the wrong way. In fact, I think I've spent my whole life do-si-doing round the wrong way.'

Victoria sat down at the large pine table and Sissy poured her a glass of strawberry milk. 'You want cookies?'

'I'm not really allowed, not before supper.'

'Well, your mom has to do some work for the police this evening so I think what I'll do is, I'll take us all *out* for supper, and when you go out for supper you're allowed cookies to keep your strength up while you're waiting for your order to arrive. How would you like to go to the Blue Ash Chili and have one of those great big chicken sandwiches with all the cheese on it?'

Victoria's eyes widened. 'Can we *really*?'

'Sure we can. It's about time we ate something unhealthy around here.'

Sissy was about to go to her room to fetch her wrap when Victoria said, 'Grandma – you just dropped one of your cards.'

She looked down. One of the DeVane cards had slipped out of the pack – but somehow it had fallen edgewise and it was standing upright in the crack between two of the wide pine planks that made up the tabletop.

'Well, that's pretty neat, isn't it? I'll bet I couldn't do that again, not in a million years!'

She hesitated for a moment, but then she plucked the card out of the crack and peered at it through her spectacles.

Une Jeune Fille Tombante, A Young Girl, Falling. It showed a girl in a yellow dress falling down a well. Her arms were upraised as if somebody had just released their hold on her, and her expression was one of absolute terror. Up above her, a man in a strange lopsided beret was grinning down at her as she fell, and throwing roses after her, as if her falling were some kind of dramatic performance.

Below her, half-submerged in the darkest depths of the well, a black creature was looking up at her expectantly, its teeth bared and its claws ready to snatch at her dress.

Sissy frowned at the card for a while and then she tucked it firmly back into the middle of the deck. *You're just a card. Don't try to get smart with me.*

'Grandma?' asked Victoria.

'What is it, sweetheart?'

'What's the matter, Grandma? That wasn't a horrible card, was it?'

'No, of course not. It was a very *nice* card, as a matter of fact. It was a little girl, jumping into some water. Hey – maybe it means that Mommy and Daddy will take you on vacation.'

But Sissy suspected that the card was yet another warning, especially since it had been brought to her attention in such an extraordinary way. How could a card fall edgewise like that, and stick in the table? It was a warning that something bloody and violent was very close at hand, and that it was going to arrive amongst them sooner rather than later. The girl, falling down the well. The black creature, waiting to tear her to pieces.

'Daddy promised he would to take us to Disney World,' said Victoria, with a mouthful of Toll House cookie.

'That would be wonderful, wouldn't it?' smiled Sissy. She rested her hand on top of Victoria's head. *Une Jeune Fille Tombante.*

The world at the bottom of the well was another world altogether, in which creatures could breathe but humans would drown. The cards were telling her that whatever was coming, it was coming from someplace different and strange – a place of reflections, and shadows, where everything was back to front, and voices argued very late at night, in empty rooms.

Molly came in from the yard, followed by Detectives Kunzel and Bellman, and Trevor.

'I'll see you later, Sissy,' she said. She picked up a green crochet shrug from the back of one of the kitchen chairs, and pulled it on. 'I don't know how long I'm going to be – maybe two to three hours, depending. You'll take care of these two for me, won't you?'

'Oh, yes,' Sissy assured her. 'I'll take care of them good. I'll feed them and I'll read them a story and I'll make sure that they wash their teeth before I tuck them into bed.'

'Ha!' laughed Detective Kunzel.

'*Momma*,' Trevor protested. 'For Christ's sake, already.'

Red Mask

They had moved Jane Becker into a private room next to the Trauma Surgery Unit. As Molly made her way along the corridor, one of the fluorescent lights was flickering, which made her feel as if she were walking through one of those Japanese horror movies like *The Ring*.

A uniformed cop was sitting on a chair outside her door, reading *Cosmopolitan*. 'All they had,' he explained, as Molly gave him a smile.

'I'll bring you a *Penthouse*, next time I come,' she told him.

The room was painted a neutral magnolia, with a large framed poster of 'Blue Grass Country' hanging on the wall. The venetian blinds had been closed but Molly could see the glittering lights of Bethesda Avenue through the slats.

A young woman with chestnut hair was propped up in bed. Although she was very pale, she had one of those faces that Molly called 'sweetly pretty.' Her pert little nose had a sprinkling of freckles across it, like cinnamon. Her eyes were mint-green and her lips were bow-shaped and very pink. But her left cheek was swollen with an angry red bruise, and she had butterfly stitches on her left eyebrow. Both of her hands were swathed in white muslin bandages and Molly could see that underneath her pink flowery hospital gown, thick padded dressings had been applied to her shoulder blades.

As Molly came in, a large black nurse was checking Jane's saline drip.

'You the artist lady?' asked the nurse.

'That's me.'

'Here,' said the nurse, and maneuvered an armchair to the side of the young woman's bed. 'But make sure you don't go tiring her out none. Her blood pressure's way too low, which means she's still in shock.'

'I'll be fine, honest,' the young woman assured her, in a high, off-key whisper.

'Oh, yeah? In my experience it's the ones who insist they're going to be fine is the ones who keel over the quickest.'

Molly propped her leather-bound sketchbook against the side of her chair and hung her satchel of pencils and pastels over the back of it.

'Molly – Molly Sawyer,' she smiled. 'I can't shake your hand, but hi.'

'Hi,' said the young woman. 'Jane Becker. Very nearly the late Jane Becker.'

'Are you sure you're ready for this?' Molly asked her. 'The police want a likeness as soon as possible, but I can always come back tomorrow morning.'

Jane Becker emphatically shook her curls. 'He killed that poor man, right in front of me, for no reason at all. Stabbed him and stabbed him and stabbed him, and then he started to stab me. I mean – *why*? I didn't even know him, and I don't think that man knew him either.'

'Well, the police can't think of any reason why he should have attacked *either* of you,' said Molly. 'The man who got killed was a realtor. George Woods, that was his name. He worked for Ohio Relocations on the nineteenth floor. Forty-one years old, with a wife and two little girls aged seven and five.'

'I'm so sorry.' Jane Becker's eyes were crowded with tears. 'Somehow it makes it so much worse, doesn't it, knowing what his name was? He wasn't just a dead man, he was George Woods.'

'Yes,' said Molly. She tugged a Kleenex out of the box on the nightstand and handed it to her. 'But doesn't that give us all the more incentive to find the guy who murdered him? Think of George Woods's family. Think of his girls. He's never going to see them grow up, and they won't even remember him. Let's try to give them some justice, shall we?'

Jane Becker nodded. 'I'll help you. I promise. I can picture that man so clearly. Like he's *there*.' She reached out with one of her bandaged hands as if he were standing right beside Molly and she could actually touch him.

Molly sat down, with her sketchbook on her knees.

'Before you start trying to describe the man who attacked you, Jane, I'd really like to know a little about *you*.'

Jane Becker blinked at her. 'Me? I'm just a legal secretary who got into an elevator and got stabbed by some psycho.'

'I know. But I want to see that man through *your* eyes. Different people see things in completely different ways, especially when they're highly stressed. If you go to court, for instance, and you listen to five eyewitnesses, you wouldn't believe that they were all describing the same crime. The perpetrators were Hispanic. The perpetrators were black. The perpetrators were white guys wearing black hoodies. They drove a blue Buick or a gray Oldsmobile or a silver Accord. They had guns, they had knives, they had baseball bats. They ran off east, they drove off west.'

'OK. I understand. But I don't know what I can tell you.'

'You can start with how old you are.'

'Twenty-five last April. Aries, although I never behave like an Aries. Like, I'm not exactly the assertive type.'

'You're single?'

A second's pause. 'Yes, I'm single.'

'Do you live by yourself?'

'For a while I did – almost eighteen months. But last October I moved back home with my mom and my dad. Oh – and my annoying younger brother Kevin.'

'And home is where?'

'Lakeside Park. I've lived there all my life. I went to Villa Madonna Academy and then to Thomas More.'

Molly thought, Quiet, conservative neighborhood, not too expensive, with mostly traditional homes. 'What made you move back?' she asked.

'I had an apartment on Elm Street, in the city. I loved it, but it was way too expensive.'

'OK . . . you like music?'

'Oh, sure. Imogen Heap, she's my favorite. *Have You Got It In You?* And Tori Amos.'

'And reading?'

'Danielle Steel. I love Danielle Steel. And *The Lovely Bones*. That was the last book I read.'

'How's your social life? Are you dating at all?'

'I go out with guys sometimes. But mostly in a gang from the office, you know? There's nobody special, not at the moment.'

'Did you *ever* have anybody special?'

Jane Becker suddenly coughed, and coughed again, and reached over for a glass of water. When she had recovered, she said, 'I don't understand the question. I mean, what does that have to do with my being attacked?'

'Jane – it's only background. It helps me to visualize the man who stabbed you in the same way that you do. You perceived him with your emotions, with who you are, as well as your eyes.'

'Can't I just describe him to you?'

'I'm sorry,' said Molly. 'I didn't mean to upset you. Sure – let's get down to business, and see if we can't bring this guy to life.'

She folded back the first page of her sketchbook and picked out a soft sepia crayon. 'What struck you about him the most? I mean – if you had to describe him to me in three words, what would you say?'

'His face. He had such a bright red face. It was so red, it was practically scarlet. It was like he was badly sunburned, or maybe he'd been drinking. And he had eyes like slits, and a mouth like a slit, too. It was almost like he was wearing a red mask.'

'Do you think he *could* have been wearing a mask?'

'Oh, no. That was his real face. But it was just so *red*.'

'Did you smell alcohol on his breath?'

'No. But he did have a smell . . . it was kind of sour, and burned. Like burned hair.'

'OK . . . he had a red face and eyes like slits. Could you take a guess at his ethnic origin? Did he look Oriental, maybe? Or Native American?' Molly's pencil was already at work, and the man's disembodied eyes were peering up at her from the page, as if they were emerging from another dimension.

'I don't know what he was. He looked *dangerous*, that's all. You ever see men like that? They're all full of tension, like those pit bull terriers, you know?'

'OK . . . how tall would you say he was?'

'At least six feet. Six feet two. Maybe a little over.'

'And how was he built?'

'Heavy, with very broad shoulders. And a thick neck. And the way he stood. Even *that* was threatening. Kind of leaning toward me, as if he was itching to be let off the leash.'

'How would you describe the shape of his face? Oval, round, or squarish?'

'Squarish. Definitely squarish. And his forehead was kind of slabby.'

'How about his nose?'

Jane Becker closed her eyes. Molly waited for her with her crayon poised over her sketchbook, saying nothing. She knew that Jane Becker could see her attacker's face as clearly as if he were standing right in front of her, and she didn't want to interrupt that moment of intense visualization. She wished only that she could share it.

'Jane?' she coaxed her. 'His nose? Was it a long nose or a snubby nose? Getting the nose right – that's real important. If you think of the way that cartoonists draw people – they always exaggerate their noses.'

Jane Becker opened her eyes again. 'I don't want to make a mistake, that's all. I was so freaked out when he was stabbing that poor man. But what if they arrest somebody and it wasn't him?'

'Jane, seriously, that's down to me. I'm the forensic artist, it's my responsibility to get it right.'

Jane Becker hesitated for a moment longer and then she said, 'OK, then, his nose was pointed, with kind of a bump in it. And he had very high cheekbones. And a big chin, with a cleft in it. I remember that. A really deep cleft.'

Molly's pencil made the softest of chuffing noises as she shaded and filled and structured, and the perpetrator gradually began to materialize in front of her, as if he were coming toward her through a hazy white fog.

'What was his hair like?' she asked.

'Reddish . . . reddish but turning gray. And cut very short. Bristly.'

Molly took out her box of pastel colors and went on sketching and shading for a few moments more. A red face, with touches of green and blue to give it depth and emphasis.

'You didn't see what color his eyes were?'

'Like I say, they were slits. All I can think of is black.'

Molly lifted up her sketchbook up and turned it around, so that Jane Becker could see what she had drawn.

Jane Becker covered her mouth with one bandaged hand. 'Oh my God,' she whispered. 'Oh my God, that's so much like him.'

'You're sure?'

Jane Becker peered at the sketch more intently. 'Maybe the cheekbones not so sharp. His cheeks were kind of fuller, not so hollow. And his eyebrows were thicker. I remember his eyebrows because they were bristly and red like his hair.'

Molly lightened the shadows under the cheekbones and made the face smoother and rounder. She quickly scribbled in some denser eyebrows, too.

'That's it,' said Jane Becker. 'That's the man who stabbed me. I can't believe how you did that.'

'I listened to you, that's all,' Molly told her. 'You told me what he looked like, and here he is. But *you* told me – Jane Becker, legal secretary who lives with her parents in Lakeside Park, and that was very important.'

She didn't say that she had made the suspect much less aggressive in his appearance than Jane Becker had described him. In spite of her prettiness, she suspected that Jane Becker had some problems relating to men. Probably not serious problems – no more than a lack of confidence, or a recent relationship that had suddenly turned sour. But witnesses' personal prejudices could dramatically distort their description of a perpetrator's appearance. Black suspects were frequently described by white witnesses as being much darker-skinned and much more physically intimidating than they actually proved to be, when they were arrested. Looking 'dangerous' didn't affect the length of a suspect's nose, or the positioning of his ears, or the color of his hair.

Molly had also made the suspect look flushed, rather than scarlet. A witness's perception of color was always intensified by fear, because it widened the pupils.

She closed her sketchbook and packed away her pencils and

her crayons. 'Thanks, Jane. You've been very brave and very helpful.'

'What happens now?' Jane Becker asked her.

'Right now I'm going over to police headquarters to put some finishing touches to this composite, ready for the media. It should be on the TV news later tonight, and the papers by tomorrow morning.'

'Do you think you'll catch him? I couldn't bear to think this could happen to anybody else.'

Molly opened her sketchbook again and looked at the face of Jane Becker's attacker. 'If this sketch is as accurate as you say it is – then, yes, I'm pretty sure we'll catch him.'

'Can I ask you one more thing?'

'Sure, of course you can.'

'Where did you find that *fantastic* necklace? I haven't been able to take my eyes off it.'

Molly lifted it up. 'It's amazing, isn't it? I got it at the Peddlers Flea Market on Kellogg. I don't suppose it's worth anything much, but I fell in love with it as soon as I saw it. It has everything, doesn't it? Suns, moons, even little animals.'

On the way out of Jane Becker's room, Molly showed the sketch to the policeman sitting outside. 'This is the guy . . . just in case he tries to get in here and finish the job.'

'Dead ringer for my uncle Herman,' said the cop. 'Be glad to pull him in for you, on suspicion.'

Hunt a Killer

By the time Molly arrived back home in Blue Ash, Sissy and Trevor were sitting in the yard (so that Sissy could smoke).

'Are you hungry?' asked Sissy. 'There's some hummus in the fridge.'

'No, I'll just have a drink, thanks. I'm pooped.'

'How did it go, hon?' said Trevor, pouring her a glass of wine.

'It was sad, as usual. Sad and horrible and pointless.'

'So how did it happen?'

Molly sat down. 'The girl was going out to get a box-lunch, that's all. She got on to the elevator on the twenty-first floor. She went down to the nineteenth and this guy from one of the realty offices got on, too. But on the next floor, they were joined by the perpetrator.

'They went down as far as the fifteenth, and then the perpetrator stopped the elevator and jammed it. He stabbed the guy from the realty office twenty-eight times, all over, including his face. Then he turned on the girl. She tried to fight him off, and then she tried to escape by pulling the doors apart, but the perpetrator stabbed her three times in the back.

'When she was pulling at the doors, though, she must have dislodged whatever it was the perpetrator had used to jam the elevator. It started to travel downward again, and at some point the perpetrator climbed out of it, and escaped.'

'Jesus, there are some crazies around,' said Trevor. 'If you can't even get into an elevator in a crowded office building, without being attacked . . .'

'Is the girl OK?' asked Sissy. 'I mean, considering what she's been through.'

'She's still in shock, but she's not as traumatized as I thought she would be. Some assault victims can't say a single word that makes any sense at all . . . sometimes for weeks. Sometimes never.'

'Did she *know* the man who attacked her?'

'Unh-hunh. She gave me a very vivid description, but he's not the kind of man that you would *want* to know, believe me. She said he was tall, and kind of blocky, but it was his face that really made an impression on her. She said that his face was very red, almost like he was wearing a red mask.'

Sissy reached across the table and picked up the DeVane cards. She sorted through them until she found *La Blanchisseuse*, the laundry woman. She passed it over to Trevor and said, 'Just as the cards predicted. A red-faced man, high up on a ladder. Of course they didn't have elevators when these cards were first drawn. A young woman, and a tub full of blood. In other words, a bloodbath.'

'Coincidence, Momma, coincidence. You're always reading things into things when there isn't anything there.'

'I don't think so. Not this time. Another card predicted that somebody would create a likeness of a man with blood on his hands, and what do you think Molly has been doing this evening?'

'Was he really so red in the face?' asked Trevor.

'That's how the girl described him.'

'Maybe he was wearing face paint. You know – trying to look like a demon, or Darth Maul out of *Star Wars*, so that he would scare people more.'

Molly shrugged. 'Maybe. But he didn't need to put on face paint to scare her. She was scared enough already. She was absolutely sure that she was going to die.'

'So what do the police think?' asked Trevor.

'Right now, nothing conclusive. They're checking out the murdered guy's background, in case this Red Mask maniac knew him and bore him any grudges. He worked in realty, so that's perfectly possible. CIS are going over the crime scene, and asking a whole lot of office workers a whole lot of questions. But there's not much more that they *can* do, not tonight.'

'Are you going to be on TV?' said Trevor.

'Not me. But my sketch is. Mind you, they've put it out on the Internet already.'

Cicadas Coming

Over the yard a three-quarters moon hung suspended, so orange that it was almost crimson. Although it was nearly 10 p.m., the air was still thick and warm. Sissy looked up to the sky and said, 'Can you feel something stirring?'

'Oh God, I hope not,' said Molly. 'Not yet, anyhow.'

'Make sure you close your bedroom window tonight, Momma,' Trevor warned her, 'And close it real tight.'

'They're only bugs, surely,' said Sissy.

'Of course they're only bugs. They won't harm you and they won't sting you. But you never came to Cincinnati in cicada season before. They come out in *billions*, and they *fly*, and they get *everywhere*.

Why do you think I've covered the pool, and hung muslin over the peach trees?'

'You never told me that they were such a nuisance.'

'I was trying to be stoical, Momma, on account of having a job here and not being able to relocate. But they get caught in your hair, they block up your ventilation, and they get spattered all over your windshield when you're driving to work. That's why we never have outdoor picnics in cicada season . . . they keep dive-bombing the potato salad.'

'The worst thing about them is the *noise*,' said Molly. 'It's the males, trying to find a mate. They screech and they screech and they never let up. That's because they know they only have six weeks to live, max.'

'Can't they be exterminated?'

'Only by digging up the whole of Greater Cincinnati to a depth of nine inches, which is where they brood. No – the only answer is to put up with them, and step on as many as you can. Or take a vacation until they're gone. Most people make a joke of them. Some people even stir-fry them and eat them with water chestnuts.'

'I think I'll pass on that,' said Sissy.

They took their glasses of wine and went inside, and Trevor closed and sealed the yard door behind them. 'By the way, Momma, if you find a couple of cicadas in your bed, don't panic. They're only sexually interested in female cicadas.'

'Don't talk dirty to your mother,' Sissy admonished him, slapping his arm.

Trevor switched on the flat-screen TV in the living room, and flicked it on to Channel 5 WLWT. 'These guys are always good for the *crime du jour*.'

They had to sit through a finance commercial for remodeling your home until it looked like a sitcom set, but then the two news anchors appeared on screen, with serious expressions on their faces. Molly's sketch of the red-faced man was displayed behind them with the subtitle *Red Mask Murder*.

'Cincinnati police tonight are still searching for a knife-wielding attacker who stabbed and killed a forty-one-year-old downtown realtor and left a twenty-five-year-old legal secretary with serious injuries.

'The vicious attack occurred in an elevator car on the fifteenth floor of the Giley Building on Race Street. When the elevator reached the lobby and the doors opened, shocked office workers were confronted by what one of them described as a "slaughter-house."'

There were jiggly hand-held interviews with Jimmy and Newton and the shirtsleeved accountant, as well as other witnesses, with police lights flashing in the background. 'Dude, the doors opened up, and it was, like, oh my God, *blood*!'

'—of course I checked the man for any signs of life, but—'

'—didn't see nobody leaving the building, nobody suspicious-looking, anyhow—'

'—quiet, hard-working family man, so far as I could tell—'

'—tragic—'

From police headquarters, a statement was given by Lieutenant-Colonel James L. Whalen, commander of the investigation bureau. He had snowy white hair and a very bronze face and he spoke in a solemn monotone, with unusual pauses.

'Despite the best efforts of the thirty CPD officers and dog-handlers who attended the scene within a matter of minutes' – pause – 'the perpetrator has still not been apprehended, and we have found no witnesses who saw him either enter the Giley Building or leave it.

'So far, we have no clues whatsoever' – pause – 'as to who might have committed this heinous act, or what his motive might have been. But the young woman who was badly injured before the assailant made his getaway' – pause – 'has helped a police forensic artist to create a very striking representation of her attacker.'

Trevor turned around and gave Sissy a look that she didn't really understand, as if he were disappointed or upset.

Lieutenant-Colonel Whalen pointed to the drawing of Red Mask. 'We are giving the suspect the nickname of Red Mask' – pause – 'because it will be easier for people to recall if they have ever seen him, or if they see him now. His face is very reddened, possibly sunburned, and his eyes are narrow.'

They were all silent as Red Mask was enlarged to fill the screen. Mr Boots whined and hid behind the couch.

'If you encounter this man, do not attempt to challenge him' – pause – 'or approach him. He is highly dangerous. Do your best not to make him aware that you have recognized him' – pause – 'and call the police as soon as you can. Do not try any heroics, even if you yourself are personally armed. We have yet to discover what his state of mind might be' – pause – 'or what weapons he might be carrying.'

Sissy stared at Red Mask's face on the television screen. In her composite, Molly had deliberately tried to tone down the sense of danger that Jane Becker had felt when Red Mask stepped on to the elevator. He was a real killer, after all, and not a villain from a comic book. But his eyes still looked dead, as if there were nobody behind them. No light, no sympathy, no human compassion. His thin lips were tilted up slightly to the left, as if he thought that his appearance on television was deeply amusing.

'Scary, don't you think?' said Molly.

'He sure is,' Sissy agreed. 'But – I don't know. I have the strangest feeling that I *know* this face . . . that I've seen it someplace before.'

'Don't see how you could have done,' said Trevor. 'You were never in Cincinnati before.'

'Well – I'm an old lady, Trevor. I've traveled far and wide and seen many strange and interesting things.'

Molly went through to the kitchen to finish clearing up. Trevor glanced over his shoulder to make sure that she was out of earshot, and then he said, 'Momma . . . I have to talk to you about this fortune-telling thing.'

'You want me to read your cards, too? Gladly.'

'No, thank you.' He paused, and blinked his eyes very quickly, the way he used to when he was a boy, and wanted to ask for pocket money. 'It's just that I think the cards are really creepy.'

'Trevor, sweetheart, they only tell us what's what. Or what's *going* to be what.'

'I don't care, Momma. They're creepy, and this is my home, and to be honest with you I don't like you reading them here.'

'Oh. I'm sorry. I didn't realize.'

'They give me the creeps. They *always* gave me the creeps, especially when I was a kid. I was scared even to *look* at them. Gravediggers, clowns, weird people walking through the woods. Strange creatures in pointy hoods, chopping their own fingers off with axes.'

'You should have said before. I never wanted to upset you.'

'Jesus, Momma. I've dropped enough hints. I don't like Molly getting involved in this police work at the best of times, especially after what happened to Poppa. I always think there's a risk of some lunatic trying to take his revenge on her. But this Red Mask thing—'

Sissy took hold of Trevor's hand. Although she was over seventy now, her eyes were as clear as his, and she looked at him with intensity and love.

'Sweetheart, it wasn't the cards that made this happen. It was going to happen anyhow.'

'Maybe it was. Maybe it wasn't. Has it ever occurred to you that you and your cards aren't just foretelling the future, they're actually *changing* it? OK – so maybe this Red Mask character was going to stab these people anyhow. But why did the police have to ask Molly to draw the composite?'

'They didn't give out her name, Trevor.'

'No. But it wouldn't take Sherlock Holmes to track down the only forensic artist in the tri-state who still uses nothing but pencils and pastels. There was an article about her in the *Enquirer* only last September.'

Sissy had turned Trevor's hand over and was delicately tracing the lines on his palm with the tip of her finger. He looked down and realized what she was doing and quickly snatched it away. 'Ho no! You're not going to give me any of your sneaky palm-readings! No way! And I don't want you telling Molly's future any more, and especially not Victoria's! Life is supposed to be unexpected, Momma. Knowing what's going to happen to you – it's unnatural.'

'I don't agree with you at all. I think it's the most natural thing in the world. I think *all* of us could do it – even *you* could do it – if only we were more in touch with everything around us.'

'We go to church every Sunday, goddamnit.'

Sissy spread her arms wide. 'I'm not talking about church. I'm talking about time, and fate, and the way that God's days and men's decisions mesh into each other, like clockwork. The trouble is, we're too busy concentrating on the little things. We have no faith any more. We've lost our sense of wonder, and we never listen.'

'OK. Listen to *what*, exactly?'

'To the warnings that we're being given, sweetheart. When something truly terrible is going to happen, you should be able to feel it coming, like an express train in the distance. The rails start singing, don't they?' She clenched her bony fist and held it up. 'Even the air starts to get tighter.'

Trevor said, 'What are you saying, Momma? That something bad is going to happen to *us*?'

'Let's pray not. But it's best to be well prepared for it, if it does.'

Giant

Sissy respected Trevor's wishes that night and left the DeVane cards untouched on her nightstand, although she was strongly tempted to try another reading. She could feel in her bones that the wheels of the world were moving beneath her, and that the next few days were going to see shifts and changes and shadows moving in contradiction to the sun.

She dressed in her long white linen nightgown and sat in front of the dressing table taking the pins and combs out of her hair, and brushing it out.

For a split second, in the shell-pink lamplight, she saw herself as she had looked when she had married Frank, and was sitting at her dressing table in Connecticut. brushing out her hair for her first night in bed with him. She still had the wide gray eyes and the delicate cheekbones, and that slightly fey, other-worldly look that had led Frank to describe her as a mermaid.

I'm still your mermaid, Frank. The girl you fell in love with, she's still here. I'm the same girl who ran barefoot through the dunes at Hyannis, that July afternoon so long ago.

Then she angled her head a little to the left, and the lamplight suddenly betrayed her. She saw the crows' feet around her eyes and the lines around her mouth, and a neck that looked like crumpled tissue paper. The cries from the seagulls faded, and the warm ocean breeze died away, and here she was in her stuffy spare room in Trevor's house, all alone now, growing older with every night that passed.

Molly knocked on her door.

'Sissy? Is there anything you need? How about a glass of warm milk?'

'A time machine would be nice. Look at me. I'll be seventy-two before I know it. How did that happen? I don't *feel* seventy-two.'

Molly came into the room and sat on the end of the bed. 'You don't behave seventy-two, either, thank God.'

'Trevor talked to me this evening. He wants me to stop fortune-telling while I'm here. He says it gives him the heebie-jeebies.'

'You don't have to stop because of Trevor. You know what *he's* like. If it can't be weighed or measured or calculated, it doesn't exist. Mind you, he makes a living out of guessing the future, just like you. The only difference is, he tries to guess what *isn't* going to happen.'

'He's frightened that Red Mask is going to find out that you drew his composite, and that he's going to come after you.'

'I don't think that's very likely. It's only happened once before. Some child molester threatened to throw battery acid at me. But I think I've protected myself the best way I know how, which is to draw a really accurate likeness of him, so that he'll be caught quicker.'

Sissy tied up her hair with a gray silk scarf. 'Did you tell Trevor about the flowers?'

Molly looked away, and didn't answer.

'I said—'

'No – no, I haven't. Not yet.'

'Are you *going* to tell Trevor about the flowers?'

'I don't know. To tell you the truth I'm kind of in two minds about it. What do you think?'

'They're a *miracle*, Molly! Somehow, you performed a miracle! He's your husband – don't you think he ought to know?'

Molly played with her necklace, so that it glittered in the lamp-light. One of her favorite mascots on it was a tiny golden Egyptian crocodile, with dark red garnets for eyes.

'I *thought* of telling him, honestly. If he had actually *noticed* them, I'm sure I would. But there they were, right in front of him – fully-grown roses and daisies and bellflowers – and he didn't even realize that they hadn't been there when he left for work in the morning.'

'Well – Trevor's the same as most men. They only see what they want to see.'

Molly said, 'It's not only that. I love him because he's so sensible, and so pragmatic. I don't think I *want* him to start believing in miracles.'

'All right, then. If that's what you think is best. Far be it from a wrinkly old mother-in-law like me to interfere in my beautiful young daughter-in-law's affairs.'

Molly wrapped her arms around Sissy and kissed her noisily on her right ear. 'You're not wrinkly and you're not as old as you think you are and I always appreciate your opinion. So there.'

With that, they started to sing *A Hard Rain's A-Gonna Fall* together, in higher and higher harmony, until they were almost shrieking.

'—and it's a hard – it's a hard – *it's a hard—!*'

Trevor opened the bedroom door. 'For Christ's sake, you two! You sound like two polecats being strangled!'

Sissy dreamed that she was very young, maybe only six or seven years old, and that she was sitting in the back seat of a large sedan with brown leather seats. She was kneeling up and watching the landscape slide past. The landscape was brown, too, and very flat – miles and miles of cornfields, all the way to the horizon. The clouds were strangely stretched out, as if they were being pulled across the sky like dark-brown toffee.

She couldn't see who was driving the sedan. He was wearing a pale panama hat with a wide brown band around it. There was a signet ring on his right hand which occasionally flashed at her, and in the center of the steering wheel there was a diamond-shaped emblem which flashed at her, too. She recognized the emblem, and now she realized which car she was in, and who was driving it. It was her uncle Henry's 1954 Hudson Hornet.

The car radio sounded as if it were playing backward – lumpy, intermittent rhythms with garbled words. '*You only saw me through a half-open door . . . I don't know what you thought that you were looking for . . .*'

'Uncle Henry,' she said, although her voice sounded fudgy and blurred.

Uncle Henry didn't turn around, but he said, 'Not far now, Sissy. Seventy miles, no more than that.'

'Where are we?' asked Sissy.

'West of the east and east of the west.'

At almost the same time, they passed a sign saying 'Entering Borrowsville, pop. 789.'

'*Was it for answers? Was it for love? Was it for forgiveness from the angels up above?*'

They drove on and on, and the brown fields continued to slide past them, mile after mile. The clouds were stretched out into long, fantastical shapes, before they slowly broke apart and drifted away. *I don't like this dream*, thought Sissy. *Something bad is going to happen in this dream.*

They passed another sign. 'Leaving Borrowsville.' And it was only a few minutes later that Sissy saw a tall figure standing by the highway up ahead. At first she thought it was a water tower. But as they came closer, and she frowned at it more intently, she began to realize that it was the figure of a man. But how could it be a man? He must be a giant, over thirty feet tall.

'Uncle Henry.'

'What is it, Sissy?'

'There's a giant.'

Uncle Henry didn't answer.

'Uncle Henry, I'm frightened of giants.'

Still Uncle Henry didn't answer.

Sissy tugged at the shoulder of his sport coat and said, much more desperately, 'I'm frightened of giants! I don't want to go past that giant! Please, Uncle Henry! Can't we go back?'

Uncle Henry slowly turned his head around. He seemed to be able to do it without moving the rest of his body. Sissy stared at him in shock. He wasn't Uncle Henry at all – not the Uncle Henry she remembered, with the circular gold-rimmed eyeglasses and the Teddy Roosevelt moustache.

This 'Uncle Henry' had a bright red face, like an enameled papier mâché mask, with thin black slits for eyes, and a wider black slit for a mouth. He had angular cheekbones and a huge chin, with a deep cleft in the middle of it, as if he had been struck with an ax.

'Can't go back now, Sissy,' he said, in the same backward-sounding voice as the songs on the radio. 'Too late now for one and all.'

Sissy started to hyperventilate. She seized the door handle and tried to open the back door, but it was locked.

'Can't go back now, Sissy. What's done is done. And now it has to be done again, and again, and again. No rest for the wicked, Sissy!'

Sissy shook the door handle again, as hard as she could, and it was then that the whole door flew off, with Sissy still clinging on to it, and bounced away over the fields, bursting through the corn stalks, tumbling over and over. Sissy landed on her back in a furrow, and the door landed on top of her with a bang.

She struggled to push the door off her, punching and kicking. But then she realized that it wasn't a door at all. It was heavy, but it was very soft and billowy. It was her patchwork comforter, and she was lying in her bed in Trevor and Molly's house.

She eased herself up into a sitting position, and coughed. It was intensely dark and outside her bedroom window she could hear that it was raining. Her bedside clock told her it was 2:11 a.m.

'You ridiculous old cow,' she admonished herself. She groped for the toggle of her bedside lamp and switched it on. No cornfields, no attenuated clouds, no giants. Only a chintz-decorated bedroom with Currier and Ives prints on the wall. 'Maybe Trevor's right. Maybe you're always reading things into things when there isn't anything there to be read into them.'

She swallowed one of her angina pills and three large gulps of water. She remembered to hang the little beaded cover over her water glass. The first night she had stayed here, she had woken up in the middle of the night and swallowed a struggling moth, along with her water.

She lay back on her pillow and thought about her dream. Or had it been more of a memory? She had visited Uncle Henry and Aunt Mattie on their farm in Iowa once, when she was about seven, but she didn't remember driving there. She recalled her mother meeting her at Penn Station when she was on her way home, so she must have traveled at least part of the way by train.

But why had she dreamed about it now? And why had Uncle Henry looked like Red Mask? And what did the giant mean? Even now that she was awake she thought about the giant and she found it frightening.

She looked over at the DeVane cards – but, no, she had promised Trevor that she wouldn't, and so she wouldn't. She switched off the light and lay there in the darkness for over an hour, trying not to think about that backward-sounding song.

Plague

Molly drew up Sissy's blind for her and said, 'Good morning, Sissy! Our visitors have arrived!'

Sissy sat up and blinked at her. Molly set a glass of orange juice on the nightstand beside her and gave her a kiss on her headscarf.

'Who's arrived?'

'The cicadas! I thought they would, when it started to rain last night. You should see the crab-apple tree!'

Sissy climbed out of bed and went to the window. From here, she could see the curving flowerbed that ran along the left-hand side of Trevor and Molly's yard. The soil around the old crab-apple tree was peppered with countless little chimneys, made of mud, and the trunk and lower branches were clustered with hundreds of glittering yellow cicada nymphs. There were even cicadas clinging to the roses and the daisies that Molly had painted.

'My *God*! There are so many of them!'

Trevor knocked on the door and came in. He was tying up his yellow necktie ready for work. '"Predator satiation," that's what the entomologists call it. *Everything* eats cicadas – birds, bats, cats – even humans. They ran a recipe in last week's *Post* for cicada stir-fry. So the cicadas make sure that their species survives by reproducing themselves by the million.'

'I thought you said they flew,' said Sissy.

'Oh, they fly all right. They're going to break out of that skin before you know it, and turn into adult cicadas with wings and red eyes. They'll stay in that tree for about a week, while they dry out and their skin grows harder, and then they'll be buzzing around everywhere and you'll be mightily sick of them. You can't even play tennis without getting four or five cicadas stuck in your racket every time you play a stroke.'

Trevor left for work, taking Victoria with him so that he could drop her off at Sycamore Community School. Although the cicadas hadn't molted yet, Sissy decided to have her breakfast indoors, in the kitchen. Molly made her some buckwheat pancakes with rosehip syrup.

'I had the *strangest* dream last night,' said Sissy, after she had finished eating. 'I dreamed I was driving across Iowa with my uncle Henry, but it wasn't my uncle Henry at all. It was that Red Mask man.'

'You're kidding me!'

'No . . . it was him all right, just the way you drew him. And he talked to me. He said what was done was done, but it had to be done again.'

'But, Sissy – *I* dreamed about him, too!'

Sissy had an odd, disorienting feeling, as if the sun had gone in, and then come out again, and the clock had suddenly jumped five minutes without her knowing where the time had gone. 'He wasn't driving a car, was he? Don't tell me he was driving a car.'

'No. He was standing in the middle of the yard, in the rain, and he was covered all over in cicadas. Like he was almost *wearing* them, like a cloak.'

'Did he say anything?'

'Unh-hunh. He just stood there, not moving. But the whole dream seemed so *real*. When I woke up, I had to go to the window to make sure that he wasn't actually there.'

Sissy said, 'How about some more coffee? You don't mind if I smoke, do you?'

'No, go ahead.'

Sissy sat on the tapestry window seat beside the open window so that her smoke would blow out in the yard. Molly brought her a mug of fresh coffee and then sat down beside her.

'I know what you're going to say,' said Molly, after a while.

'So . . . *you're* a mind-reader, too?'

'No, but as it happens, I agree with you. Especially since we both had those dreams.'

'I promised Trevor that I wouldn't.'

'I know. But Trevor's not here, is he, and what Trevor doesn't know won't hurt him. Whereas something that *we* don't know might very well hurt *us*.'

Sissy crushed out her cigarette in a blue earthenware ashtray. 'All right,' she said. 'But *please* don't tell Trevor. I don't want him to think that I don't respect him, because I do.'

She went to her bedroom and brought in the DeVane cards. They sat down together at the kitchen table and Sissy laid them out in the Cross-of-Lorraine pattern. She was telling Molly's fortune so she chose *La Fleuriste* for her Predictor card, the Florist. The card showed a bare-breasted young woman in a diaphanous empire-line dress and a huge bonnet laden with flowers and apples and bunches of grapes. She was walking in between two lines of red chrysanthemums, sprinkling them with a golden watering can.

In the background, a young man dressed in fool's motley of yellow and blue was pushing a wheelbarrow, and on closer inspection Molly could see that the wheelbarrow was heaped up with human body parts – arms and legs and decapitated torsos, all spattered with blood.

In the distance, on a hillside, she could just make out the crosses and monuments of a cemetery.

The young man himself appeared to be wearing a spiky hat, or maybe his hair had been waxed up into points. But again – when she examined the card more closely – Molly realized that it wasn't a hat and it wasn't his hair, either. He had ten or eleven large kitchen knives embedded in the top of his head.

On the far side of the gardens, beyond the chrysanthemum beds, there were rows of beehives. They were being tended by monks, whose faces were concealed under bell-shaped muslin nets.

As she dealt out the cards, Sissy said, 'Lay your hand on top of your card and ask it a specific question. Don't tell me what the question is, the cards will answer for you, not me.'

When she had finished, Sissy picked up three cards and arranged them in a fan shape in front of her, face down, so that all Molly could see was the blandly-smiling face of *La Lune,* the Moon, on the reverse side of each of them. She touched each card, one after the other.

After almost half a minute of silence, Molly said, 'Well?'

Sissy looked across the table at her, and the sun reflected in the lenses of her spectacles, so that she looked as if she were blind. 'Are you *sure* you want me to give you this reading?'

'Why? What's wrong? Nobody's going to *die* or anything, are they?'

'I don't know. The cards are being very evasive. Maybe such-and-such a thing is going to happen or maybe it isn't. It always makes me very uneasy when they come up like this.'

'Well, tell me anyhow, Sissy. Come on, they're only cards.'

Sissy picked up *La Fleuriste*. 'I see some warnings. I'm not entirely sure what all of them are. But just take a look at your Predictor card. Here's a pretty young woman who can bring flowers to life – that's you. But there's pain and death in her garden, too – chopped-up bodies, all being carted off to the cemetery.'

'This young man with knives in his head – what does that mean?'

'He's *Le Pitre*, the Clown. He represents laughter and happiness and friendship. But somebody has stabbed him in the head. Whoever he is, his attacker is deliberately trying to spread fear and suspicion, and to make people mistrust each other. A killjoy, in the very worst sense of the word.'

'And these beekeepers?'

'There's no doubt what *they* mean. The cards may not be ready to tell us *what's* going to happen. But they're pretty darn sure about *when.* The beehives are an indication of a swarm of insects, and you only have to look out of the window to see what's happening in your own backyard. So whatever's going to happen, I think it's going to happen pretty soon – if not today.'

Molly nodded toward the three cards laid out in a fan shape. 'And these cards? What do they say?'

Sissy turned over the card on the left. 'This tells you why your future is going to turn out the way it is. This is something you've done already, so there's no changing it, and no going back.'

'*Le Porte-Bonheur*, the Charm?'

The card showed a young man walking through a forest, carrying a tall staff with a jeweled eye on top of it. On either side of the path, the wriggling tree roots had become transformed into snakes, and were standing erect as if they were about to strike.

'This is your ability to draw things and make them come to life. The cards seem to think that it comes from some kind of talisman, just like this staff.'

'I don't have anything like that,' said Molly. But then she pressed her hand against her necklace and said, 'I mean, there's *this*. But it's nothing special. I only paid fifty-five dollars for it, and they threw in a couple of diamante barrettes as well.'

'When did you buy it?'

'Two weeks ago, at the Peddlers' Market. There was all kinds of great stuff there. I saw this amazing copper fire screen with fairies on it. I nearly bought that, too.'

'Did they know where the necklace came from? It's not like any necklace I ever saw before.'

Molly lifted it up and peered at it. 'Me neither. It looks like something that her grandma must have put together herself, piece by piece. Look at this little face, all carved out of ivory. And this lizard. They're incredible.'

'It could be that it carries some kind of power,' said Sissy. She held out her right hand and showed Molly the amethyst ring that she wore on her middle finger. 'My mother gave me this, and I've always been convinced that it helps me to tell if people are telling me the truth. When they lie, the stone grows darker. Sometimes it almost turns from purple to black.

'Mind you, a *person* can be a good-luck charm, too. Your flowers have only come to life since *I've* been here – have you thought about that? It could be our natural chemistry that's doing it. Our life force, the two of us together. Our charisma.'

'What are the other cards?' asked Molly.

Sissy turned over the right-hand card. '*Le Marionettiste*, the Puppeteer. This is what today is going to bring.'

The card showed a young, shabbily-dressed man in a tricorn hat sitting on a wooden bench. He was holding the strings of two dancing marionettes – a ballet dancer with an ostrich plume in her hair, and a soldier with a bushy moustache and a bright blue tunic. The room in which he was playing with these marionettes was very gloomy, and they were illuminated only by a single lantern.

Close behind him, in the shadows, a man in a gray hooded cloak was standing, his arms crossed, holding a large butcher's boning knife in each hand.

'I don't understand this one at all,' said Molly.

'I'm not sure I do, either,' Sissy admitted. 'I think it's one of those predictions that we won't understand until it's actually happened.'

'A man's going to stab a puppeteer?'

'Remember that these cards were drawn over two hundred years ago. A puppeteer could represent all kinds of things, like an aerobics instructor, or a human resources manager. Or a politician, maybe. Anybody who controls other people's lives.'

'OK . . . and the last one?'

Sissy was sensitive enough to know already what the last card was, and she was reluctant to turn it over. She could tell Molly a white lie about its meaning, she supposed, but she doubted if Molly would believe her, and what was the point? She had laid out the cards in order to find out what was going to happen to them, and the more they knew, the better prepared they would be.

Apart from that, her mother's amethyst ring would darken, and she always believed that the cards themselves were aware of how truthfully they were being interpreted. Next time she tried to use them, they would stay silent, and give her no guidance to the future at all. They would be nothing but brightly-colored pasteboard, with incomprehensible pictures on them.

She turned the card over. It was solid scarlet, with no illustration on it. *La Carte Ecarlate*, the Scarlet Card.

'And what does that mean?' asked Molly.

'Mostly it means overwhelming rage. You know, like "seeing

red." But it can also mean blood. A whole lot of blood. So much blood that it almost drowns us.'

Molly sat staring at the card but she didn't touch it. 'Do you know what my question was?' she asked Sissy.

'You don't have to tell me if you don't want to, especially if the cards have answered it for you.'

'I asked if Red Mask was going to murder anybody else.'

The Seventeenth Floor

The next morning was bright but hazy, and very humid. Jimmy arrived at the Giley Building nearly an hour earlier than usual – so early that Mr Kraussman, the super, had to unlock the front doors for him. Mr Kraussman was keg-shaped, with a blue bald head and rolls of fat on the back of his neck, and a green-checkered shirt so loud that it was deafening.

He took out the goetta sandwich that was stuffed in his mouth and said, 'Jimmy! *Ach du lieber Gott!* You get to work any sooner, you'll meet yourself leaving last night!'

Jimmy maneuvered his silver Mutant mountain bike into the lobby. 'Thanks, Mr Kraussman. I have to finish this dumb animation. I tried to knock it off last night but I kept on falling asleep.'

'So what you animating now? Not more of those singing diapers?' He waddled ahead of Jimmy, jingling his keys. 'Singing diapers! I'll tell you something, *my* kids' diapers never sang, but they sure did hum!' He laughed raucously at his own joke, and then he gave a deep, swamp-like sniff.

'This time it's pop bottles,' Jimmy told him, as he folded his bike and stowed it in the utility closet, amongst the mops and the sweeping brushes and the buckets. 'Line-dancing pop bottles.'

'Please?'

'Pop bottles, Mr Kraussman, that line dance. We have a major presentation at eleven, and that gives me less than three-and-a-half hours to finish about five hours of rendering.'

'It's a tragedy,' said Mr Kraussman. 'To think that a great artist like you, he can only make his living with – whatever it is, dance-in-the-line pop bottles.'

'Mr Kraussman, I'm not Leonardo da Vinci. I'm an animator, that's all.'

'Hey – that picture you drew from my little Freddie, you can't tell me that isn't great art. I hang it in my living room, pride of place.'

'Well, I'm glad you liked it. He's a real cute kid, your little Freddie.' Jimmy didn't mention that a huge booger had been protruding from little Freddie's left nostril all the time that he had been drawing him, and that he had been sorely tempted to include it in the finished portrait, in vivid booger green.

Jimmy crossed over to the elevator bank. The elevator in which George Woods and Jane Becker had been attacked was still cordoned off with yellow police tape, and the elevator next to it was labeled *Out Of Order*, but the third elevator was working. Jimmy pressed the button and waited, while Mr Kraussman stood uncomfortably close to him, smiling at him for no apparent reason at all, and continuing to sniff. Like so many Over-the-Rhine residents, he suffered from Cincinnati Sinus.

'Hey – maybe you could draw Mrs Kraussman, too!'

Jimmy said, 'Sure thing, if I can find the time.' *And if I can find a sheet of paper wide enough.*

The elevator arrived and Jimmy stepped on to it.

'Maybe for our ruby wedding, August twelfth!' Mr Kraussman suggested, just before the doors juddered shut. 'Not for free! I pay you top dollar!'

As the elevator car clanked slowly upward, Jimmy leaned back against the mirrored wall and closed his eyes. He felt exhausted. He had been working on the Sea Island Cranberry Soda animation for over six weeks now, seven days a week, and some nights he had still been hunched over his computer at 2 a.m. But it was a critical pitch for the company that employed him, Anteater Animation, and if they landed the account he knew he was in for a more-than-generous bonus. He might even be able to take his girlfriend, Devon, to Disney World.

Jimmy was skinny and slight, two months shy of his twenty-ninth birthday, with curly black hair, a very pale face, and a beaky nose. Devon said he reminded her of a heron. He didn't mind because Devon was just as skinny as he was, if not skinnier, and even though she was pretty, *she* had a beaky nose, too.

This morning Jimmy was wearing his Cincinnati Reds cap (peak sideways) and a white T-shirt with *2007 Cornhole Champions* printed on the back in red, as well as baggy red shorts and big silver Nike TN8 trainers.

The elevator shuddered to a stop and he opened his eyes. He was just about to step out when he realized that he had reached only as far as the seventeenth floor. The corridor in front of him was blue-carpeted, unlit, and strewn with crumpled-up paper. The corporate signboard on the opposite wall had nothing on it but empty screw holes.

Jimmy stuck his head out of the elevator to see if there was anybody there. But the corridor was empty, and the entire floor was silent, except for a faint tapping sound, like a faucet dripping. *Tap* – pause – *tap*. Then – *tap*.

He pushed the button for the twenty-third floor. The elevator doors started to close, but then they jolted open again, with a loud bang which made Jimmy jump. He could hear a harsh squealing noise from the elevator's winding mechanism, and the entire car started to shudder violently, as if the gears were jammed. He could smell overheated oil, and scorched dust, too.

He stepped quickly out of the elevator car and into the corridor. He had seen too many movies in which elevators dropped all the way down to the basement, full of screaming people, and he had heard that when they hit the bottom, people's shinbones came bursting right out of their knees.

Almost immediately, though, the elevator doors closed behind him. He pushed the button again, but they refused to open. He jabbed and jabbed, but then he heard a smooth whining sound, and the indicator showed that the elevator was continuing its upward journey, without him.

'*Shit*,' he said. He jabbed the button a few more times, but the elevator didn't respond. He waited until it went all the way up to the twenty-fifth floor, but even when he called it again, it stayed there.

'Shit, man. This is total shit.'

He had no choice: he would have to take the stairs. He just hoped the doors hadn't been locked to keep out squatters.

He walked along the corridor toward the main office area. The floor was divided into nearly a hundred cubicles, with built-in desks. In some cubicles, graphs and sales charts and Post-it notes were still stuck to the walls. Some of them even had family photographs. Smiling boyfriends, children sitting in paddling pools, dogs.

Jimmy negotiated his way between the cubicles, his satchel slapping against his thigh. He held one hand up in front of his face, because the early-morning sun was shining on the buildings on the opposite side of Race Street, and dazzling him. He began to cough, as he always did when he was stressed.

He reached the double doors which led to the staircase. He pulled the handles, but as he had feared, they were locked.

'*Shit!*' He peered through the wired-glass windows and he could actually see the staircase.

He rattled the doors violently. He tried barging them, with his shoulder, and then he kicked them, as hard as he could. But they were solid oak, with ten-lever locks, and he knew that he didn't have a chance of breaking them open.

He took out his cell phone. No signal. Double shit. But maybe this was a dead zone, here by the staircase. He crossed over to the window. He looked down, and he could see the early-morning traffic and the sidewalks crowded with hurrying office workers. They looked tiny and insignificant, but at least they weren't trapped in here, on the seventeenth floor, like a fly in a jelly jar. He tried his cell phone again but there was still no reception.

He circled slowly around the office, but wherever he went he still couldn't pick up a signal. He even went into one of the cubicles and picked up the phone from the desk, but of course that was dead. Dead like the withered pot plant that stood beside it, abandoned and neglected.

He would have to go back to the elevator. Maybe he could bang on the doors and Mr Kraussman would hear him.

But when he was only halfway across the office, he heard a quick, rattling noise, somewhere off to his left. He stopped and listened, and then he heard it again. *Trrrrrrrttt!* like a giant cicada, flexing its tymbal. He was very short of breath now, and he couldn't stop himself from coughing again.

Trrrrrrrttt! Now the rattle was off to his right. He turned around, and around, but there was nobody there – nobody that he could see, anyhow.

Trrrrrrrttt! Trrrrrrrttt! Trrrtt-trrrtt-trrrtt!

Jimmy turned around again, and then he said, '*Jesus!*'

Only twenty feet away from him, a man was standing in one of the cubicles, so that he was visible only from the chest upward.

He was tall and heavily-built, but because of the sunlight that shone through the windows behind him, Jimmy couldn't see his face.

'Hey,' Jimmy wheezed. 'You scared the shit out of me, dude.'

The man stayed where he was, and said nothing.

Jimmy pointed back along the corridor. 'Stupid elevator's stuck. I keep pushing the button but it won't come back down. And the doors to the stairs are locked.'

Still the man said nothing; and still he didn't move.

'Like – how did you get here, dude?' Jimmy asked him. 'Is there another way out? Another staircase or something?'

Silence.

'Come on, dude, I really need to get out of here! I have all of this work to finish . . . that's the whole reason I came in so early!'

Jimmy coughed once, and then again, and then he went into a spasm, and had to rummage inside his satchel for his inhaler. He took two deep squirts of salbutamol, and then he closed his eyes and counted to five. But when he opened them again, the man had disappeared. He looked around, his eyes still watering, trying to suppress any more coughs.

'Excuse me? Excuse me, sir? Are you still here?'

A pause, and then *trrrrrrtttt!* on the opposite side of the office.

'Excuse me, sir, I seriously need to find a way out of here! I could lose my job if I don't get up to my office!'

Trrrrrrttt!

It was no use. The man was either some kind of nutjob or else he was deaf and dumb, or maybe he was one of those street people who refused to talk to anyone but their own kind. Jimmy started to walk back along the corridor, glancing behind him now and again to make sure that the man wasn't following him. Maybe the elevator was working now – or even if it wasn't, maybe he could make enough noise to attract Mr Kraussman's attention.

He reached the elevator. The indicator was still pointing at the twenty-fifth floor. He pressed the button and held his finger there. *Please, God, come down and get me out of here.*

At first nothing happened. He took his finger off the button and then he pressed it again. There was a moment's pause, and then he heard the elevator mechanism whining, and the indicator crept down to the twenty-fourth floor.

Jimmy coughed, and took another puff from his inhaler. The indicator came down to the twenty-third floor, and then the twenty-second.

'Leaving so soon?' said a thick voice, close behind him.

He jerked sideways, almost losing his balance. The man was standing less than five feet away from him. He was even bulkier than he had appeared when he was standing in the cubicle, and much more threatening. It was the way he was standing, slightly tilted forward as if he were straining at a leash, his head lowered between his shoulders, his arms crossed over his chest.

He was wearing a red shirt, but his face was even redder. It was tight-skinned, like a mask, with slits for eyes and a slit for a mouth. It had a sheen to it, too, as if it were varnished. But, strangely, it looked *blurred*, as if Jimmy were staring at him through a smeary window.

Jimmy opened his mouth and then closed it again. He almost blurted out, *'You're him, aren't you? Red Mask? The guy who stabbed those people in the elevator?'* But the words got tangled up in his throat and all he could manage was a cough.

The elevator indicator went *bing!* Jimmy glanced upward and saw that it had come down as far as the nineteenth floor.

'Do I *scare* you?' asked the red-faced man. 'You look for some reason like you're gravely alarmed.'

Jimmy said, 'I'm just – I just want to get out of here, is all.' He could hear his own voice and it didn't even sound like him. More like a frightened twelve-year-old. 'I have all of this work to do, you know? All of this animation. If I don't get it finished on time—'

'Animation, eh? Bringing things to life?'

Jimmy nodded. The elevator indicator went *bing!* as it reached the eighteenth floor.

'No going back, is there, once you've brought something to life? What's created is created. What's done is done. Like genies, released from their lamps. Or cats, let out of their bags.'

'I'm sorry,' said Jimmy, 'I'm really not too sure what you're trying to say to me, sir. But it looks like the elevator's finally decided to behave itself, and I'm going to have to say *ciao*. And very interesting to meet you. And, you know, *hasta luego*.'

The elevator indicator went *bing!* and to his supreme relief, the doors slid open smoothly.

'What's done is done, son,' said the red-faced man. He was tilting forward even more aggressively, even though his feet hadn't moved. 'And once it's *been* done, it has to be done again and again. No rest for the wicked, that's what they say, isn't it? No peace for the innocent, neither.'

Jimmy stepped backward on to the elevator. 'I really don't know what they say, sir. But it's been very enlightening. Or something like that. So long.'

He pressed the button for the lobby and the elevator doors began to close. *Don't jam this time, please. Just close, and close tight, and let me be carried safely out of here.*

The doors closed. The elevator sank. Jimmy had never said a prayer of thanks before, but he said one now. *Dear God, thank you for fixing the elevator and saving my ass. I shall never doubt Thee again, ever. In fact, I shall walk up every one of the two hundred thirty-five steps outside the Immaculata church on Mount Adams and say, 'Thank you, Lord,' on every single step.*

He went up close to the mirrored wall and peered at himself. He thought he looked surprisingly unruffled, considering how scared he had been. But he would have to decide what he was going to do next. He would have to call the police, and tell them that Red Mask was hiding out on the seventeenth floor. And then what? Go back to his line-dancing pop bottles, as if nothing had happened?

The elevator went *bing!* and stopped on the sixteenth floor. The doors slid back, revealing another abandoned reception area, with a sign saying Kings Communications, Inc. This floor was much gloomier than the floor below, because all of the blinds had been drawn. There were stacks of plywood chairs all the way along the corridor.

'Come on, for Christ's sake,' said Jimmy, and prodded the button for the lobby.

The doors began to close, but as they did so, he heard a rushing noise, like somebody running. He prodded the button again, but he was too late. The red-faced man came hurtling through the gap between the doors, with both arms raised high above his head. In each hand he was holding a large triangular butcher's knife.

Jimmy ducked to one side, and lifted his left elbow to protect himself. But the red-faced man attacked him with unstoppable fury. He stabbed him in the elbow, and then the forearm, and then his other knife slashed Jimmy's right cheek.

To his surprise, Jimmy didn't feel that he was being stabbed, only struck, and he reached up and tried to twist the knives out of the red-faced man's hands. But the red-faced man kept on stabbing and stabbing, and the blades sliced right through Jimmy's fingers, and the heel of his hand, and blood was spraying everywhere.

The tendons in Jimmy's wrists were cut through, and his hands helplessly flapped like red rubber gloves. The red-faced man stabbed him in the forehead, and in the nose, and took a slice out of his chin. Then he stabbed him simultaneously in both eyes, and blinded him.

Jimmy fell sideways to the floor. All he could hear was the pounding of his own blood as it rushed through his eardrums, and the faintest of chopping noises. He didn't feel any pain, only a vague discomfort at being jostled so often, and a deep coldness in his stomach.

'Where am I?' he whispered, through bloodied lips.

A voice very close to his ear said, 'Hell, son. Where you belong.'

Signs and Wonders

They heard about it on the TV news as Sissy was making lunch: a Swiss cheese and ciabatta sandwich, with plum tomatoes.

'This just in,' announced Marcia LaBelle on WLWT. 'A twenty-eight-year-old man has been found stabbed to death in an elevator car in the Giley Building in downtown Cincinnati – less than twenty-four hours after the knife attack in the same building which left one man dead and a young woman seriously injured.'

'Molly! Did you hear that?' Sissy called out. She picked up the remote and turned up the volume.

'A police spokesperson said that it is still too early for investigators to determine if the murder was committed by the same assailant. However, she admitted that the attacks bore "several distinct similarities."

'The victim will not be named until next of kin have been informed, but Channel Five news has learned that he was an animator who worked for the computer graphics company Anteater Animations on the twenty-third floor of the Giley Building.'

Molly was standing in the kitchen door now, still holding her paintbrush. 'Oh God. I know a couple of artists who work for Anteater. Klaus and Sheila. I hope it wasn't Klaus. I'd better call.'

Marcia LaBelle said, 'Still wanted by police in connection with yesterday's stabbings is this man,' and Molly's composite picture of Red Mask suddenly filled the TV screen. 'Detectives have dubbed him Red Mask, because of his florid or sunburned or possibly grease-painted face. They warn anybody who sees him not to approach him but to call nine-one-one immediately. He is almost certainly armed, and extremely dangerous.'

Sissy sat down on one of the kitchen chairs, feeling hot and dithery and distressed. 'An animator, that's what she said.'

'That's right,' said Molly. She lifted the phone off the wall and punched out the number of Anteater Animations.

'But an *animator*. And what did the cards show us? A puppeteer. Somebody who brings little figures to life.'

Molly said, 'Busy,' and punched redial. 'Still busy.'

'Why didn't I make sure that the cards gave me more information?' said Sissy. 'You don't know how *guilty* I feel.'

'Sissy – there was no way you could have predicted exactly who was going to be killed, was there? Or exactly where? Or exactly when?'

'But there was! If I had only *persisted*, I probably could have found out that the attack was going to happen in the same place as yesterday's murder, and what time of day it was going to happen. I turned up the Blood Card, didn't I? So I knew that there was going to be more killing, and I knew that it was going to happen very soon. I could have warned the police, couldn't I? I might have been able to save that young man's life!'

'Sissy, for God's sake, you can't blame yourself.'

'But I *can*, Molly, and I *do*! I was blessed with the gift of foresight, and that makes me responsible for using it, and using it wisely, and to protect innocent people from evil, if I see evil coming their way.'

'All right. So what are you going to do?'

'I'm going to read the cards again, and if they warn me that there's going to be even more killing, I'm going to call that detective friend of yours.'

'Mike Kunzel? To be fair, Sissy, I very much doubt if Mike will believe you. You know how skeptical he is.'

'I don't care if he believes me or not, so long as there's a chance that I can prevent any more innocent people from being murdered.'

'Well, you do what you feel you have to do. Damn it, still busy. I wonder if I still have his home number.'

While Molly tried to get through to Klaus, Sissy went to her bedroom and came back with her cards. She cleared the table and wrapped their sandwiches in foil. Neither of them had any appetite now.

At last, Molly got through to Klaus's girlfriend, Anita. She came off the phone looking relieved.

'It wasn't Klaus. It was a young guy called Jimmy Moulton. That's all she knows. Apparently this Jimmy was the first person to arrive this morning, so whoever killed him must have been hiding in the building all night, waiting for him.'

Sissy was laying out the Cross of Lorraine. She turned over *La Blanchisseuse*, the Laundress with her washing tub brimming with blood. Then she turned over *L'Avertissement*, the Warning. This card showed a party of finely-dressed people approaching a wooden bridge – men, women and children. A man with wild hair and tattered clothes was standing in front of the bridge with his hand raised, as if he were warning the party not to cross. The bridge's handrails were entwined with what appeared to be red climbing roses, but when Sissy took off her eyeglasses and examined them more closely, she realized that they were severed human hands, of varying sizes – some large, some very small – smothered in blood.

In the background, on a hill, stood two crosses, in the shape of Xs, with two men nailed to them.

The last card was *Le Cache-Cache*, the Game of Hide-and-Go-Seek. A group of hunters were making their way through an oak forest, holding up lanterns. They had dogs, too. But the oaks in the forest all had distorted human faces, and their branches were upraised arms with spidery fingers. One of the oaks looked as if it were about to seize one of the unsuspecting hunters from behind, and many of the trees had human legs dangling from them, as if dozens of previous hunters had been hoisted upward and lynched.

Molly leaned over Sissy's shoulder. 'So you're going to show these to Mike Kunzel, are you? And what are you going to tell him?'

'I'm going to tell him that the killer hasn't stopped killing yet, not by a long way, according to these cards. In fact he's going to kill more and more people every time. I'm also going to tell him that he and his men need to be very careful when they go looking for him. You see this *Cache-Cache* card? This means that the hunters are going to become the hunted. They're going to suffer a whole lot of casualties before they find Red Mask. That's if they find him at all.'

'Well, you can try,' said Molly. 'But like I say, Mike Kunzel is one of these people who won't believe that a stove is red-hot until he's sat on it to make sure.'

Sissy said, 'There's so much detail in these cards . . . times, dates. There's a sundial in this picture, pointing to quarter after ten o'clock. And there are five magpies sitting on that signpost. That means the fifth month, May.'

'Sissy – *I* believe that you can predict what's going to happen. But what I'm trying to tell you is, it's going to take so much more to convince Mike.'

'I'll write down everything that I can, and then maybe you could take me to police headquarters.'

'Sissy—'

'People are going to be killed, Molly! People are going to die! And I'm the only person who can stop it from happening! I have to *try*, goddamnit!'

'OK,' Molly agreed. 'But take my advice, and try to make your predictions sound very straightforward. Don't tell Mike that five magpies means May. And don't mention *any* kind of magic.'

It took Sissy over an hour to study the cards in detail, noting every single nuance, such as distant castles with flocks of rooks around them, and two-headed cats, and peasants sleeping under hayricks. She couldn't interpret all of the signs, though, and she began to feel that the cards were deliberately trying to frustrate her.

She sat on the tapestry window seat overlooking the yard. The cicada nymphs were beginning to molt, breaking out of their skins and stickily emerging with red eyes and black bodies and wings. Their discarded remains floated to the ground, so that the soil around the maple tree was littered with hundreds of papery shells.

Molly brought her a glass of wine. 'How's it going?'

Sissy held up her legal pad. On it, she had written *Red Mask: Predicted Behavior Patterns* and underlined it seven times.

'Is that all?'

'I can't do it, Molly. Not *logically*. I know what the cards are telling me because I know what they're telling me. But I can't explain it to anybody else. Why do five magpies mean May? Because they do, that's all. I can't tell you why.'

Molly sat down beside her. 'All right. But even if you can't explain *how* you know what Red Mask is going to do next – what do you think he's going to do?'

'He wants to kill dozens more people, I'm sure of it. He has the taste for it now. You see this card? You see this man in the background, stuffing himself with tripe? From what the cards are telling me, I'm kind of surprised that Red Mask only killed one person today. He *enjoys* stabbing people. He relishes the blood and the close physical contact and the power that it gives him over his victims. And for some reason he's very vengeful, very self-righteous. He believes that he's totally justified in committing all of these murders.

'The cards are telling me something else, too. Red Mask wants to be recognized. He wants to be *notorious*. He wants everybody in the city to be frightened of him. I think he's going to contact the police or the media before too long, and start making threats. Look here – this man shouting from the top of a tower.'

'And the roses? *These* roses are really gruesome, aren't they – these ones like bloodstained hands?'

Sissy took out a cigarette and lit it. 'I'm not sure about the roses yet. But they show up in practically every card, don't they? So they must be significant. I get the feeling that the cards are trying to tell me that I'm missing something really obvious, but I can't for the life of me work out what it is.'

The phone warbled. Molly picked it up and said, 'Sawyer residence.'

'Molly? It's Mike Kunzel.'

'Mike? You must be psychic. I was just about to call you.'

'Really? I guess you've heard there's been another homicide at the Giley Building.'

'Yes – yes, I did. It's so horrible. The young guy who got stabbed, Jimmy Moulton? – he worked with some friends of mine in the same animation studio.'

'Well, it was pretty damned brutal, I can tell you. Worst stabbing I've ever seen, bar none.'

'Do you think you're looking for the same perpetrator?'

'We haven't finished the forensics yet, but personally I'm ninety-nine percent sure of it.'

'My mother-in-law thinks it is.'

'Your mother-in-law?' Pause. 'You mean your mother-in-law who tells fortunes?'

'That's the one.'

'Well, it's reassuring to know that we're on the right track.'

'Mike – she's read the cards, and she believes she knows what Red Mask is going to do next. She might even be able to help you to find him.'

'Molly, with respect, I'm looking for evidence here, not conjecture.'

'I'm not talking about conjecture. Sissy doesn't do conjecture. Sissy reads the cards and interprets what they tell her about the future. And what they've been telling her about Red Mask, and his whole state of mind – well, I've told her that you probably won't believe any of it. But don't you think it's worth your listening to what she has to say? Remember that her late husband was a police detective. She won't deliberately waste your time, I promise.'

'You realize what will happen if the media find out that I've been talking to a fortune-teller? I'll be back on traffic duty before you can say *Crossing Over With John Edward*.'

'The media *won't* find out. And what do you have to lose?'

Detective Kunzel was silent for a moment. Then he said, 'OK, Molly. I need you down here anyhow, so you might as well bring her with you. We have a witness here who says he caught a glimpse of the perpetrator and I'd like you to see if you can rustle up another composite.'

'You're still at the Giley Building?'

'That's right. There's a unit on its way right now to pick you up.'

Molly hung up the phone.

Sissy said, 'Thank you for standing up for me. You were great.'

'I've told you. *I* believe in you. I always have. But I can't guarantee that Mike Kunzel is going to be impressed.'

Sissy said, 'Give me a minute. My hair's such a mess.'

'Your hair is *fine*.'

'How can you say that? My hair's *always* a mess. My hair is the Battle of the Wilderness, reenacted in hair.'

She stood in front of the mirror next to the door, trying to rearrange the pins and the combs that kept her hair up in a wild, lopsided bun.

'I'm really concerned about this Red Mask character,' she told her reflection.

'What's to be concerned about?' said Molly. 'All you have to do is tell Mike Kunzel what you saw in the cards. It's up to him if he believes you or not, which he probably won't.'

'But supposing Red Mask finds out what I've done? You can see how vengeful he is.'

'How can he possibly find out? Mike Kunzel's not going to tell anybody that you talked to him, that's for sure, and nobody else will, either.'

'I don't know. But there's something about Red Mask that's really beginning to disturb me. It's not like my usual readings. Usually, I pick up some sense of who people are. I can sense if they're artistic, or if they're more practical. I can sense if they're confident, or shy. Sometimes I can even tell what kind of family they came from, and if they had any brothers or sisters. But Red Mask . . . he doesn't give me *anything*. Blankness. Black. Nothing at all, except anger, and *revenge*, and this terrible thirst for blood.'

'Sissy, they'll *catch* the guy. They're bound to. They'll catch him and they'll lock him up and they'll probably give him a lethal injection.'

Sissy took hold of her hands and squeezed them. 'I'm sorry. I see these signs and these warnings and I usually read too much into them. You're absolutely right.'

The door chimes sounded. 'That must be our ride,' said Molly. 'And remember – no magpies.'

The Red Secret

A uniformed policeman took them through to the lobby, where Detective Kunzel and Detective Bellman were talking to two crime scene investigators, one of them black and gray-haired, like Morgan Freeman's overweight cousin, the other blonde and bespectacled and thin as a stick insect.

'Molly, thanks for coming down,' Detective Kunzel greeted her. 'And – *ah* – thanks for bringing your mother-in-law.'

'You're more than welcome,' Sissy told him. 'Anything I can do to help.'

Detective Kunzel led Molly to the super's office. It was built into the right-hand side of the lobby, in a curve, with windows that looked right across to the elevator bank. Inside, Mr Kraussman was sitting at his desk, which was heaped with invoices and newspapers and his half-eaten goetta sandwich in a crumpled foil wrapper. On the wall in front of him he had pinned up photographs of his wife and his children and his family schnauzer and a photograph of himself, standing next to a giant statue of Paul Bunyan and his blue ox, Babe, somewhere in rural Wisconsin.

'Molly, this is Mr Herbert Kraussman. He's the super here at the Giley Building. Mr Kraussman, this is Molly Sawyer, our forensic sketch artist.'

Mr Kraussman stood up, wiped his hand on the front of his shirt, and held it out. 'Like on TV, right? I tell you what the guy looked like, you make a drawing.'

'That's right, Mr Kraussman. That's exactly what I do.'

'I don't know what I can tell you, ma'am. Like I said to this detective here, I only saw him for just one blink. *Blink!* And then he wasn't there no more.'

'Well, you might surprise yourself,' said Molly. 'Your brain, it's like a camera. You may not *think* you saw very much, but in fact you saw everything. It's a question of getting you to picture it in your mind's eye, and describe it to me. Do you mind if I sit down?'

'Oh – forgive,' said Mr Kraussman, and lifted a blue plastic box of dusters and cleaning sprays from a wooden armchair on the opposite side of his desk. Molly sat down and propped her sketchpad on her knee.

'We'll leave you to it, then,' said Detective Kunzel. He turned uncomfortably to Sissy. 'Maybe you and I can discuss the future.'

They walked out into the lobby. The doors to the third elevator had been wedged open, and Sissy could see that the interior was spattered all the way up to the ceiling with blood. Morgan Freeman's cousin was kneeling on the floor of the elevator car, taking photographs, and with every flash the elevator car appeared to jump. His skinny blonde partner was dusting the mirrors for fingerprints, and another young CSI with a Zapata moustache was measuring the lobby with a laser. Detective Bellman and half a dozen other police officers were gathered around a makeshift table, studying the architect's plans for the Giley Building.

'You think the killer is still here?' asked Sissy.

'Almost sure of it. The elevator doors opened, and Mr Kraussman saw the suspect look out. Like he says, though, it was only for a split second. Then the doors closed again and the elevator went back up and stopped at the seventeenth floor, which is where we found it with the victim's body inside. No sign of the suspect, of course.

'No other exits were open at the time. There's an emergency fire door in back, and a service door for laundry and deliveries and such, but at that time of the morning the service door was locked and chained, and the emergency fire door has a seal on it which you need to break to open it.

'So the logical conclusion is that the suspect is still hiding on the premises someplace, which is why we're carrying out a floor-by-floor search. It's a complicated old building with all kinds of attics and storage spaces and closets and cubby-holes, but we have seventy-seven officers deployed, and two dog-handlers, so if he's here, then we'll find him.'

Sissy lifted her head. The lobby was echoing with conversation and footsteps and camera shutters clicking and somebody hammering. Detective Bellman called out, 'Mike! Mike, c'mere, would ya?' and another officer said, 'You're breaking up, Stan, I can't hear you,' as he talked to one of the dog-handlers on his radio.

But Sissy closed her eyes and allowed her sensitivity to rise upward, as if she were asleep, and her spirit was rising from her body on a fine golden chain. It rose past the art-deco chandelier with its amber glass diamonds, and up through the combed-plaster ceiling, ascending through the building floor by floor.

She felt the police officers who were searching the offices, and even saw the flicker of their flashlights. She felt the dogs panting, and the dogs, who were much more sensitive than their handlers, stopped and turned in bewilderment as her presence passed them by.

She went all the way up to the twenty-fifth floor, and into the roof space, where the water tanks and the elevator winding gear were housed. She could have risen further, through the coronet-shaped roof, and seen the whole of Cincinnati spread around her, with its waterfront office buildings and its giant ballpark, and the wide hazy curve of the Ohio River, with all of its bridges. But she allowed herself to sink down again, all the way back to the lobby, and opened her eyes.

Detective Kunzel had been talking to Detective Bellman. 'Are you OK there, Mrs Sawyer?' he asked her. 'Thought you were kind of meditating there, for a moment.'

'He's not here,' said Sissy, emphatically.

'Please?'

'Red Mask. He's not here. I would have sensed him, if he was.'

'With all due respect, ma'am,' Detective Bellman put in, 'there's no way he could have gotten out. He *has* to be here.'

'I don't care what you say. He's not.'

'So what makes you so sure about that?' asked Detective Kunzel.

'Detective Kunzel, I was born with certain sensitivities, and certain abilities, and while they're very difficult to explain to other people, they're as natural to me as seeing and hearing and smelling. He's not here any more. He's gone. I don't sense him in the building anywhere.'

'Whatever – we still have to complete our search. At worst, we can find out how he managed to get out of the building without anybody seeing him.'

'He's going to kill again,' Sissy told him. 'He has the appetite for it now. And next time, he's going to kill three or four people, or even more.'

Detective Kunzel and Detective Bellman exchanged meaningful glances.

'And, what, your cards told you this?' asked Detective Kunzel. 'Or did you use your crystal ball instead?'

'You can mock me all you like,' said Sissy. 'Crystal balls are wonderful for telling the future. They're very far-seeing, much more far-seeing than cards or tealeaves.'

'So what's his motive?' Detective Bellman put in.

Detective Kunzel shook his head in exasperation, so that his jowls wobbled, but Detective Bellman said, 'No, come on, Mike . . . Mrs Sawyer has taken the trouble to come down here and tell us what she sees. I'd like to hear it. Hey, my grandmother used to read my palm.'

'Who needs fingerprints, and DNA, and witness evidence?' asked Detective Kunzel. 'Let's just issue the whole department with ouija boards.'

Sissy was unfazed. Frank had been equally skeptical about her psychic sensitivity, even when she had guided him to a hit-and-run suspect who was hiding in a disused laundry in New Canaan, and when she had warned him about a fatal shooting at a local store, even before it had happened. So if Detective Kunzel didn't want to believe her, that was his privilege. But she was sure that Red Mask wasn't here, in the Giley Building

– just as she was equally sure that he was going to commit more murders.

'I told Molly – I was very surprised that he killed only one person today. The cards say that he's going to escalate his attacks very quickly. As for his motive, he's taking his revenge for something that he perceives to be a serious injustice. He believes that he was taken advantage of, and badly wronged. He believes that the fear and suffering that he had to endure entitle him to punish anybody and everybody, even if they weren't personally involved in this injustice.'

'Do you have any idea where he's gone?' asked Detective Bellman. 'Like, I know some psychics can see through a suspect's own eyes, and identify the place where they're hiding out. There was this one movie I saw, the psychic heard bells, and they found the suspect hiding in this church.'

'That was a *movie*, Freddie,' said Detective Kunzel, with exaggerated patience. 'And it wasn't bells, it was train whistles, and he was hiding in a barn.'

'It was bells.'

'Frankly, I don't give a rat's ass if it was the Cincinnati Symphony Orchestra. It was fiction and this is R-E-A-L. Mrs Sawyer here cannot possibly have any idea where Red Mask has gone to.'

'Well, you're right,' said Sissy. 'I don't. You know – I've never known a subject like him. I can feel his anger. I can feel his need for revenge. But I can't feel *him*, not at all. I don't have any sense of his personality whatsoever.'

Detective Kunzel laid his hand on Sissy's shoulder. 'Thanks for trying to help, anyhow. I just wish that more of the good people of Cincinnati were as concerned about helping us to catch criminals as you are.'

'There's one more thing, Detective,' said Sissy.

'Hey, call me Mike, please.'

'Red Mask wants notoriety. He's probably seen himself on the TV news already, and in the papers. He's going to be in touch with you, personally. He's going to start giving you advance notice of what he's going to do next. He wants to start his own personal reign of terror.'

'All I can say is, he knows my number.'

At that moment, Molly came out of Mr Kraussman's office with her sketchpad. Without saying a word, she folded it back and showed them her drawing.

Detective Bellman whistled. 'Same guy. Never saw two composites look so much alike.'

The sketch depicted a red-faced man with bristling hair and a sloping forehead, glaring out of the narrow space between two elevator doors. He had sharp, angular cheekbones and a prominent chin, with a sharp cleft in it. The only difference between this sketch and the sketch that Molly had drawn from Jane Becker's description was that his eyes appeared to glitter, as if he were feeling triumphant.

'Right,' said Detective Kunzel. 'Good job, Molly. Why don't you take that over to headquarters and have them send it out to the media?'

Morgan Freeman's cousin came rustling up to them in his blue Tyvek suit. 'Got you some footprints this time, detective.'

'Any idea what size?'

'Ten, I'd say. Very broad foot. But the soles didn't have no pattern on them, nothing at all. Not even stitching.'

Detective Bellman said, 'Any footprint is better than no footprint. That first stabbing, there was all this blood on the floor, and the perpetrator didn't leave a single footprint, nowhere.'

'Correction,' said Morgan Freeman's cousin. 'He may have left a footprint but we were unable to tell if he did or not. Half of the office staff trampled in and out of that elevator, followed by half of the homicide unit. By the time they were through, the whole place looked like one of those Arthur Murray dance lessons.'

'Bernard here is very hot on crime scene integrity,' said Detective Bellman.

Molly said to Sissy, 'Are you coming to police headquarters with me, or would you rather go back home? I shouldn't be longer than an hour.'

'I'll go home,' said Sissy. 'Victoria will be back at three thirty, won't she? I can give her some milk and cookies.'

'Trevor can do that. He can't cook, but he can pour milk and take cookies out of the cookie jar.'

'I'd still like to be there,' Sissy told her. *Just to make sure that she's safe.* She still didn't understand the significance of the girl in the yellow dress falling down the well, and the man in the beret throwing roses after her, and it worried her.

'I'll have an officer take you home,' said Detective Kunzel, and beckoned to one of the uniforms standing by the main doors.

'*We're here*,' somebody whispered, very close to Sissy's right ear.

Dying in the Dark

'What?' she said, turning around. But there was nobody within twenty feet of her.

'Please?' said Detective Kunzel.

'I distinctly heard somebody speak. A woman, I think. She said, "We're here."'

'An echo, I guess. You go with this officer and he'll take good care of you.'

'*Don't leave us. We're here.*'

Sissy lifted one hand and said, 'Ssh! There she was again! She just said, "Don't leave us."'

Detective Kunzel looked around. 'There's no woman here, Mrs Sawyer. I think your ears are playing tricks on you.'

But Sissy could sense the woman now. She could almost feel her breath against the side of her neck. The woman was black, and she was middle-aged, and she wore upswept eyeglasses. Her name began with an 'M' or an 'N.'

And she was here.

Sissy began to circle around the lobby, her hand still lifted, listening.

'*Don't leave us. For pity's sake, please don't leave us.*'

Molly said, 'Sissy, what is it? Are you OK?'

'She's very close,' said Sissy, distractedly. 'She's trying to tell me where she is.'

There was a sharp clatter as two crime scene investigators adjusted the tripods that supported their floodlights. Sissy said, '*Ssh!*' and Detective Bellman called out, 'Hey, people! Can we have a little quiet in here for a moment?'

'*We're here,*' the woman whispered.

'Where?' Sissy coaxed her.

'*Please don't leave us. It's dark and it's cold and I can't see nothing. The others I think they both dead, Henry and Lindy, or else they real close to it.*'

'What's your name, sweetheart?' Sissy asked her. Detective Kunzel looked at Molly and raised his left eyebrow.

'*Mary. Mary Clay.*'

'Well, you just hang on there, Mary, because I can hear you and I'm going to find you.'

'Mary?' said Detective Kunzel. 'Who the hell is Mary?'

'What's the last thing you remember, Mary?'

'*We is all finished up cleaning on the twenty-second floor. We is waiting to go up to Mr Radcliffe's. The doors opened up. I didn't know this one was working, says Henry.*'

'The elevator . . . you're talking about the elevator?'

Detective Kunzel turned to Molly. 'Does she always talk to herself like this?'

But Molly said, 'Ssh . . . I've seen her do this before. Whoever she's talking to, she can hear them and they can hear her, even if we can't. Astral conversation, that's what she calls it.'

'You mean like Patricia Arquette, in *Medium*? Talking to dead people, and people who aren't even there?'

'Well, something like that. More like broadband, only psychic.'

Sissy stopped circling around now, and stayed where she was, in the center of the lobby. 'You're close, Mary, I can feel you.'

'*Lindy says it looks like it's working now. So in we step and the doors close.*'

'What then, Mary?'

'*Elevator gives a kind of a bang and it scares the daylights out of us. Now it starts to move, but jerky. And it ain't going up, like we want it to. It's going down. And now there's another bang, and it's stopped. Why's it stopped? Don't tell me we're going to be trapped in here. I can't stand being all closed in like this. I even get the claustrophobia when the church is crowded, and I have to step outside and take in some air.*'

Mary was breathing hard now, and her voice began to rise in panic.

'*The doors is opening up. Which floor we on? I don't know which floor we on. But we don't even get a chance because he comes rushing in like a mad person and he's stabbing at us with two big knives and Henry drops down to his knees with blood spraying out of his neck and Lindy falls backward and then he's stabbing at me and I can feel the knives chopping into my shoulders and into my arms and then it's all black.*'

Sissy closed her eyes again. She could sense that Mary was

very badly hurt, and that she was dying. That was the reason she could hear her. Her spirit was already leaving her – floating away from her material body in skeins of light.

'Mary?' she said. 'Mary, can you hear me?'

'*Please come find us*,' Mary whispered. '*Don't let me die in the dark. My kids. My mother*.'

Sissy walked slowly toward the center elevator, the one with the *Out Of Order* sign. She pressed both hands against the doors, and took a deep breath, and held it, and then another. She heard somebody say, '*Mary? Is that you, Mary?*' A different woman, older. Without turning around, she called out, 'Mike!'

Detective Kunzel hurried up to her and jabbed at the elevator button. The doors refused to open, but he shouted out, 'Kraussman! Hey, Kraussman! Somebody get that goddamned super for me!'

Mr Kraussman came out of his office, blinking.

'Get these elevator doors open, and get them open now!'

'OK, for sure. I got a key.'

He came hurrying across with his bunch of keys jingling, knelt down in front of the elevator. He unlocked the hoistway doors, and wound them open, but the doors to the elevator car were still firmly closed.

'You wait, I bring crowbar!'

He returned to his office and came back with a crowbar and a tire iron. He handed the tire iron to the burliest of the uniformed officers, and between them, inch by inch, they forced the elevator doors apart.

As they were opened wider and wider, the doors gave out intermittent groans, as if they were in pain. A little at a time, the floodlights began to illuminate the interior of the elevator car. It was wall-to-wall red.

Three people were huddled on the floor – two women and a man. All three of them were wearing pale blue coveralls, but they were soaked and spattered in so much blood that they looked as if they had been attacked by an action painter with a bucket of scarlet paint.

'*Gott in Himmel*,' coughed Mr Kraussman. 'It's the cleaning crew.'

'Paramedics!' bellowed Detective Kunzel. 'Paramedics, and quick!'

Mr Kraussman swayed and stumbled, as if somebody had pushed him. 'I thought they finish up hours ago. Most nights, they're all through by two. I thought they went home. I swear it.'

'Hey, steady,' said Detective Bellman. 'This wasn't your fault.'

Detective Kunzel hunkered down beside the elevator and pressed his fingertips against the victims' carotid arteries, one after the other.

'That's Mary,' said Sissy, trying to stop her voice from trembling. 'The one in the middle, with the eyeglasses. Is she still alive?'

Detective Kunzel felt for Mary's pulse a second time, but then he shook his head. 'They're all deceased, all three of them. I'm sorry.'

'Just before she passed over, do you know what Mary told me? She said that she didn't want to die in the dark.'

Molly put her arm around Sissy's shoulders and gave her a sympathetic squeeze. 'At least you found them.'

Detective Kunzel stood up. 'I don't know how you did that, Mrs Sawyer, but I have to admit that I'm impressed.'

'If only I'd heard her sooner.'

'By the look of her injuries, Mrs Sawyer, I don't think she could have survived, even if you had.'

Detective Bellman was clearly upset, and kept blowing out his cheeks. 'Guy's a total maniac. I never saw anybody with so many stab wounds, ever.'

'You know what nice people these were?' said Mr Kraussman. 'Always smiling. Always got time for laughing. What kind of person would want to hurt them so bad?'

'You were right about one thing, Mrs Sawyer,' said Detective Kunzel. 'Red Mask *did* kill more people this time. Molly – how about you take that composite over to headquarters pronto? The sooner we get it out to the media the better. We have to nail this bastard before he attacks anybody else.'

'I just wish I could sense where he went,' said Sissy. 'I've tried and I've tried – but nothing.'

'Come on, Sissy,' Molly told her. 'You're in shock. We all are. Why don't you let the officer drive you home? Make yourself some of that chamomile tea.'

Sissy nodded. She was more frustrated than distressed. Usually, she could feel where somebody had gone, because everybody left a psychic wake behind them – a shivering in the air, a refraction in the daylight – in the same way that everybody left their scent or their footprints behind them. Sometimes, if a person was very angry, or agitated, they left a trembling in the air which could persist for hours.

But Red Mask had vanished without a trace, as if he had stepped out of the world altogether, and closed the door behind him. No emotion, no after-image, no distortion in the daylight. Not even the faintest of distant echoes.

The Voice of Unreason

Sissy and Molly were about to push their way through the revolving door when three paramedics came bustling through, so they had to step back. As they did so, Detective Kunzel's cell phone played *Hang On, Sloopy*.

Detective Kunzel said, 'Kunzel.' Then, 'Who?' Then, 'Who is this?' Then he lifted his hand and called out, 'Molly! Mrs Sawyer! Hold up a moment!'

Reluctantly, they returned. The paramedics were already kneeling by the bodies in the elevator, double-checking that none of the three victims showed any signs of life. Sissy looked away, but not before she noticed Mary's upswept eyeglasses, with congealing blood on the lenses, lying on the floor.

Detective Kunzel had switched his phone to speaker. A grating voice was saying, '*—too late now for one and all—*'

'It's him,' mouthed Detective Kunzel.

Sissy said nothing, but stood closer so that she could hear the voice more clearly.

'*What's done is done, and it can't be undone, no matter what. And it has to be done again, and again, until amends are made, and dues are paid, and justice is satisfied. No rest for the wicked, Detective. No rest for the guilty, neither.*'

'What do you want?' asked Detective Kunzel. 'If we knew what you wanted, maybe we could come to some kind of compromise.'

'*You can't compromise when it comes to justice. You can only take what's due to you, until justice has been satisfied.*'

'So what do you believe is due to you? I'm pretty sure that we could work something out, if only I knew what it was.'

'*Do you know what I lost, Detective? I lost my happiness. I lost everything that made me what I was. My self-confidence, my very identity. I lost* me.'

'So what are you trying to tell me? That you've taken the lives of five innocent people, just because your ego took a bruising? That doesn't sound like checks and balances to me.'

'*You don't think so? You wait. Tomorrow, even more innocents are going to meet their Maker. And the day after that, even more again. It's going to be a massacre, Detective, and the people of this city should be warned about it. You need to tell them that Red Mask is hell-bent on justice, and that none of them is safe.*'

'Red Mask? That's the name that *we* thought up for you. How about telling me your real name?'

'*Red Mask will do fine. Red Mask is what you decided to call me. Red Mask is what I am.*'

'How about a first name? I can't call you "Red Mask" all the time, can I?'

'*You can call me anything you like. I'm not choosy. You can call me the Elevator Murderer or the Butcher's Knife Maniac or the Scarlet-Faced Slasher. You can call me Sudden-Death-on-Legs if you want to. All's I'm saying is, the people of Cincinnati should be warned what I intend to do to them.*'

'Listen to me—' Detective Kunzel began, but then they heard a sharp click, followed by a buzzing noise.

'Hey – are you still there?' Detective Kunzel demanded. 'Red Mask? Are you still there?'

'I think he's said all he needs to say to us,' Sissy put in. 'For the time being, anyhow.'

Detective Kunzel said, 'You guessed that he was going to call me, didn't you?'

'I didn't *guess*, Mike. I *knew*. It was forecast by the cards, very specifically.'

'I don't suppose the cards told you his home address? Hey – sorry. I didn't mean to be sarcastic.'

'Actually, no, you don't have to apologize. The cards often give me a strong sense of where people live. Which neighborhood, anyhow – which general locality – even if they don't actually give me a street number. But for Red Mask – they've given me nothing. Not even which side of the river he comes from. And they haven't explained his motive. They've told me *what* he's going to do, yes. But they haven't given me even the slightest inkling *why*.'

Detective Kunzel turned to the officers who were gathered all around him. 'Anybody pick up anything from that conversation? Accent? Speech mannerisms? Anything at all?'

'Sounded local to me,' said Detective Bellman. 'But he's kind of sissy for a serial killer, don't you think? All that stuff about losing his happiness. "I lost *me*." Sounded like something out of a woman's magazine.'

'He's educated,' said one of the uniformed cops. 'He's trying to talk tough and streetwise, but I'd lay bets that he's been through college. It's the words he uses. And he didn't cuss once.'

'Age?'

'Difficult to say, but I think he's younger than he's trying to make out. Mid- to late-twenties, maybe. He's straining his voice to make it sound gruff.'

'This I do not like at all,' said Detective Kunzel. 'I prefer mad-dog psychos to educated misfits. Remember the Lincoln Penny Killer? Never caught him. Smartest serial murderer we ever had to deal with.'

'Who was he?' asked Sissy.

'Copycat killer. *Historical* copycat killer. Cut off three women's heads, to imitate the murder of a girl called Pearl Bryan in 1896 – Cincinnati's most notorious homicide. Pearl Bryan's head was never found. We never found these women's heads, neither.

'It's kind of a tradition when people visit Pearl Bryan's grave they leave pennies with the Lincoln side up, so that poor Pearl will have a head when it comes to Resurrection Day. The Lincoln Penny Killer always left a penny where his victims' heads had been. Kind of an intellectual joke.'

Sissy said, 'If only we could find out why Red Mask is feeling so vengeful.'

'Who knows?' asked Detective Kunzel. 'Look at Columbine. Look at that shooting at Virginia Tech. There wasn't any why. The perpetrators had giant-sized chips on their shoulders, that's all.'

'I think I need to ask one of his victims,' Sissy told him.

'Please? Apart from that one girl, what's-her-name, Jane Becker, all of his victims are dead. And Jane Becker's told us everything she witnessed, which wasn't very much.'

'Maybe the other victims saw more.'

Detective Kunzel's eyes narrowed. 'What are we talking about here?'

'A séance, I think you'd call it. I can talk to people who have passed over, Mike, especially if they feel an urgent need to explain what happened to them, which many of them do.'

'I see. Well, I guess you can try. But I can't officially involve the homicide unit in anything like that.'

Sissy cocked her head to one side. 'I wouldn't expect you to. I'm just pleased that you don't seem quite so skeptical any more.'

'Hey – don't think for one minute that you've made me a true believer. I still think that the future doesn't happen till it happens, and I still think that when you're dead you're dead. But after what you did here today – let's say that I have more of an open mind. Maybe you *can* sense things that other people can't. Maybe you *can* guess how tomorrow is going to turn out.'

'Who was Red Mask's first victim?' asked Sissy.

'He was a realtor called George Woods,' said Molly.

'Do you have an address for him?'

'Sure,' said Detective Kunzel. He took out his notebook, licked his thumb, and leafed through it. 'Here you are – 1445 Riddle Road, Avondale. There's a phone number, too. I mean, his address is no secret, it was in the papers, and the number's listed in the phone book, but don't tell Mrs Woods that I gave them to you, will you?'

'I'll be very discreet,' Sissy assured him. 'She may not agree to my holding a séance, but I doubt it. In all my years I've only had a handful of out-and-out refusals. Most people will do anything to hear their loved ones again.'

Detective Kunzel turned to Molly. 'Can she really do it? Like, if I wanted to talk to my pops . . .?'

'You always told me you *hated* your pops,' said Detective Bellman. 'You always said he was a world-class word which I can't use in front of present company.'

'I did. I did. But I never got the chance to tell him to his face, before he died, and I would give anything to be able to do that.'

Three men and two women from the coroner's office were wheeling in gurneys to take away the three victims in the elevator.

Sissy lifted the little silver-and-pearl cross she wore around her neck and said, 'Goodbye, Mary, rest in peace. Please forgive me for letting you die in the dark.'

The Magic Garden

Sissy and Molly kissed on the steps of the Giley Building. The street outside was crowded with squad cars and ambulances and television vans, as well as scores of rubber-neckers. From the hubbub of excitement going through the crowd, anybody would have thought that they were expecting the imminent arrival of a famous movie star.

'Cincinnati sightseers,' said Molly, in disgust. 'Look – I'll see you later, Sissy. Take care of Victoria for me. And Trevor. Well, I know you've been taking care of Trevor all of your life.'

Molly climbed into one of the squad cars, to be taken over to Cincinnati police headquarters on Ezzard Charles Drive. A big, heavily-built officer with curly white hair was waiting to escort Sissy down the steps to another squad car, to drive her back to Blue Ash.

She settled into the back seat. The interior of the squad car smelled strongly of cheeseburger.

'Excuse the fragrance, lady,' the officer apologized. 'I haven't eaten in six hours straight. Not even a candy bar.'

As he pulled away from the curb, he opened up a yellow polystyrene box and lifted out a twelve-ounce cheeseburger, and took an enormous bite.

'I'm sorry, you know, but my captain thinks I'm what? The starving millions in Africa? I always say you gotta eat to function. Nobody can function on an empty stomach.'

'Well, you're right,' said Sissy. She was looking out of the window, but she couldn't help sensing the officer's heartbeat.

Bom – pause – *badom* – pause. Clogged arteries. She could feel them. She could feel a pain clutching at her left arm, too, as if she were just about to have a heart attack.

'Got this at Zip's,' he said, holding it up. 'Best damned burgers in Cincinnati.'

'All the same,' Sissy told him. 'You should watch what you eat, and how you eat it.'

'Lady – I wish I had the luxury. If I had the luxury, I wouldn't be eating no cheeseburger in no squad car. I'd be sitting down proper with my napkin tucked in my collar and I'd be eating T-bone steak and mashed potatoes and plenty of gravy, with a plate of hot corn-bread on the side, and blueberry pie and ice-cream for dessert.'

'What's your name?' Sissy asked him.

'You want to know my name? It's Gerald. Gerald Clyde. Forty-one years old, proud father of three little girls.'

'You want to see your little girls grow up, Gerald?'

'Excuse me?'

'You have a health crisis coming,' Sissy warned him. 'You really need to ease up and visit your doctor for a physical.'

The officer stared at her in his rear-view mirror. 'Lady, I'm a little stressed is all. Maybe a touch overweight. Otherwise, I'm two hundred percent fit. I could stop this car right now and do ten one-arm push-ups on the sidewalk.'

'I'm sorry,' said Sissy. 'It really is none of my business, is it? It's just that I get these very strong feelings about people.'

'Oh, yeah?'

'Really – don't take any notice. I'm only a silly old woman, that's all.'

The officer chewed his cheeseburger slower and slower. 'You got a feeling about *me*?' he asked her. 'Like, what?'

'Please, I shouldn't have said anything. I'm upset, that's all. Seeing those people murdered—'

'I know. It's tough.'

The officer drove for three or four minutes in silence. Then he said, 'You feel there's something wrong with me? Like I'm sick or something?'

'No. Really. Forget it, please.'

They stopped at the intersection of Madison Road and Dana Avenue. The officer turned around in his seat and for a split second his face was transformed. His eyes were rolled up into his head, showing nothing but white, like snooker balls, and his lips were white, too, as if he had been drinking bleach.

Then he said, 'Believe me, lady, I take care of myself. So don't you worry. I eat plenty of fruit. And yogurt, too. And I spend fifteen minutes every day on the treadmill.' And his face returned to normal, red-cheeked, blue-eyed, and grinning. Before the signals changed, he took another large bite of cheeseburger.

* * *

When Sissy arrived back at Blue Ash, Trevor and Victoria were already home. Victoria was watching *School of Rock* in the living room, while Trevor was out in the backyard, sweeping up dried cicada skins. The trees and the bushes were still clustered with hundreds of glistening cicadas, gradually drying out in the afternoon sun. Mr Boots came wuffling up to greet her, licking her hand.

'How was it?' asked Trevor.

'Bad. Horrible. He didn't only kill that poor young man. He killed three office cleaners, too.'

'Molly told me, on the phone. She said you heard his voice, too.'

Sissy nodded. 'It's so terrible. He seems to want revenge on anybody and everybody, and I still can't understand why.'

'Come on, Momma. You shouldn't let it worry you so much. It's not *your* responsibility to catch him.'

'But if I can *help,* Trevor—'

'Momma . . . the cops know what they're doing. They'll track him down sooner or later, and they won't need fortune-telling cards or séances.'

'Oh, I see. Molly told you about the séance?'

'Of course she told me about it. But, you're a seventy-one-year-old woman. I can't stop you, can I? No matter what I think about this talking-to-the-dead stuff.'

Sissy laid her hand on his arm, very gently. 'Just like your father. He refused to believe in spirits even when I got through to his sister Joan and she told him where her diary was hidden.'

Trevor scooped up the last of the cicada skins and dead leaves on to a piece of cardboard, and tipped them into the trashcan. 'Hey – have you seen these?' he asked Sissy, and pointed to the roses and the hollyhock and the Shasta daisy. 'They're beautiful, aren't they? I don't know how, but I never even saw them grow.'

'They're miraculous,' said Sissy.

'I was thinking of cutting the roses before the cicadas suck the life out of them.'

'Why not? I'll put them in a vase for you.'

Trevor took out his pocket-knife and cut each of the roses at the bottom of the stem. 'They're wonderful, aren't they? They remind me of New Milford. You remember, the roses that Dad used to grow, around the porch.'

'Yes,' said Sissy. 'I remember.' And for a moment, she thought she could see Frank standing under the vine trellis, but it was only a trick of the sunlight and shadow.

They went back inside, into the kitchen. Sissy looked in the cupboard next to the sink and found a narrow glass vase. Victoria came in and watched her as she arranged the roses with a few ferns around them.

'How was school today?' Sissy asked her.

'OK.'

'Just OK?'

'I was tired. I nearly fell asleep in geography and Mr Pulaski came right up behind me and clapped his hands together to wake me up.'

'Why were you so tired? Didn't you sleep well last night? After all that spaghetti you ate, I thought you would have slept like a pig in clover.'

'I slept OK, but I had too many bad dreams.'

'Bad dreams? What about?'

'I dreamed that a giant was chasing me.'

Sissy placed the vase of roses on the hutch. 'A giant? What did he look like?'

Uncle Henry, I'm frightened of giants. Uncle Henry, can't we go back?

'I didn't see. It was much too dark and I was running away as fast as I could run.'

'The giant didn't catch you, did he?'

'No. I made myself wake up. I said, "There's no such thing as giants," and I felt better after that. But then I fell asleep again and I dreamed that I was falling down this dark hole, like Alice in Wonderland.'

'What *horrible* dreams! I'm not surprised you were tired.'

'Maybe I should pop a couple of Valium before I go to bed tonight.'

'"Pop a couple of Valium?" – I don't think so. But I could make you a nice warm mug of malted milk.'

The phone rang. Trevor came back into the kitchen and answered it, but then he handed it to Sissy. 'It's Mike Kunzel, for you.'

Sissy said, 'Mike?'

'Hi there, Mrs Sawyer. Just thought you'd like to know that you were right. We searched the Giley Building from the roof to the basement. Every office, every closet. We even checked the garbage chutes. No sign of Red Mask anywhere. No fingerprints, either, and the footprints were a bust.'

'Did you manage to work out how he could have gotten away?'

'My guess is he walked straight out the front door while the super was dialing nine-one-one. It's amazing what people don't notice when they're panicking.'

'So what are you going to do now?'

'There's nothing much we *can* do, except to keep on looking for him, and appeal to the public to keep their eyes open, too. By the way, Molly left about fifteen minutes ago. She's a really great artist, that girl.'

'Yes, she is,' said Sissy, looking at the roses on the hutch. 'Even better than you know.'

Trevor said, 'What?'

'Nothing. Molly should be home soon. Do you want me to make you some supper? How about some fried chicken, with salad and French fries?'

'No, no. I'm good. I had lunch at Nick and Tony's with a guy from Brussels. Euro Investments . . . they're looking for a foothold here in the States.'

'Trevor—'

'Yes?'

She wanted to tell him how special he was, and how special Molly was, and Victoria, too, but for some reason she couldn't find the words. She was feeling protective, but she didn't think that Trevor would appreciate her mothering him, not right now. He was a man, after all. Whatever happened to him or his family, he had to take care of them the way he thought best.

'Don't say I'm just like Dad,' said Trevor. 'You always say that, but Dad was Dad and I'm me. Dad took risks. I only calculate them.'

'I was only going to tell you that I'm proud of you. Is that such a crime?'

He held her close. It made her aware of how frail and ribby she was. 'No, that's not a crime.'

Victoria said, 'Giants *must* be real, don't you think? If they're not real, who made them up, and why did everybody believe them?'

'If I knew the answer to that, honey,' said Trevor, 'I'd be a very wealthy man.'

About ten minutes later, Molly arrived home, looking pale and fractured. She lifted her fringed satchel over her head and hung it over the back of a kitchen chair.

'Boy, I am *totally* pooped. Drawing that Red Mask . . . for some reason it took *so* much out of me.'

'Well, he's not a very pleasant character to think about, is he?' said Sissy. 'Leave alone *draw*.'

'I don't know. It was more than that. It was like he was staring at me out of my sketchpad and saying, "Go on, then, let's see how much life you can breathe into me."'

'How about a glass of wine?' asked Sissy.

'No, I think I'll take a shower first. I feel kind of *tainted*, you know, like he's been pawing me.'

'He's only a drawing, hon,' said Trevor. 'You shouldn't let yourself get so upset.'

'I know . . . but while I was drawing him, I kept thinking – OK, that's it, I've finished. But then I felt like I had to shade his eyebrows some more, and thicken his hair, and change the expression in his eyes. By the time I *was* finished, he looked so much younger – and, like, *pleased* with himself. And pleased with *me*, too.'

Sissy took hold of her hand. 'Come on, sweetheart. It was really traumatic, what we saw today, all of those people dead. And in a way – when you were drawing him – it was like you were face to face with the man who murdered them, wasn't it?'

'I guess so. Yes, it felt like that.'

Trevor put his arm around her shoulders and gave her a squeeze. 'From now on, you stick to drawing fairies, OK?'

'OK,' Molly smiled. Then she said, 'Victoria – did you finish your homework?'

'Yes! It was cool. It was all about cicadas. I *love* cicadas.'

'I'm glad somebody does. They're starting to fly already, and when the police officer was driving me home, they kept going *splatter-splatter-splatter* all over the windshield.'

Without taking a breath, Victoria said, 'Cicadas live underground for seventeen years, feeding on the sap from tree roots. Then they tunnel their way out so that they can reproduce. They have yellow skins, which are very tough. The men cicadas make their mating calls by flexing their stomachs and some of them are as loud as a hundred decibels.'

'What about the women cicadas?' asked Sissy.

'They never make any noise at all.'

'See?' said Trevor. 'The perfect species.'

'After they mate, the men cicadas drop down dead.'

'I agree with you,' said Molly. 'The perfect species.'

She turned to leave the kitchen, and it was then that she noticed the vase of roses on the hutch. She gave Sissy a quick, quizzical look and said, 'Did *you* cut these roses?'

'Trevor did,' said Sissy, as calmly as she could. 'Pretty, aren't they?'

'Strange thing was,' said Trevor, 'I never even noticed them growing.'

'Really?' asked Molly. 'I don't know how you could have missed them.'

'Well, *I* never noticed them, either,' said Victoria.

Molly lifted up the vase and gently touched the roses' petals, stroking them between finger and thumb. Sissy could tell that she was upset. These were a miracle, created out of pencil and ink, not just a table decoration.

Sissy looked at her wryly. *Miracles are miracles, Molly. If we knew how they happened, they wouldn't be miracles. They would only be tricks.*

Strange Chorus

That night, Sissy dreamed that she was driving across Iowa again, in her uncle Henry's Hudson Hornet. The radio was playing that strange, lumpy, backward-sounding music, and outside the windows the landscape was revolving like a huge turntable.

'Uncle Henry?'

But Uncle Henry didn't turn around. He just kept on driving, tapping his wedding band on the steering wheel in time to the music. *I saw you yesterday . . . you were standing by the wall . . . I thought I recognized you but I didn't, not at all . . .*

The clouds were sepia, as if they were driving through an old photograph. Sissy could see a dark shadow on the eastern horizon – a shadow which rose higher and higher, like a swarm of locusts. Locusts, or cicadas.

I was quite certain that I recognized your face . . . but when you turned your head around I saw nothing, only space . . .

About a half-mile up ahead, she saw a huge figure standing by the side of the road, silhouetted against the last pale wash of daylight. It must have been all of thirty feet tall. She knelt up on her seat and tapped Uncle Henry frantically on the shoulder.

'Uncle Henry. There's a giant. I'm frightened of giants.'

Uncle Henry didn't answer.

'Uncle Henry! Please! Can't we go back?'

Insects started to patter against the windows, leaving brown-and-yellow splashes and broken wing segments, which fluttered in the Hornet's slipstream.

'Uncle Henry!'

At last Uncle Henry turned his head around. But it wasn't Uncle Henry. It was Red Mask, with a triumphant shine in his eyes.

'No peace for the wicked, child! No mercy for the innocent, neither! What's done is done, and can't be undone!'

The insects pattered against the windows, harder and harder, until they sounded like hail. 'Uncle Henry' kept on driving, but he didn't turn back to see where he was going. He just kept grinning at Sissy, as if he were daring her to try and stop him.

Sissy let out a piercing scream. She screamed louder and louder and higher and higher, but all 'Uncle Henry' did was to roar back at her, just as loud, until she was deafened. The song on the radio stopped, and the interior of the car was filled with screeching, high-pitched static.

She opened her eyes. She wasn't screaming any more, and 'Uncle Henry' was gone, but the static continued, on and on, interspersed with weird swooping sounds.

'My God,' she said to herself. 'The cicadas.'

She climbed unsteadily out of bed and opened her blinds, lifting one hand to shield her eyes from the early-morning sunshine.

The yard was crowded with thousands of cicadas, all calling for their mates. Most of them were still clinging to the trees and the bushes, but scores of them were flying around, and some of them were pattering against her windows, as they had in her dream.

Molly came into her room, wearing a pink silk headscarf and a pink nightshirt. 'Got your wake-up call, then?' she smiled.

'I never realized they were going to be so goddamned *loud*. I don't know how you stand it.'

'At least it happens only once every seventeen years. They have a joke in Cincinnati – two cicadas sitting in a bar, and one says to the other, "Seventeen years wasted if we don't get lucky tonight."'

Sissy said, 'How about I make us some coffee? And maybe some eggs. We didn't eat anything yesterday, did we?'

'Sure, that would be terrific.'

They went through to the kitchen. Mr Boots was still asleep in his basket. The cicada chorus didn't seem to bother him at all. Outside, cicadas were clustered all around the window frames. Trevor had sealed up the ventilator above the cooker hob with a circle of cardboard and several layers of duct tape. He had also attached a cardboard flap to the bottom of the back door, and duct taped over the keyhole.

Molly opened the fridge. She took out a carton of cranberry and pomegranate juice and poured a glass for each of them. As she was about to drink it, she said, 'What did you do with the roses?'

Sissy turned toward the hutch. The glass vase was still there, but all it contained were two drooping ferns. She shook her head and said, 'I haven't touched them.'

'Neither have I. Maybe Victoria took them. She's crazy about brides and weddings at the moment. I'll bet she wanted her Barbie to have a bouquet.'

Sissy spooned coffee into the percolator. 'You're still not going to tell Trevor where they came from?'

'I don't see what good it would do.'

'I don't really see what *harm* it would do.'

'Oh come on, Sissy. You know Trevor. He needs to be in control of things. That's why he doesn't like your fortune-telling cards. They're not logical and he doesn't understand how they work. If I told him that I could create real flowers just by drawing them . . . it would make him so wary of me. He would feel like there was a part of me that he could never reach, and I don't want him to feel like that.'

Sissy switched on the percolator. 'I think I'll brave the bugs and go for a cigarette.'

'Well, they're disgusting, and they're noisy, but they won't hurt you. Just don't let them get caught up in your hair.'

'Don't! Maybe they'll do what Frank and Trevor never could, and persuade me to give up smoking.'

Wrapped up in her green satin bathrobe, and wearing Trevor's adidas running shoes in case she trod on any cicadas, Sissy went outside, with Mr Boots following close behind. Here in the yard, the mating chorus was even harsher and even higher, and the swooping noise sounded even more weird, like a musical saw.

She flapped a few of the cicadas away with her hand, but one of them persisted in perching on her shoulder, prickling her with its tiny claws, and staring at her with its scarlet, wide-apart eyes.

'My God, look at *you*,' she said. 'You must have been feeding on sap from the ugly tree.'

She lit a cigarette and blew smoke at the cicada, and it whirred away, flying only an inch away from Mr Boots's nose. Mr Boots snapped at it, but only because it had surprised him. He had tried to eat a wasp once, and ever since then he had treated anything that buzzed or hopped or chirruped with the utmost caution.

The radio-static noise went on and on, and Sissy couldn't stop thinking about her dream. She very rarely had recurring dreams, and even when she did, it had been months or even years in between each dreaming. She had to assume that this was more than a dream, it was a warning, or an omen – either from her own subconscious, or from somebody else's spirit. The giant standing by the road could be some kind of a symbol. But a symbol of *what*? And why did he seem so terrifying?

A flurry of cicadas flew up in front of her, like the locusts in her dream. And it was then that she saw the flowerpots on which they had been feeding. The five roses were standing there, nodding in the morning sunshine, along with the hollyhock and the Shasta daisy. They were all intact, as if Trevor had never cut them.

Sissy felt a tight shrinking sensation in her scalp. These roses couldn't be real roses, after all. They must be something else altogether. A mirage? An hallucination? She couldn't understand it.

'Molly!' she called. 'Come out here! What the *hell* do you make of this?'

Molly stared at the roses for a long time. 'I don't know. How could that happen?' She took hold of one of the stems and tugged at it. 'It's firmly rooted, just like it was before.'

Sissy looked around, frowning. 'When you painted them, did you imagine them here – in this particular flowerpot?'

'Yes, I did. Even this first rose, the one I was painting for *Fairy Fifi*.'

'Maybe they *have* to come back here, because this is the only place that they really exist.'

'I don't know what you mean.'

'Well, neither do I, to be frank. But let's try something. Let's cut them again, and see if they come back here a second time.'

Molly looked dubious. 'Maybe we should just leave them alone. This whole thing is beginning to give me the willies.'

'Molly – think of what the cards predicted. Violence, and bloodshed. And you could be involved in it somehow. The sculptor, the artist, the creator of likenesses – that's almost certainly *you*.'

'Maybe Trevor was right. Maybe I shouldn't have done that Red Mask composite.'

'I really don't know. But I still think that the roses are the key to all this. If we can understand how and why these flowers come to life, it may help us to keep you safe.'

Mr Boots was chasing after cicadas, jumping up and down at them as they scattered into the air, but being careful not to catch any in his mouth.

'OK,' said Molly. 'I'll bring some scissors.'

Sissy smoked while Molly cut the roses again. They took them back inside and arranged them in the vase in the same way that they had been arranged before. They had just put them back on the hutch when Trevor came in, his black hair tousled, yawning.

'First chance I get for a couple of hours' extra sleep and what do I get? Ten thousand horny cicadas singing outside my window.'

'Your mom's making eggs. Do you want some?'

'Coffee first. Black. I need to jumpstart my heart.'

Killing Time

Chrissie Wells climbed out of the back of the taxi and caught her purse on the door handle. As she struggled to disentangle it, she dropped her cell phone and the folder of papers that she was carrying under her arm. The morning breeze caught them and blew them across the sidewalk.

When she had managed to untwist her purse and pick up her cell phone, she frantically gathered up her scattered papers, bending over again and again like a dipping bird, until she split the seam at the back of her red cotton skirt. The taxi driver waited for her with an expression on his face like St Sebastian, martyred with a hundred arrows.

Chrissie fumbled in her purse, took out a twenty and accidentally dropped a shower of loose coins on to the taxi's front seat. The taxi driver gave her a ten and said, 'Don't worry about a tip, miss. I'll pick it up later, off the floor.'

As usual, Chrissie was running late. She always seemed to be running late, no matter how early she set her alarm. She felt that she had been born out of synch with the rest of the planet – fated to miss every bus she wanted to catch and every appointment she was supposed to keep. She never arrived at concerts on time, and had to wait in the foyer until the interval. She was always hurrying, always hot, always out of breath, and still she couldn't catch up.

She bustled up the steps of the Giley Building but she was stopped in the entrance by two police officers.

'Morning, ma'am. Need some ID, if that's OK.'

'ID?'

'Driver's license. Anything like that.'

Chrissie opened her purse and dropped her file of papers again. One of the officers bent down and picked it up for her. She rooted through every compartment inside her purse and finally managed to pull out her Cincinnati Public Library card.

'OK, that'll do it,' said the officer. 'You don't look much like a serial killer anyhow.'

'You haven't found him yet? I didn't have time to catch the news this morning.'

'No, ma'am. But we will. You can be damn sure of that.'

Chrissie pushed her way through the revolving doors. All three elevators were working now, and the left-hand elevator still had its doors open. Chrissie called out, 'Hold it, please! Hold it!' and click-clacked her way across the lobby. By the time she had reached the elevator, however, more than a dozen people had crowded into it, and there was no more room, especially for a size fourteen.

The occupants of the elevator stared at her balefully, as if to say, don't even *think* about trying to squeeze your way in. Then the doors closed, and they were gone.

Chrissie pressed the button for another elevator. As she did so, she was joined by five more office workers, secretaries and junior executives, two of them carrying cappuccinos, and one of them holding a brown paper bag which smelled strongly of hot pastrami.

'I'm not too happy about this,' said one of the cappuccino-carriers.

'You're not too happy about what, for Christ's sake?' his friend gibed him.

'You know—' and the cappuccino-carrier nodded toward the elevator doors and made a stabbing gesture in the air.

'Oh, come on,' said his friend. 'The cops went through this entire building with a fine-tooth comb. The guy's probably three states away by now.'

To her horror, Chrissie saw her boss coming in through the revolving doors. Elaine Vickers, dark and sleek and black-suited and highly unforgiving. By now, Chrissie was supposed to be up in the conference room, with all of her paperwork prepared and the page proofs for next season's catalog all laid out. And herbal tea on the table, too, with Elaine's favorite wafer-thin almond biscuits.

She pushed the elevator button again and again. The elevator indicator read four, three, two and then stopped. *Please, God, hurry*, Chrissie prayed. She could see that Elaine had stopped to talk to two women in the middle of the lobby. If the elevator arrived now, she might just miss it, and Chrissie could get to the conference room with seconds to spare.

The elevator doors opened. Inside, there were two technicians from the elevator company, with part of an electric motor on a trolley. They maneuvered it around, slowly and awkwardly, while one of them held the doors open. *Please God, hurry*. Elaine had finished her conversation now, and was walking toward the elevator bank with her usual fashion-runway prowl, one stiletto shoe in front of the other.

The technicians managed to trundle their trolley out of the elevator, and Chrissie immediately stepped on, followed by the other five office workers. Elaine was less than thirty feet away now. 'Twenty-one, please,' she told the man with the brown paper bag.

Elaine raised her hand, and the man with the brown paper bag kept his finger on the 'Open Doors' button. Chrissie stared at the back of his neck and thought, *You are going to die for this. You are going to die for this and go to hell.*

'Twenty-one, please,' said Elaine, as she stepped inside. The doors closed, and the elevator began to rise. Chrissie stayed right at the back of the car, trying to keep herself concealed behind one of the cappuccino-carriers. But when she turned sideways, she realized that Elaine could clearly see her in one of the mirrors.

She thought, *Positive action. Don't show Elaine that you're intimidated.* She excused herself and jostled her way around the cappuccino-carrier.

'Good morning, Elaine.'

Elaine's scarlet lips puckered up until they looked like a poisonous rosebud. One eyebrow arched.

'How was *your* traffic this morning?' Chrissie asked her, trying hard to sound nonchalant. 'The I-75 Bridge – what a nightmare. My taxi didn't move for over twenty minutes.'

'I live in Mount Adams, if you remember,' said Elaine. 'I don't use bridges.'

'Oh, so you do. Right next door to Vidal Sassoon. And *Mrs* Vidal Sassoon.'

'How long will it take you to get the presentation ready?' asked Elaine.

'Fifteen minutes, tops. It's shaping up so well. The cardigan range . . . I have three fabulous new colors to show you.'

Elaine turned to stare at her directly. Her eyes were unblinking. Very quietly, so that nobody else in the elevator could hear her, she said, 'This can't go on, Chrissie. You know that as well as I do.'

'Elaine—'

'Every time you're late, Chrissie, every time you miss a meeting, that's an act of disrespect to everybody you work with. We respect you. Why don't you respect us?'

Chrissie's mouth opened and closed. 'It's *time*,' she said. 'I don't know. No matter what I do, it refuses to behave itself.'

'*Time* won't behave itself?' Elaine repeated.

'The clock jumps, when I'm not looking. It's three thirty. I look up five minutes later, and it's almost five. And I'm sure my watch goes faster than anybody else's.'

Elaine was about to say something when the elevator came to a stop, and the doors slid open. The corridor outside looked dark and deserted.

'Fourteenth floor, anybody?' asked the man with the brown paper bag.

'Nineteenth, I want,' said a tall black man.

'Nothing here, anyhow,' said one of the cappuccino-carriers, peering out. 'This used to be Atlas Carriers, before they moved out.'

The man with the brown paper bag pressed the button for nineteen. The doors closed again, and the elevator continued to rise. But this time it didn't stop at all.

'Hey, I said the nineteenth!' the black man protested.

'I pressed it for the nineteenth. It should have stopped.'

The black man pushed his way forward and jabbed the button. No matter how hard he jabbed it, however, the elevator continued to rise smoothly upward – twenty-two, twenty-three, twenty-four – all the way up to the twenty-fifth floor, where it stopped. The doors, however, didn't open.

'This goddamned building,' said one of the cappuccino-carriers. 'We should sue the managers, you know that? They must have broken every safety regulation in the book.'

'Use the emergency phone,' said Elaine. The black man opened the hatch and took out the red receiver. He held it up to show her. The wire was cut.

One of the cappuccino-carriers handed his cup to his friend, and took out his cell phone. 'These building managers . . . when I take them to court, they're going to go bankrupt, I'm telling you. I'm going to sue them for everything. Criminal negligence, false imprisonment, you name it.'

He prodded at his cell phone and held it to his ear. 'No goddamned signal. Anybody else got a signal?'

They all took out their cell phones, but none of them showed any reception.

'Isn't that just wizard! We're stuck here until somebody realizes that we haven't showed up for work! And knowing *my* secretary, that will take till lunchtime!'

Elaine said, 'Isn't there a way to force these doors open?'

'With what, exactly?'

'Well, let's bang on them, and shout. Somebody must hear us.'

'OK. Let's bang on them, and shout.'

The tall black man clenched his fists and hammered on the doors. 'Help!' he bellowed. 'Help! We're trapped in the elevator! Help!'

The rest of them joined in, although they were embarrassed by the different pitches in their voices.

'Christ,' said the man with the brown bag. 'We sound like a crateful of frightened chickens.'

'Wait,' said the black man, lifting up his hand. They waited, and listened, but there was no response. Only the moaning of the wind down the hoistway, and the sad, distracted singing of the elevator cables. A distant echo of elevator doors, opening and closing, and *hummmmm.*

'OK – let's try it again.'

He hammered on the doors with even more fury. 'Help! We're trapped in the elevator! Help!'

They listened again, but still nobody answered.

'This is *ridiculous*!' snapped Elaine, but she sounded more frightened than angry.

At that moment, the elevator gave a violent jerk, and dropped downward two or three feet, and then stopped. All of them cried out in alarm, and one of the secretaries burst into tears. 'Let me out! Let me *out*! I have to get out!'

'It's OK,' the black man reassured her. 'All elevators have emergency brakes. They can never drop all the way down.'

'Well, that makes me feel a whole lot better – *not*,' said one of the cappuccino-carriers.

The elevator gave another jerk, and dropped a further two feet, and then another, and another. With each jerk, they all shouted out, in a terrible off-key chorus.

Chrissie had wanted to go to the bathroom even before she had arrived at the Giley Building, and now she wet herself. Only a little, but enough to make her feel even more terrified and out of control.

'We need to shout again and go on shouting,' said Elaine.

The black man yelled out, 'Get us out of here! Get us out of here!' and thumped on the doors with both fists, denting the metal.

The elevator dropped at least fifteen feet, and then stopped with a sickening thump, sending them all sprawling and splashing hot coffee all over them. Before they could manage to stand up, it dropped again, and stopped; and then again. They had no choice but to crouch on the floor on their hands and knees, while the elevator took them down and down in a series of staccato jolts – sometimes six inches and sometimes as much as twenty feet. By the time they were down to the ninth floor, they had stopped shouting and moaning and crying for help. They simply knelt on the floor, grim-faced, each of them silently praying that the elevator would reach ground level without dropping too fast.

They passed eight – seven – six – five. Just past five, they dropped over thirty feet, all the way down to the third story, and when the elevator came – *bang!* – to a halt, Chrissie was flung against one of the junior executives and knocked her forehead against his teeth. Blood ran into her eyes, so that she could hardly see.

The elevator fell past three – two – one, but as it did so it slowed down to a shuddering crawl. When it reached basement level it was sinking so gradually that they hardly felt it come to a standstill.

'We've stopped,' said the black man. 'Thank God we've stopped.'

They clambered to their feet. One of the junior executives pressed the button for the doors to open, but they stayed firmly closed.

'Now we should shout,' said the black man. 'They must be able to hear us down here.'

'*Help!*' shrilled out one of the secretaries. '*Help, let us out of here!*'

But then, quite unexpectedly, the doors slid open. There was a split second's hesitation and then a figure in red rushed into the elevator with two butcher knives in his upraised hands, chopping and stabbing at them in a frenzy. They staggered back, screaming, tumbling over each other in confusion. But the figure kept on stabbing and hacking until blood was flying everywhere, like a dark red rainstorm.

Bloodbath

At almost the same time, in the new Four Days Mall on Fountain Square West, Marshall Willis and his fiancée Dawn Priennik were leaning over the counter at Newman's Jewelry, trying to decide which wedding bands to buy.

Marshall favored a wide band with diamond-shaped facets on it, 'so it kind of catches the light,' while Dawn preferred a thinner band with alternating twists of yellow and white gold.

'There's no law which stipulates that a married couple are obliged to wear matching bands,' said the jewelry store assistant, his bald head gleaming under the spotlights. 'After all, sir's fingers are very generously sized. Compared to madam's, that is.'

It wasn't only Marshall's fingers that were generously sized. He was generously sized all over – six feet three inches tall with a rugged head that looked as if it had been hacked in a hurry out of hardwood, a massive neck, and a chest as deep as a bison's.

Dawn, on the other hand, was tiny – only five feet two inches tall, with long shiny chestnut hair and a round, Kewpie-Doll face. She had long black eyelashes which blinked like hummingbirds, especially when she was excited. Her two most prominent features were her breasts, which filled her little pink vest to bursting point. Marshall had paid for her breast enlargement last April, as a birthday gift. Dawn's mother, disgusted, had said that it was a gift for himself, rather than her.

'I'm pretty much set on matching bands,' said Marshall. 'When you have matching bands, it shows people, like, we totally belong to each other.'

'But we *know* we totally belong to each other. Why do we need to prove it to anybody else?'

Marshall slowly shook his head. Now he was showing his dark, possessive side. He had given Dawn much bigger breasts, but if he caught any man ogling her, he would instantly confront him. 'You checking out my girl? Well, take a good look, dude, because that's the last thing on this earth you're ever going to see.' And if Dawn even smiled at anybody else, he would slap her when he took her home and accuse her of acting like a 'two-bit back-alley whore.' He would always apologize afterward. He would always bring her flowers. But he would always do it again.

'Maybe we should go for a latte or something and talk it over,' Dawn suggested. She could see that Marshall was working himself up into one of his gnarly moods – moods which he always blamed on everybody else. 'Now look what you fricking made me do!' he always used to protest, after he had kicked over the television or thrown his supper up against the wall or grabbed Dawn so hard that he had bruised her upper arms.

Dawn's mother said that Dawn was crazy to marry him – crazy. He was a brute. Worse than that, he was a childish brute. But Dawn loved him and knew how gentle and thoughtful he could be. He *was* childish, yes. But that made her all the more determined to protect him. It wasn't his fault that the world was so much against him.

They left the jewelry store and walked across the balcony toward the elevators. The Four Days Mall was only eighteen months old. It was shiny and marble-clad and smelled of women's perfume and new leather belts, and the aroma of freshly-ground coffee. The central atrium rose five stories to a clear glass ceiling, so that the center was flooded in brilliant natural sunlight, and everything sparkled. Four floors below them, a stainless-steel fountain represented the *Orleans*, the first steamboat to sail up the Ohio River to Cincinnati, in 1811.

Four glass-walled elevators slid up and down the outside of the building, giving their occupants vertiginous views down to Race Street and Seventh Street. From the top floor, they could even see the river, which glittered in the morning sun, and Covington, Kentucky, on the opposite side.

The doors of the nearest elevator opened and Marshall and Dawn stepped on to it. Dawn immediately went to the rail and peered down at the traffic below. 'Look! They're like little toy cars!'

'Oh, really?' said Marshall. He had never liked heights, and he stayed well back.

For a few seconds they had the elevator to themselves, but just before the doors closed, a crowd of eight or nine noisy teenagers piled their way into it, hooting and laughing and jostling each other.

One of the boys had a pale spotty face and a Cincinnati Reds baseball cap with the long black peak turned sideways. He produced a pink girl's thong from out of his sweatshirt pocket and whirled it in the air. It still had the price labels attached. 'Hey – see what I just boosted!'

'Oh, *Mikey*!' shrilled one of the girls. 'Aren't you going to try it on for us?'

Another boy wrapped his arm around Mikey's shoulders and said, 'You never told us you were a cross-dresser, Mikey! I woulda bought you a peephole bra for your birthday, instead of that T-shirt!'

'Get outta here, Tyler, it's a present for Linda.'

'Oh, *sure* – Linda! I'll bet she got tired of you wearing her panties, that's all, so you had to buy some of your own!'

'Hey, cool it, guys,' said Marshall. 'We got a lady in here.'

The boy in the Cincinnati Reds cap swiveled his head around, mouth open, blinking. 'Lady? Where? Where? I don't see no lady.'

Marshall grabbed hold of the front of the boy's sweatshirt, and almost lifted him off his feet. 'Don't get funny with me, punk. This lady is my fiancée, OK? And you treat her with respect.'

The other teenagers, far from being intimidated, started to jeer. 'You hear dat, punk? Dis lady is my fy-ance!'

Marshall swiveled around to confront them, still gripping the boy's sweatshirt. 'You want trouble, you dickweed? Is that what you want? Believe me, I can give you trouble.'

'*Woooooooo!*' the teenagers howled at him.

Dawn said, 'Come on, Marshall, leave the kid alone. He didn't do nothing.'

'Yeah, Marshall!' said the boy in the Cincinnati Reds cap. 'Leave the kid alone. I mean, who do you think you are, Marshall? The Incredible Bulk?'

Marshall shoved the boy so that he lost his balance and slammed against the opposite wall of the elevator car.

'Hey, you psycho!' yelled one of the teenagers.

Marshall shoved him, too, and he staggered back against the rest of the teenagers, and one of the girls fell against the window, bruising her shoulder.

'Marshall!' Dawn pleaded, frantically tugging at his arm. 'Marshall, leave them alone!'

The boy in the Cincinnati Reds cap pointed his finger at Marshall and shouted, in his half-broken voice, 'That's it, man! I'm going to call the zoo, man, and have you put back where you belong! In with the goddamned gorillas!'

Marshall gripped the boy's sweatshirt again, and shook him. As he did so, the elevator reached the third floor and the doors opened. A crowd of shoppers was waiting to get on, fathers and mothers and children carrying balloons. But when they saw Marshall and the boy struggling together, they all held back.

One of the teenage boys shouted, 'Let's get out of here, man!' and a girl screamed, 'Call the cops! Somebody call the cops! This guy's gone crazy!'

Before any of them could move, however, a bulky man in a black suit shouldered his way through the crowd of shoppers and stepped on to the elevator, pushing the button for the first floor. A smart young woman, emboldened, tried to follow him, but the man held his arm out to keep her back. '*Hey!*' she said, but the doors closed, and the elevator continued on its way downward.

The man looked at Marshall, and then at Dawn, and then at

each of the teenagers, very deliberately, as if he were sizing them up. His face was so red that it looked sunburned, or varnished, and he had bristly red hair. His eyes and his mouth were like slits cut into a Japanese mask. He was shorter than Marshall, and not so bulky, but he had an almost tangible aura of menace about him. Marshall relinquished his hold on the spotty boy's sweatshirt and took a cautious step back, with his hands held up in surrender.

'Just a little disagreement, man. Nothing to get worked up about.'

'He attacked me!' put in the spotty boy. 'He was going to frigging kill me!'

The man stared at Marshall, expressionless.

'And you're – what?' Marshall asked him. 'Security or something?'

'Security?' asked the man, in a hoarse, foggy whisper. 'You should be so lucky.'

'Then what? These kids were disrespecting my fiancée, and I was teaching them a lesson, that's all. Not only that, they've been shoplifting. You don't believe me? Make them turn out their pockets.'

'Do you think I care?'

One of the teenage boys pointed at Marshall and said, 'This guy's a nut! You going to arrest him? He started pushing us around for no reason at all!'

But Marshall was confused. 'I don't get it, man. If you're not security, who the hell are you?'

'You wouldn't believe me if I told you.'

Dawn was clinging to Marshall's arm and she wasn't going to let him go. She had suddenly realized where she had seen the man's face before, on the TV news.

'*Marshall!*' she breathed. '*It's him!*'

Marshall wasn't listening to her. He was too busy challenging the red-faced man. 'What? Come on, man. What the two-toned hell is going down here?'

'It's the Red Mask guy!' Dawn hissed at him, but Marshall still wasn't giving her his full attention.

'You want to know what's going down?' grinned the red-faced man. 'More of the same. More of the same! *That's* what's going down.'

'More of the same frigging *what*?'

'You should lock him up!' said one of the girls. 'You should lock him up and throw away the key!'

'Hey – what's done is done,' the red-faced man interrupted her. 'But that doesn't mean we can't seek retribution, does it? You make your bed, you gotta lie in it. No rest for the wicked. Not ever. No forgiveness for the innocent, neither.'

'What the hell are you talking about?' Marshall challenged him.

Dawn said, 'Please . . . we don't want to make any trouble. None of us. Let's all get out of the elevator and forget it, what do you think?'

'What do I *think*?' said the red-faced man. 'What do *I* think? I'll tell you what I think. Now is the time for a little natural justice. Now is the time and today is the day for the settling of old scores. Wouldn't you agree?'

'I don't understand what you mean,' Dawn told him. 'I'm sorry, but I just don't. What justice? What old scores? We don't even know you!'

With a sharp squeal, the elevator came to a halt, halfway between the third and second floors.

'Hey!' Marshall protested. 'We want to get the hell out of here, that's all.'

'Come on, man,' said the boy in the Cincinnati Reds cap. 'If this guy is willing to forget it, then we will, OK? Just let us out.'

The red-faced man said, 'Sorry, folks. This is the end of the ride. For you, anyhow.'

He crossed his arms, reaching inside the left-hand side of his coat with his right hand, and the right-hand side of his coat with his left. There was a moment in which all of time seemed to stand still, and even sound was suspended, too. Marshall suddenly thought, *Cross-draw, like an old-time gunslinger.*

With a harsh metallic *zhhinnggg*! the red-faced man drew out of his coat two huge triangular-bladed knives, and held them high above his head.

'Come on, man,' said Marshall. 'This has stopped being amusing, OK?' He took a step toward the red-faced man, with one hand lifted.

Dawn screamed out, 'Marshall! No! He's the Red Mask guy!'

But she was a fraction of a second too late. As Marshall turned his head, the red-faced man stabbed him straight through the middle of his upraised palm. Then, without hesitation, he stabbed him in the shoulder.

The teenagers shouted out, 'Whoa!' and 'Jesus!' and one of the girls let out such a high-pitched scream that it was almost beyond the range of human hearing. Dawn clung to Marshall's arm and said, 'Marshall? *Marshall*!' but then the right side of her face was suddenly sprayed in blood.

The red-faced man stabbed Marshall again and again – his hands, his arms, his shoulders. Marshall grunted with every stab, but although he was so badly wounded, he lunged forward with his head down and football-tackled the red-faced man around the hips, hugging him tight.

The red-faced man didn't hesitate. He stabbed Marshall in the back of the neck, between the atlas and the axis vertebrae, with an audible *chop* that severed his spinal cord. Marshall dropped heavily on to the floor, and the red-faced man turned around to face the rest of them, whirling his knives in both hands.

The teenagers were going mad with panic, shouting and beating on the doors and climbing up on to the handrail. Dawn backed away from the red-faced man, shuddering with fear, until she was pressed up against the window. He stepped over Marshall's body and approached her, with both knives raised.

'Don't hurt me,' she begged him.

'What? Couldn't quite hear you, darling, what with all these squealing piglets in here.'

'Please don't hurt me. I only came here to choose my wedding band.'

The boy in the Cincinnati Reds cap was trying to edge his way round behind the red-faced man, but the red-faced man quickly turned and jabbed at him with one of his knives. 'Going someplace, kid? Weren't thinking of *jumping* me, were you, by any chance?'

'No! *No*. We just want to get out of here, sir! We don't want to die!'

'Nobody ever does, kid. Nobody ever does. But if you're brought to life, no matter how, that's the only destiny that's open to you, in the end. No wonder folks rail at God, for their existence.'

'Please don't hurt me,' said Dawn. Tears were running down her cheeks, streaked with black mascara. 'I promise I won't give evidence against you. I promise. I'll say that it was all Marshall's fault. He provoked you. He attacked you. He was like that, always angry. Always setting on people.'

The red-faced man appeared to think for a moment, although his slitted eyes gave nothing away.

'How old are you?' he asked Dawn. He had to raise his voice to make himself heard over the whimpering, weeping teenagers.

'Eighteen and a half,' said Dawn. She managed a sloping, hopeful smile, as if the red-faced man would let her live if he realized how young she was.

'Eighteen and a half,' the red-faced man repeated. Then he said, '*Freak!*' and stabbed her in the chest with both knives. Her implants burst, and the right-hand knife penetrated her heart.

She stared at him for a moment as if she couldn't understand what had happened to her. Then he wrenched out both knives and let her drop to the floor.

Ned Jennings was walking along Seventh Street taking photographs when he looked up and noticed the red glass elevator.

Ned was an arts student from Xavier University, curly-haired, with thick-rimmed eyeglasses and a fawn corduroy coat. He was compiling a photographic study of Cincinnati's art-deco architecture. He had already photographed the Union Terminal and the Lazarus Building and several office buildings, and he was trying to make up his mind if he should include pictures of the Four Days Mall, since the architects had deliberately embellished the frontage with art-deco-style brickwork, as a tribute to Cincinnati's architectural glory days.

He looked up and saw that one of the glass elevators that ran up and down the exterior of Four Days Mall was stopped between floors. Not only that, all of its windows were streaked with red, as if somebody inside it were furiously painting them.

He was about to carry on walking when the palms of two white hands appeared through the paint, pressed hard against the glass. Then half of a face appeared, too. A young girl, it looked like, and although Ned couldn't hear, her mouth was wide open as if she were screaming. She was only visible for two or three seconds, then she disappeared, leaving two smeary handprints and a distorted impression of her right cheek.

Ned hesitated. He couldn't work out what he had actually seen. Vandals? Some kind of promotional stunt? But who would vandalize a glass elevator in broad daylight? And if it was a promotional stunt, what was it meant to promote?

If he hadn't seen that girl's hands and face, he would have walked on. But he entered the mall and approached two security guards who were standing by the *Orleans* fountain, chatting to three young women.

'I think something weird is happening in one of your elevators.'

One of the security guards cupped his hand to his ear. 'You think what?' The mall was echoing with piped music and the footsteps of hundreds of shoppers and the clattering of water in the fountain.

'It looks like somebody's painting the windows with red paint. And I think there's a girl trapped inside there who's in some kind of trouble.'

'Red paint? What do you mean, red paint?'

'Well, I don't know. It *looks* like red paint.'

'OK. Which elevator?'

The security guards walked over to the elevator bank with Ned following close behind them. A small knot of shoppers were gathered outside the right-hand elevator, and as the security guards approached, an elderly man in Bermuda shorts said, 'Out of order. Looks like it's stuck between floors.'

One of the security guards went up to the elevator doors and pressed the button. There was a juddering noise, but nothing happened.

'Better call Wally,' he told his colleague.

'Maybe you should phone the police,' Ned suggested. 'I couldn't exactly see what was happening in there, but this girl looked really upset.'

'George, why don't you go outside and take a look?'

Ned said, 'At first I thought it might be some kind of advertising display.'

'Unh-hunh. Nobody told me about no advertising display, and if nobody told me about no advertising display, then there ain't no advertising display.'

One of the security guards walked out into the street, but as he did so the elevator's indicator light suddenly blinked three and two and then one.

'George! It's OK! It's working now!'

They waited for the doors to open, but after a short pause the elevator continued down to P1, which was the first parking level. The security guard pushed the button again, however, and the indicator showed it coming back up again.

There was another pause, longer this time, but then the elevator doors opened. Inside, it glowed a dull crimson, like a small hexagonal chapel with red stained glass windows.

The security guard stepped forward, and then he stopped and said, 'Holy Mother of God!' The floor of the elevator car was heaped with bodies. Arms and legs all tangled together, so that it was almost impossible to tell how many people had been killed, except for their faces, which were pale and serious, like medieval saints.

Behind the Mirror

A little after 11 a.m., a heavy bank of charcoal-gray clouds passed over Cincinnati from the south-west, very low, and a warm rain started to fall.

'At least it keeps the bugs from flying,' said Molly, as they drove along I-71 toward the Avondale turnoff. All the same, when she turned on the wipers, there were enough splattered cicadas on the windshield to smear it with two semicircles of brown and yellow viscera.

Sissy said, 'I wish I could shake off this feeling.'

'What feeling?'

'I don't know. It's not what you'd call a premonition. It's more like "What's wrong with this picture?" – as if there's something out of place, and it's right in front of my nose, but I can't see it for looking.'

Molly was wearing a black silk headscarf tied around her head pirate-fashion, with small silver coins dangling from it. Sissy thought that she looked more like the young Mia Farrow than ever. Sissy herself had dressed in a long-sleeved crimson dress, with large red chrysanthemums all over it. She wore long dangly earrings, which Frank had always called her 'chandeliers.'

Molly said, 'Don't tell me. You read the cards again before we came out?'

'I was just wanted an update.'

'OK. And?'

'They're still saying the same. The Warning, the Game of Hide-and-Go-Seek. And the Blood Card, too.'

'No new clues?'

Sissy shook her head. 'I've never known the cards be so unhelpful. It's like somebody saying to you, "Don't go out tomorrow, whatever you do, you'll regret it," but refusing to tell you why.'

They turned off I-71 and made their way toward Riddle Road. It rained harder and harder, with misty spray drifting across the street in front of them. The windshield wipers were flapping furiously from side to side, but they could barely keep up.

As they reached the Woods house, however, the rain abruptly stopped, and by the time Molly had parked her Civic in the driveway, the sun was beginning to shine through the clouds, and sparkle on the cedar trees that sheltered the house on either side.

Avondale was a quiet, old-style neighborhood, and 1445 Riddle Road was a solid, old-style house, with three stories and a long verandah that ran all the way across the front. Molly and Sissy climbed the steps to the front door. It was painted dark purple, and there was a brass knocker on it in the shape of a grinning face – a clown, maybe, or a joker.

Molly knocked and the door was opened almost immediately. They were greeted by a thin, nervous-looking woman with a blonde bob and short-sleeved black dress; and a young girl clutching a black toy rabbit.

'Mrs Woods?' Sissy smiled. 'I'm Sissy Sawyer. This is my daughter-in-law, Molly.'

'Come on in,' said Mrs Woods. 'And, please, call me Darlene.'

She led the way into a large living room, furnished with two antique sofas and four spoonback chairs. On the left-hand side of the room there was a handsome antique fireplace, with fluted columns, and a wide, gilt-framed mirror hanging above it. On the right-hand side there was a dark mahogany sideboard, with a collection of nineteenth-century silver – jugs and candlesticks and decorated tankards.

Between the sofas there was a low, glass-topped table with magazines and antique crystal paperweights on it, as well as a bronze statuette of a leaping horse. But it was a small pedestal underneath the window that caught Sissy's attention. It was draped in a black velvet cloth, and on it stood a photograph in a silver frame of a smiling, broad-featured man, with a lick of brown hair across his forehead.

All around the photograph tiny seashells had been arranged in flower patterns, as well as multicolored candies, and glass beads – the tributes paid by two small girls to their murdered father.

'I don't really know how much I can help you,' said Darlene.

'Oh, I'm sure you can,' Sissy told her, 'and we can help *you*.'

She looked around the living room, trying to sense any presence of the late George Woods. It wasn't easy, because she could feel all of the hundreds of people who had lived here since the house was built. She could almost hear them shouting and laughing and singing as the years had flickered by – birthdays, Thanksgivings, Christmasses and weddings. She could also feel the stillness of death.

'Amanda,' said Darlene, 'why don't you take Floppy upstairs to your room? I have to talk to these ladies for a while.'

'May I have a cookie?' asked Amanda.

'Sure you can, sweetie. But just one.'

'May Floppy have a cookie, too?'

Darlene shook her head. 'Floppy can share yours. It's going to be lunchtime soon.'

When Amanda had gone, Darlene said, 'Please . . . do sit down. I have to tell you that I was kind of knocked off balance when you called me. You know – what you said to me about talking to George.'

'I'm not a con artist, Darlene,' Sissy told her. 'I've been holding séances ever since I first discovered that I could contact people who have gone beyond. I've never asked for money or any kind of recompense and I never will.'

'You said that you and – Molly, is it? – you said that you were working with the Cincinnati police.'

'I'm a forensic sketch artist,' Molly told her. 'After a crime's been committed, I interview witnesses and then I try to draw a likeness of the person who committed it.'

'I understand,' Darlene nodded. 'I've seen people doing that on *CSI*. But why do you need to talk to George?'

Molly said, 'There was only one witness to George's murder, and that was a young girl who was also stabbed, so she was in pretty deep shock. Red Mask struck a second time – at least, we believe it was him. But again there was only one witness, and this witness had already seen my picture of Red Mask on TV, so his recollection could well have been compromised. Witnesses bend over backward to be helpful, but sometimes they're *too* helpful, if you see what I mean. They try to tell you what they think you want to hear, instead of what they actually saw.'

'The more witnesses we can talk to, the more accurate Molly's picture will be,' said Sissy. 'That's why we need to contact George.'

'Is it really possible?' asked Darlene. 'My mother used to go to a medium to talk to her older sister. She said she had long conversations with her, but I can't say that I ever completely believed her. I thought it was no more than wishful thinking.'

Sissy took hold of Darlene's hand and gave it a reassuring squeeze. 'It *is* possible, for sure. But let me say this: if it upsets you in any way at all, Molly and I will just get up and go and you won't have to see us ever again.'

'Will *I* be able to hear him?'

Sissy nodded. 'More than likely. But you have to realize that not all gone-beyonders *want* to talk to the people that they've left behind – not directly. They're usually anxious to spare them from any more grief. It's not exactly an easy experience for them, either, to see everything they lost, when they passed over, and to talk to a loved one they'll never be able to hold in their arms again.'

Darlene looked across at the photograph of her late husband on the pedestal by the window. 'All right,' she said, at last. 'What do we have to do? Hold hands or something?'

Sissy said, 'You can, if you think that it will help you to concentrate. But it isn't necessary. If George is here, if he's able and willing to talk to us, then he will. All you need to do is to think of him – how you best remember him. Try to remember what he looked like. Try to remember what he *felt* like. Imagine he's still with you. Imagine he's still alive.'

Sissy opened her floppy tapestry bag and took out four small pouches, which she set down on the glass-topped table. 'Blood root, celandine, chicory and pennyroyal,' she explained. 'I don't know whether they really work or not, but they're supposed to help the gone-beyonders to find their way through.'

She took out a red candle, too, in a round stone holder, and lit it with her cigarette lighter. The candle had a strong, cloying scent, like rotting peaches.

'Now, you're thinking about George, aren't you?' she asked Darlene.

Darlene nodded.

'Close your eyes if it makes it easier. Try to imagine that he's here, standing in this room, watching you.'

Darlene closed her eyes. She was silent for a short while, and it was obvious from her tightly-clenched fists that she was concentrating deeply.

'George,' she whispered. 'George, where are you, darling? Come talk to us.'

Sissy joined in. 'George, we need to ask you some questions. Come on, George, Darlene's here, waiting for you.'

Nearly a minute went by. Darlene said, 'Please, George. I miss you so much. The girls miss you so much. I need to tell you that I still love you, and I always will. I need to hear you say that you still love me.'

Sissy suddenly saw a distortion in the air, in front of the fireplace. She looked meaningfully at Molly, and inclined her head toward the distortion, and Molly saw it, too. It looked as if the fluted pillar on one side of the fireplace were slowly rippling, as if it were under water.

The mirror above the fireplace began to darken. Sissy touched Darlene on the arm and said, '*Look.*' The reflection of the living room grew gloomier and gloomier, and as it did so, a man's face began to appear, pale and staring, like a face from a long-forgotten photograph. His eyes were smudged and the rest of his features were blurred, but Darlene immediately rose to her feet and held out one hand toward the mirror, and her eyes filled up with tears.

'George! It's George! Oh my God, how did you do that? *George!*'

Sissy stood up, too. Molly looked up at her in alarm, but Sissy said, 'Don't be frightened. It's only his image. He's using the mirror's memory . . . the impressions that he left on its silver backing, when he was alive.'

All the same, Sissy could feel George's presence as strongly as if he were standing right in front of her, although his personality was jumbled and bewildered and he was still in state of shock. She approached the mirror, and concentrated on calming him down. *Steady, George, steady.*

'George, can you hear me?' she said. 'My name is Sissy Sawyer. I'm a friend of Darlene's.'

George's head moved jerkily, and his lips moved, but all Sissy could hear was a distant, strangled sound, like a loudspeaker announcement on a windy day.

'George, I need to ask you some questions about how you were killed.'

More strangled noises – but then, unexpectedly, and very clearly, the word '*Sorry.*'

Sissy laid her hand on Darlene's shoulder. Darlene was weeping quite openly now, and she had to wipe her nose with the back of her hand.

'George, can you hear me, George?' Sissy asked him. No matter how distressed Darlene was, she couldn't allow George to fade away – not yet, anyhow, not until she had talked to him – because she might never be able to call him back. Like so many gone-beyonders, he could well find this contact with his past life so painful that he never wanted to repeat it.

'George, darling,' said Darlene. 'George, I miss you so much.'

'*—miss you too – and Kitty, and Amanda—*'

'Oh, George.'

'What happened, George?' Sissy interrupted. 'Can you remember the man who stabbed you?'

George's image suddenly shuddered, but then it came back into focus. '*—it was all so* – sudden – *didn't—*'

'The man who attacked you, George. Can you tell me what he looked like?'

'*—stabbed me and stabbed me – strange thing, though – I didn't feel it – didn't feel anything—*'

Molly stood up now. 'George, my name's Molly.'

George stared at her as if he thought he ought to know who she was.

'I'm an artist, George. If you tell me what the man looked like, I can make a drawing of him, and help the police to catch him.'

'*—just started stabbing me—*'

'Was he white? Was he black? What kind of clothes was he wearing?'

'*—couldn't see too clearly – all I saw was that knife—*'

'George, listen to me,' Molly insisted. 'Was he taller than you? How would you describe his build?'

George turned toward Darlene. His expression was one of infinite regret. '*—I'm so sorry, Darlene – how can you ever forgive me?*'

'George, it wasn't your fault. I don't blame you.'

'*—if only I hadn't—*'

'It wasn't your fault, George. How were you to know that he was going to get on to that elevator with you?'

'*—not that – she—*'

George's image in the mirror began to shudder. Darlene said, 'No! No, George, don't go!' and she went right up to the fireplace and pressed her hands and her forehead against the glass. 'No!' she sobbed, as her own reflection grew clearer and brighter, and the living room reappeared behind her. 'Please, George, we haven't talked at all!'

Sissy gently put her arm around her. 'He's gone, Darlene. For now, anyhow. It's as much of a strain for the gone-beyonders to talk to us as it is for us to talk to them. But he won't be far away, ever. So long as you go on thinking about him, and remembering what he was like, and how much he loved you, he'll always be close to you, I promise.'

Darlene turned away from the mirror, distraught. Her two palm-prints remained for a moment, like ghosts, and then they faded, too.

'He didn't have to say he was sorry,' she said. 'Why did he keep on saying he was sorry?'

'Well . . . often a gone-beyonder will feel guilt for having died, and leaving his family to fend for themselves. Just like his family will blame him for dying, even though it wasn't his fault.'

Darlene pulled a Kleenex out of a decorative box on the table, and wiped her eyes. 'Do you think I might be able to talk to him again?'

'I hope so. Especially since he's so regretful. But give him some time. If you like, I could come back in a week or so, and we could try again.'

Darlene nodded. 'I'd like that. Now – how about a drink? I could really use something to steady my nerves.'

'A little too early for me,' said Sissy. 'But coffee would be good.'

Darlene went through to the kitchen, leaving Sissy and Molly still standing in front of the mirror.

'That was incredible,' said Molly. 'You actually made him *appear.* I've never been so frightened in my life.'

'He was *desperate* to appear, that's why. Absolutely desperate. He needed Darlene to see how sorry he was.'

'If he'd committed suicide, maybe I could understand it. But sorry for being *murdered*?'

'Well, you're right, of course,' said Sissy. She held out her hand with the amethyst ring that used to belong to her mother. The stone was still shiny but it had turned black as a stag beetle. 'Our friend behind the mirror was lying to us.'

'Lying about what? He didn't *say* very much.'

'Well, let's think about it. Number one – he said that the stabbing happened really quickly. Number two – he said that he didn't feel any pain. And number three, he said that he didn't have a chance to see the man's face.'

Molly frowned. 'Jane Becker said that it happened really quickly, too. And she said that she didn't feel any pain, not until afterward. But she *did* see Red Mask's face, and very clearly.'

'So maybe George saw his face, too, but for some reason of his own he doesn't want to admit it. Maybe George recognized him. Maybe it wasn't a random stabbing, after all. Maybe Red Mask killed George deliberately.'

'But if that's true – why did he go on to kill that young artist guy, and those three cleaners?'

Sissy dropped her pouches of herbs back into her purse, and blew out her candle. 'I don't have any idea,' she admitted. 'And I don't think the cards do either. We're dealing with something really strange here – something that's way beyond my experience.'

Darlene came back into the living room, carrying a tray with three cups of coffee on it. As she put it down, Sissy noticed that one of the cups already contained a large measure of amber liquid. She didn't blame Darlene at all. For months after Frank had been killed, she herself had opened a bottle of Jack Daniel's whenever her loneliness became unbearable.

'I'm still shaking,' said Darlene, sitting down and filling up their cups with hot black espresso.

'George is probably shaking, too,' said Sissy. 'Being dead, that doesn't exempt us from feeling any emotion. Love – hate – pleasure – they don't all stop because we die.'

'Do you think he still loves me, as much as I love him?'

'I think he bitterly regrets that he's left you.'

Sissy sipped her coffee. As she did so, she noticed that Darlene kept glancing up at the mirror, as if she half-expected George to reappear. Sissy wished that he would. She had so many more questions to ask him. In particular, *What are you so darned sorry about, George?*

Red Mask Panic

On their way back home they stopped off at the Rookwood Pavilion in Norwood so that Molly could buy some more crayons and paints from an artists' supply store called Arts Of

Gold, and some purple beaded cushion covers from Stein Mart. Then they bought themselves strawberry ice-cream cones and walked through the mall, window-shopping.

'So where do you think we go from here?' said Molly.

'I'm not sure yet,' Sissy admitted. 'But I do think that George told us something important. Or rather, he *lied* about something important.'

'But he's dead. Why should he lie about anything? What would be the point?'

'People usually lie because they've done something that they're ashamed of.'

'Being murdered is nothing to be ashamed of.'

'Yes, but *why* was he murdered?'

They were looking at summer dresses in T.J. Maxx when Molly's cell phone warbled. She answered it and said, 'Yes,' and then, 'Yes,' and then, 'Oh God, not again.'

'What's happened?' Sissy asked her.

'Red Mask,' said Molly. 'He's killed seven more people in an elevator at the Giley Building. But it looks like there's a copycat killer, too. Eleven people were stabbed in an elevator at the Four Days Mall, but almost at the same time.'

'There are *two* Red Masks?' said Sissy. 'That's just terrible. How can there be two of them?'

'Mike Kunzel says he has witnesses. Three people survived – one at the Giley Building and two at the Four Days Mall. He wants me to go to the hospital and talk to them. He says they all described a red-faced man with two knives.'

'This is just awful. No wonder the cards predicted so much blood.'

'Do you want to come with me?' asked Molly. 'Maybe if you sit in while I'm drawing my composites, you might get some kind of insight.'

'Sure, yes, I'll come along.'

They walked back to Molly's car. The skies had cleared now, and a gilded sun was shining, but the morning was still steamy, and thousands of cicadas were chirruping in the trees that surrounded the parking lot. They drove out of the gates, splashing through the puddles, and headed toward Allison Street.

Molly turned on the radio. On 700 AM, a reporter was talking to Lieutenant-Colonel Whalen, the commander of the investigations bureau.

Lieutenant-Colonel Whalen sounded shaken. 'It's far too early for us to say exactly who we're looking for. It could be a copycat killer, yes. But then again it could be an organization of two or more terrorists. Whoever it is – and whatever perverted purpose they have in mind – they are obviously determined to cause as much panic and disruption as they can.'

'But what would you say to the general public in Cincinnati?' asked the reporter. 'What special precautions would you advise them to take?'

'We all need to keep our eyes open. We all need to be aware of what these men look like, and to check out our fellow passengers whenever we step on to an elevator.'

'But if we can't be sure of our safety in a glass-paneled elevator that's in full view of two crowded streets and a crowded shopping mall . . . where can we?'

'Right now, I'd advise Cincinnatians to stay on a high level of personal alert no matter where they're going or what they're doing. Riding in elevators, walking in the park, going out shopping – even at home. So far, yes, these men have attacked people only on elevators. But we have no guarantee that they won't diversify their assaults, and we have no idea when, or where, or even if they are planning to strike again.'

'So you couldn't even guess at a motive?'

'Not yet. It's perfectly possible that the perpetrators have an agenda which makes some kind of twisted sense to them. Last year, if you remember, James Kellman shot two innocent children on a bus because he thought they were laughing at his private thoughts. But – no – we have no idea at this time why any of these people were attacked.

'All I can say on behalf of the CPD is that their loved ones have our deepest sympathy.'

Chrissie had survived. Elaine had been stabbed in the face with both knives at once and had fallen backward, with Chrissie underneath her. Chrissie had been stabbed three times in the left arm, and once in the left leg, above the knee – but even though the blade had penetrated so deeply that the point had momentarily stuck in her thighbone, it had missed her femoral artery by a quarter of an inch.

She was sedated and confused, and her eyes kept roaming around the room as if she were fearful that her attacker was suddenly going to reappear.

But Molly kept on saying, 'You're safe now, Chrissie. He's gone, and he won't be coming back. I promise you.'

'I was so scared. He kept shouting, *"Wicked! wicked!"* He was trying to kill all of us.'

'I know. That's why I need you to tell me what he looked like.'

'His face. His face was so *red*. It was like he was burned.'

Molly held up one of her Caran d'Ache crayons. 'Was it red like this?'

'No. It was redder than that.'

Molly held up another crayon, torch red. 'How about this?'

Chrissie nodded. 'That's how red he was. And his *eyes*. It was like he had no eyes at all.'

Sissy sat on the opposite side of the hospital bed, a little way back. She could feel Chrissie's fear, as tight as an overwound clock. But, oddly, she had no sense of Red Mask himself, only emptiness. It was just as if Chrissie were describing a figure that she had seen in a nightmare, rather than a real person.

Usually, when she talked to women who were being intimidated or beaten, she could pick up a distinct sense of the people who were frightening them so much. Bullies and abusing husbands lived inside their victims' consciousness, possessing them like malevolent spirits. But Chrissie's description of Red Mask evoked nothing at all. Blackness. Coldness. No more soul than a cicada.

She moved her chair closer to the bed and reached out for Chrissie's hand.

'Do you mind?' she asked her.

'Of course not,' said Chrissie.

Sissy turned Chrissie's hand over and examined her palm. She had a long, double lifeline, which meant that she had an outstanding resistance to negative events in her life, and would live to a very old age – even though there were two significant breaks in it. The first of those breaks was probably an indication of the knife-attack that she had just suffered. The other showed that she had another life-threatening incident in store for her, when she was very much older, but she would survive that, too. Maybe an accident, maybe an illness.

Her line of Venus was perforated, which revealed sensitivity and a willingness to listen to other people's problems. But her line of Apollo was short and broken, meaning that she was a dreamer and a procrastinator, who lacked concentration.

Her Fate line, though, was highly unusual. It had a complicated whorl in it, which Sissy had only seen once before, on a woman who had claimed that a statue in the ornamental gardens in Darien, Connecticut, had spoken to her, and given her a warning that her daughter was about to die.

The whorl meant that Chrissie had witnessed a highly potent psychic phenomenon – something which most people would never witness even if they lived a hundred lifetimes. A miracle.

Molly was quickly sketching the face of Chrissie's assailant. His head looked slightly narrower than her previous two drawings of Red Mask, and his cheeks were more chiseled, but there was no question that it was the same man.

When she had finished, she lifted up her sketchpad and turned it around so that Chrissie could tell her how accurate it was. Chrissie immediately turned her head away. 'That's him. Please, I don't want to look at it. That's exactly him.'

Sissy held Chrissie's hand between hers, and said, 'Don't worry. You're never going to see him again. Your palm tells me that you're going to be happy and healthy and live for a very long time. Oh – and apart from that – you're going to have at least five children.'

Chrissie opened her mouth in disbelief. 'Five children! But I'm not married yet! I don't even have a boyfriend.'

'You will. You see your mount of Venus here, just below your thumb? It's very high and rounded, which means that you're going to have a passionate love life and a very satisfying marriage. And five children, one for each finger.'

Molly stood up. 'My mother-in-law is never wrong, believe me. Madame Blavatsky was nothing on her.'

Chrissie said, 'Thank you. And I really hope you catch this psycho.'

Sissy and Molly glanced at each other. Chrissie hadn't yet been told that there had been *two* attacks in the city center that morning, almost simultaneously, and that both of them had been carried out by a red-faced man.

'We'll catch him,' Molly reassured her. 'You just worry about getting yourself better.'

They were about to leave the room when Chrissie said, 'Oh – there's one more thing that I remember. The man – he had a piece missing from his ear.'

Molly stopped. 'A piece missing from his ear? What do you mean?'

'It was his right ear, like a triangular piece missing from his earlobe.'

'You want to show me on this drawing?'

'OK.'

Molly kept most of the man's face covered while Chrissie penciled in a V-shaped nick.

'That's good,' Molly told her. 'That's very distinctive. That should help the police a lot.'

Chrissie looked across at Sissy. 'You're sure I'm never going to see him again?'

'Never,' said Sissy. 'Cross my heart and hope to die.'

They managed to talk to one of the teenage boys who had been stabbed in the glass elevator at the Four Days Mall. His name was Ben and he was seventeen years old and very spotty and skinny, with black hair that stuck up like a yard broom.

When the red-faced man had started stabbing, Ben had crouched down in one corner of the elevator with his hands covering his face. He had been stabbed through his hands seven times, and his left cheek had been sliced open right to the bone, but he had been lucky that the knives hadn't penetrated his eyes.

'It was like his face was painted red, you know? He scared the crap out of me, if you must know. This one dude was telling him back off and everything, but he pulled out these knives and nobody stood a chance.'

'Was he tall, medium or short?'

'He was, like, *humungous*.'

'How about his face? Was it squarish, or long, or oval?'

'He looked like the Hulk. Like, if the Hulk was red instead of green, that's exactly what this dude looked like.'

'Did you notice anything about his ears?'

'His ears? I wasn't looking at his frickin' ears, ma'am – excuse my French.'

Sissy said, 'Would you do something for me, Ben?'

'Sure, whatever.'

She opened her purse and took out the deck of DeVane cards. Ben watched her, baffled, as she sorted through them. She found *L'Apprenti*, the Apprentice, which she picked as Ben's Predictor card. It showed a young man in a long leather apron sawing wood in a carpenter's workshop. At the far end of the workshop three latticed windows gave out on to a garden. In each window stood a naked girl with braided hair – a brunette covering her eyes, a blonde covering her ears, and a redhead covering her mouth, like the three wise monkeys. They represented the young man's inexperience.

She laid the card on the bed, and then offered the rest of the pack to Ben. 'Choose four cards. Any cards, it doesn't matter.'

Ben looked up at the Chinese-American nurse who was filling in his notes. She shrugged as if to say, 'Go ahead . . . it's fine by me. A little fortune-telling never hurt anybody.'

He picked four cards, which Sissy set around the Predictor card at all four points of the compass.

'This is behind you,' said Sissy, pointing to the card below the Apprentice. 'You had a spat with a girl you really care about.'

Ben stared at her. 'How do you *know* that? Have you been talking to my folks?'

Sissy smiled and shook her head. 'It's true, then?'

'I broke up with my girlfriend at the weekend. We kept fighting all the time.'

'All right,' said Sissy, and pointed to the card on the left. 'This is your ambition.'

The card was *Le Violoniste*, and showed a young man in a green velvet suit playing the violin in front of an audience of various animals – dogs, goats, llamas and leopards – all of which were also dressed in human finery.

'You want to be a musician,' Sissy told him. 'A rock guitarist, if I'm guessing correctly. And you and your girlfriend used to fight because she was jealous of all the girls who hung around whenever you played.'

'This is incredible,' said Ben.

Sissy pointed to the right-hand card, *Le Marcheur*. A thin man in a triangular hat was walking down a muddy country road. It was teeming with rain, and the man's only companion was a bedraggled black dog.

'This is what lies ahead of you, Ben. Success won't come to you easy. You'll have to travel a long, long way to achieve your ambition, and you'll get very depressed and frustrated. But you should make it in the end. See this break in the clouds? You'll get a break one day, when you least expect it.'

Ben said nothing to that, but pointed to the last card, at the top. 'What does this one mean?'

'*Le Témoin*, the Witness. That's you, and what happened to you today.'

'I don't get it.'

The card showed a man in a pigtailed wig and a frock coat, stepping back from a picture frame with one hand raised as if he were trying to shield his eyes. But the picture frame, although it was elaborate, with curlicues and bunches of grapes carved around it, was empty.

Sissy picked it up and scrutinized it carefully. 'I'm not so sure that I get it, either.'

Molly said, 'Let me see,' and Sissy handed it to her.

'It's a man looking at nothing,' she said, and handed it back.

'Exactly,' Sissy agreed. 'But he's obviously frightened of it, isn't he – even if it *is* nothing.'

Drawing a Blank

Outside Ben's room they came across Detective Bellman, talking to a pretty blonde female officer in uniform. Detective Bellman looked very tired. His mussed-up hair was even more chaotic than usual and his hula-girl necktie was askew.

'Hi, Molly. You got your descriptions?' he asked.

Molly folded back her sketchpad so that he could see the two composites that she had drawn. Detective Bellman flicked from one to the other, and said, 'Sure looks like we got ourselves *two* Red Masks, don't it?'

Sissy said, 'You're absolutely certain that one man wouldn't have been able to carry out both of these attacks?'

'No way. The stabbings in the Giley Building took place at approximately a quarter after nine. The Four Days assault started at nine eighteen. Even Spiderman couldn't have made from the Giley Building to the Four Days mall as quick as that. It's way across the other side of Fountain Square.'

'Something's *very* strange about this,' said Sissy. 'I saw this TV program once about serial killers. Sometimes they have admirers who hero-worship them and commit more murders in the same way, don't they? Almost like a tribute. But if these two attacks happened at pretty much the same time, that can't have been a coincidence, can it? If there *are* two Red Masks, they must have worked this out together.'

'That's just about the same conclusion that we came to,' said Detective Bellman. 'These killings weren't random. They were planned – premeditated.' He checked his watch. 'Listen – we should get these composites back to headquarters so that you can finish them off and we can release them to the press. Do you need a ride?'

An hour later, in the brightly-lit art studio on the fourth floor of Cincinnati police headquarters, Sissy stood by the window sipping a cup of weak lime tea while Molly finished shading and coloring her composites of the two Red Masks.

'Look at this beautiful day,' said Sissy, looking down on Ezzard Charles Drive, and the sparkling traffic below her. 'You wouldn't think, would you, that something so horrible had happened? Not today. This is one of the Lord's good days.'

Molly said, 'Bad things always happen on beautiful days. I've been to so many funerals, you know, and it's never been raining, like it does on TV. The sun is always shining and I always look at the casket and think to myself, excuse me, recently-deceased person, why aren't you here to see this wonderful weather? But I think I'd have a hell of a shock if they answered me.'

The door opened and Detective Kunzel came in. He looked even more exhausted than Detective Bellman. One of his shirt-tails was hanging out and his chin was prickly with white stubble.

'Hey, Molly,' he greeted her. 'How's it going with the composites?'

'Hey, Mike,' said Molly, using her thumb to rub vermilion pastel on to Red Mask's cheeks. 'Can you give me five more minutes? I'd like to put a bit more depth into this.'

'It's OK, Molly, you got time. The news bulletin isn't scheduled to go out until a quarter after one.'

He collapsed into a chair opposite Sissy and ran his hand over his short-cropped salt-and-pepper scalp. 'How about you, Mrs Sawyer? Do you have any ideas? Right now, I could use all the help that I can get.'

'Oh, really? Even if it comes from beyond?'

'I don't care if it comes from Indianoplace, so long as it gives me a lead.'

'Indianoplace?'

'Indianapolis,' Molly explained. 'Where nobody never knows nothing about nothing. According to these know-all Cincy folk, anyhow.'

Detective Kunzel sniffed, and loudly blew his nose on a Kleenex. 'Goddamned sinuses,' he complained. Then he said, 'You want me to be totally frank with you? I don't have any idea if we're dealing with two perpetrators dressed up the same, working some kind of premeditated plan, or identical twins, or a guy who can be in two different places at the same time.'

'I really have no suggestions at all,' said Sissy. 'None that make any kind of sense, anyhow.'

'Try me.'

'Well, if you look back into the early days of American spiritualism, in the days of the Pilgrim Fathers, there were several recorded instances of people being seen in different locations at the same time. But they were only *visions,* you know? They frightened people, for sure, but they didn't hurt anybody, and they never caused anybody any harm. They would never have stabbed anybody. I didn't think that spirits were capable if doing that.'

'I was only kidding, Mrs Sawyer. This has to be two different guys, right?'

'I don't really know. I mean – probably. I mean, yes.'

'So how about motive? Any spiritualistic ideas on that?'

'I think Red Mask might have had a logical motive to begin with, but not any more. It seems to me like he's taking his revenge on anybody and everybody. He's angry at them simply because they exist. And he seems to have found an accomplice who feels the same way.'

Detective Kunzel raised his eyebrows. 'Do you have any idea *why*?'

'Not really. Nothing that makes any sense.'

'Your cards aren't telling you?'

Sissy shook her head. 'Usually, the cards are very specific. But not this time – not about Red Mask. I might have to try some other form of divination, like coffee grounds, or fortune sticks.'

'OK . . . if there's anything you need, just let me know.'

He stood up. As he did so, his cell phone played *Hang On, Sloopy*, and he rummaged around in his coat pockets until he found it.

'Kunzel,' he said. Then, almost immediately, he covered his cell phone with his hand and said, 'It's Red Mask.'

He switched on the loudspeaker so that Sissy and Molly could hear his conversation, too. It was the same Red Mask – harsh and indistinct, with a noticeable Cincinnati accent. He sounded even more pleased with himself than he had before.

'*So, how are you feeling now, Detective? A little anxious, maybe?*'

'Anxious? I'm not *anxious*, you sick bastard. I'm blazing mad. You and your friend, you're nothing but a pair of sadistic morons. Me and my people, we're going to hunt you both down, don't you have any mistake about that, and we're going to make sure that you get what you deserve. A nice fat bolus of potassium chloride, one for each of you.'

There was a pause. Then, '*Friend? What are you talking about, Detective? I don't have any friends. That's the story of my life. I lost everything, including myself.*'

'If you don't have any friends, who stabbed all of those innocent people at the Four Days Mall this morning?'

'*I did, Detective. It was me. The Glass Elevator Executioner.*'

'OK, then. Who killed those people at the Giley Building?'

'*Guilty, I'm afraid. That was me too. The Bloody Basement Butcher.*'

'Not a chance. You couldn't have committed both of those attacks. Not humanly possible.'

'*You said it, Detective.*'

Detective Kunzel took a deep breath. Then he said, 'Listen to me, whatever you call yourself. What will it take for you to stop these killings?'

'*Aha! You seriously want to know?*'

'Of course I want to know. If you have a grievance – if there's something we can work out between us – why don't we try? I've said this to you before, haven't I? You got a problem? I'm prepared to listen.'

'*Is that what they taught you at negotiation school? Talk reasonable to your perpetrator, and hold out an olive branch?*'

'I want you to stop slaughtering innocent people, that's all.'

'*Oh, I will, Detective. I promise you.*'

'OK, then. When?'

'*When the streets of Cincinnati are flooded with blood. When the cemeteries are too crowded to take any more bodies and the crematorium ovens are so clogged up with human ashes that their fires go out. Then I'll stop. Maybe.*'

'Maybe' was followed by an emphatic click, as Red Mask abruptly hung up. Detective Kunzel lowered his cell phone and said, 'Shit.' Then he turned to Sissy and said, 'Sorry, Mrs Sawyer. Didn't intend to offend you.'

'Don't mind me, Detective. I would have said something a whole lot worse.'

'He's taking the credit for both of those attacks. But he couldn't have been in two places at once.'

'No, he couldn't,' Sissy agreed. 'On the other hand, I think he might have given us a very important clue.'

'Oh, yes? What, exactly?'

At that moment, however, Detective Kunzel's cell phone rang again. 'Yes, sir,' he said. 'Right away, sir. OK.'

He stood up and said, 'Captain wants to see me, so I'll have to catch you later. Molly, if you can finish up those composites quick as you can. And – Mrs Sawyer – if you can work on those theories of yours, wacky or not.'

He left, closing the studio door behind him. As soon as he had gone, Sissy said, 'Where do you keep your originals?'

'What do you mean?'

'Your original sketches. Where do you keep them?'

Molly pointed toward a gray steel plan cabinet on the opposite side of the studio. 'They're all in there. Why?'

'Show me the second sketch you made of Red Mask. The one you drew when that young Jimmy Moulton and those three poor cleaners got killed.'

Molly went across to the cabinet and opened the third drawer down. She took out a yellow manila folder marked *Red Mask Composite/Kraussman* and the date that she had drawn it. 'Here,' she said, and handed it over.

Sissy opened it. It contained nothing but a blank sheet of white cartridge paper.

'Oh,' said Molly. 'The media guys probably borrowed it to make some more copies and forgot to bring it back. They're always doing that. Unless they put it in the wrong file.'

She took out the folder in which she had filed her first Red Mask composite – the one she had drawn from Jane Becker's description. She opened it up, but that contained only a blank sheet of cartridge paper, too.

'Don't tell me the media guys borrowed *that* one, too.'

Molly lifted up the sheet of paper and examined it closely. 'No, they didn't. This is the same sheet of paper I drew it on. Look – those are my initials in the bottom right-hand corner, M.S., and a little picture of a saw, for Sawyer. And here are my initials on this Kraussman composite, too. Except there's no composite on either of them, is there? They're blank.'

Sissy pressed her fingertips to her forehead, and momentarily closed her eyes. 'It's the same as the roses,' she said, slowly. 'It's exactly the same as the roses.'

'What?'

She opened her eyes again. 'You painted the roses and they faded from the paper but they grew for real out in the backyard.'

'You're not saying that when I drew Red Mask—'

'The same thing happened. I'm sure of it. You drew him, and your drawings came to life.'

'Oh, Sissy, that's not possible. That simply can't happen.'

'It happened with the roses, didn't it? And those other flowers you drew? It even happened with that ladybug. And you drew Red Mask *twice*, didn't you? So now we have *three* Red Masks, the original one who murdered George Woods, and two more copies, drawn by you. *That's* how he was able to kill those people at the Four Days Mall at the same time as he was killing those people in the Giley Building.'

'I can't believe it. It's like some kind of a nightmare.'

'It's not a nightmare, sweetheart. It sounds impossible, but it's the only explanation that makes any kind of sense.'

'So where is he? Or *them*, if there are three of him?'

'I don't know where the real Red Mask is. But I'd guess that at least one of your drawings is hiding someplace in the Giley Building.'

'But the police searched the Giley Building, didn't they, with dogs? And you tried to find him there, too?'

'I know. But if he's only a drawing so he doesn't have a soul that I can sense and he doesn't have a human scent that the dogs could pick up.

She lifted up Molly's sketchpad. Molly's drawing of Red Mask stared back at her, his eyes dead and his expression unreadable. 'I couldn't sense him when I talked to that poor girl Chrissie, either. All I could feel was coldness, emptiness. Nothing at all. And what happened when I asked young Ben to pick out a card? He chose a picture frame with no picture in it.'

Molly said, 'What about these two new composites? If the same thing happens—'

'We'll have to destroy them. Burn them. We can't have *five* Red Masks roaming around the city. It'll be carnage.'

'But what am I going to say to Mike Kunzel? He wants to put these out on the news in twenty minutes' time.'

'Tell him you're not happy with them. Tell him you spilled coffee on them, anything. He can always put out a copy of your first drawing of Red Mask. It's the same man, after all.'

Molly hesitated. Then she ripped the two composites of Red Mask from her sketchbook and noisily crumpled them up. She held them over the metal wastebasket while Sissy took out her Zippo lighter and set fire to one corner. Molly dropped them in, and they watched them flare up and crumple into wrinkled black ash.

'I hope we're not making a mistake,' said Molly.

'Better to be safe than very, very sorry,' said Sissy. 'Besides, we'll soon find out when we go looking for them.'

'Excuse me? When *we* go looking for them?'

'The police will go on hunting for the first Red Mask, won't they? The real one? But how are the police going to find two living drawings? And even if they can, how are they going to arrest two men who don't really exist?'

'I don't know, Sissy. But when it comes to that, how on earth are *we* going to find him – or *them*? And supposing we do, what then?'

'Like I told you,' said Sissy, 'it's the roses.' She opened her purse and took out her deck of DeVane cards. 'The roses are the key to all of this. They have been, right from the start.'

'I don't understand.'

'In every single card that I turned up since you painted that Mr Lincoln rose, there are roses. They're like a code. If we can work out what the cards are telling us, then I think that we'll find out how to find Red Mask. Or Red Masks, plural.'

'Sissy – I don't think that we should even *think* about finding them. Honestly – it would be way too dangerous.'

'If we don't do it, who will? Who's going to believe us? Can you imagine Mike Kunzel's face if we told him that he has to go looking for two living sketches?'

As if on cue, Detective Kunzel came back into the studio, with his mouth full of Whatchamacallit. 'Those composites ready?' he asked. Then he coughed and waved his hand from side to side. 'What the hell have you been doing in here? Building a campfire?'

'Sorry,' said Sissy. 'Slight accident.'

The Hooded Guest

They drove back to Blue Ash in a hailstorm of cicadas – smashing themselves against the windshield like the locusts in Sissy's dream. Molly had to use the washer spray again and again so that she could see where was going.

'These bugs are beginning to get seriously horny,' she complained.

'Just goes to show you, doesn't it? Sex is a matter of life or death, even for bugs.'

'*Especially* for bugs. Even if they don't get squished all over my windshield, and they manage to find themselves some lady cicadas, they're all going to drop dead anyway, just as soon they've done their reproductive duty.'

When they reached home, they discovered that the backyard, too, was teeming with cicadas. Molly picked up an old squash racket and swung it from side to side, swatting them out of their way. Mr Boots followed her, jumping up and barking.

The roses were still nodding in the sunlight, even though scores of cicadas were crawling all over the flowerpot. Sissy lit up a Marlboro and stood looking at them, blowing smoke out of her nostrils.

'I still think they're a miracle,' she said.

'Yes,' Molly agreed. 'But that doesn't make them any less scary. It's a pretty fine line between miracle and nightmare, don't you think?'

Sissy thought, *In one sense these roses are real.* Their thorns had pricked her thumb and drawn real red blood, just as Red Mask's knives had cut real people's flesh open. Yet they weren't real at all. They couldn't be. They had been created out of nothing but pencils and paint.

Maybe they were like ghosts, or the spirits of dead people appearing at a séance. Maybe they were only *visiting* this reality. But ghosts could be exorcized and the spirits of dead people could be sent back to the world of shadows. Maybe these roses could be sent back to the two-dimensional world of paper, where they truly belonged.

And if the *roses* could be sent back, maybe the two living drawings of Red Mask could be sent back, too.

Sissy was almost certain now that *this* was what the DeVane cards had been trying to tell her. Their predictions had been terrifying and strange, but if she and Molly could discover the secret of the roses, maybe they could change the future. Maybe there didn't have to be any more killing. Maybe the two Red Masks who had committed this morning's murders could be returned to the sketchpad on which they had been created, and their likenesses torn out, and burned, and their ashes scattered for ever.

Molly said, 'It's hot. I'm just going inside to change. How about a glass of wine?'

'Why not? It might lubricate the old psychic mojo a little.'

Sissy sat down under the vine trellis. Trevor had cut the roses with his pocket knife, but somehow they had managed to reappear here in the flowerpot. He had cut them, but they were only *images,* after all, not real flowers at all, and images belonged where their creator had imagined them, just as spirits belonged in the world beyond.

Molly had created them, so Molly was the only one who could make them vanish.

Mr Boots made one of those mewling noises in the back of his throat. He was hot and tired, and the cicadas were beginning to annoy him. Sissy ruffled his ears and said, 'Never mind, mister. They'll soon be gone.'

Molly came back out, wearing a tight pink T-shirt and white shorts and carrying two large glasses of chilled Zinfandel. 'So, have you managed to break the code yet?'

'Not really. But I'm beginning to think that *you* have to cut the roses. You personally, because you painted them. And I also think that when you cut them, you have to use the painting of a knife, rather than a real one.'

'The *painting* of a knife?'

'Trevor used a real knife, but real knives exist only in *this* reality – not "painting reality." He could imagine the roses being cut, and so they were, for as long as he kept his attention on them. But as soon as he turned his attention to something else, the illusion ended, and the roses returned here, to this flowerpot, just as you had first painted them.'

'Well, I'm not sure what the *hell* you're talking about, but I'll give it a try.'

'It's simple. If an artist painted a picture of us sitting together in this yard, and then he stabbed the picture with a knife, neither of us would be hurt, would we, either in *this* reality or the painting's reality? But if the artist took his paints and altered the picture so that you were stabbing me, and I was bleeding, then my image would be injured, wouldn't it, even if the real me wasn't?'

Molly shook her head. 'Sometimes, Sissy, you leave me way, way behind. You know that?'

'No – it's not difficult to understand. Think of *The Picture of Dorian Gray*. The real Dorian Gray stayed young and handsome, didn't he, while his portrait grew old and ugly? There are two different realities – *real* reality and *painting* reality. I know *Dorian Gray* is only a story, but Oscar Wilde is supposed to have borrowed it from a famous incident that happened in Paris in the eighteen-hundreds. A cardinal had a secret passion for a prostitute, so he had her portrait painted and then he blessed it. She stayed beautiful and unblemished for over thirty years, until she died. But when they found her portrait, hidden in her attic, it was supposed to have looked so hideous that men actually vomited when they looked at it.

'There are other stories, too, of real people getting lost inside paintings, and I don't think they're all hokum, either. If you go to the Whitney Museum in Stamford, in Connecticut, they have this huge painting of a family of colonists saying grace. I've seen it for myself. It was painted in 1785, but there's a man sitting at the head of the table wearing a 1940s suit and a wristwatch. They've had dozens of experts test that painting, but there's no question about it. The man with the wristwatch was painted at the same time as everybody else in the picture.'

'OK,' said Molly, although she still didn't sound convinced. 'I guess that makes some cockeyed kind of sense. I'll see if I can paint a knife.'

They went back inside the house. Molly took one of her steak knives from the wooden block on the kitchen counter, and then she went through to her studio and pinned a clean sheet of art paper to her drawing board. Sissy stood beside her as she deftly drew a pencil sketch of the steak knife and painted it with watercolors.

They stood and watched the painting for almost ten minutes, but even when it had dried, it refused to disappear.

'Maybe I've lost the magic touch,' said Molly. 'Maybe it only works with living things, not inanimate objects.'

Sissy looked around the room. 'What's different?'

'Nothing's different.'

'Those are the same paints you used before?'

'Same paints, same brushes. Same paper.'

'I don't know what it is. Yes, I do. You're not wearing your necklace.'

'No, I took it off when I changed.'

'Last time you were wearing your necklace. And you were wearing it when you drew those pictures of Red Mask, too. The cards showed you with a talisman, remember, something to make your drawings come to life. Put it on, and try painting that knife again.'

Molly went to her bedroom and came out with her necklace. It looked dull and cheap when she was carrying it – nothing but a jingling collection of glass beads and tarnished mascots – but when Sissy helped her to fasten it around her neck, it started to sparkle.

'I said it had power, didn't I? And you're definitely the person who makes it come to life.'

Molly sketched and painted the steak knife a second time. While she watched her, Sissy was strongly tempted to light another cigarette, but she didn't want to smoke in the house, even if Molly was relaxed about it. Trevor could smell cigarettes, even if she had smoked them days ago, just the way that Frank had been able to.

They waited. The air conditioning rattled and the cicadas ceaselessly chirruped. Five minutes passed and the steak knife remained on the paper, without a hint of it fading.

'Maybe you're right, and it doesn't work with inanimate objects.'

'No – look!'

As the seventh minute passed, the steak knife's handle gradually began to fade. After eight minutes, there was nothing left but the faint outline of the blade. After nine, that was gone, too, and the paper was blank.

Sissy touched the paper with her fingertips. She felt nothing at all, not even the inherent *sharpness* that a real knife would have left behind it. The paper was completely empty, in the same way that Red Mask was empty. No knife. Not even an absence of knife.

The two of them went back outside. The yard was teeming with cicadas, all glistening in the early-afternoon sun, but there was one distinctive shine which they both saw at once. It was the steak knife, lying on the table.

'You did it,' said Sissy.

'The necklace did it, not me.'

'I'm sure you did it together, the necklace *and* you. Just like my mother's ring won't go dark on its own, the necklace doesn't work unless you're wearing it. You're an artist. You're a brilliant artist, and the necklace *knows* that you are.'

Molly reached out and picked up the steak knife. She ran her fingertip down the blade, and said, 'Ouch. Just like the real thing.'

'Well, let's see how it cuts these roses.'

Molly knelt down on one knee and cut the roses as close to the soil as she could. She smelled them, and then offered them to Sissy, so that she could smell them, too.

'Nothing,' said Sissy. 'No fragrance at all. If anything, they smell like paper.'

Molly took the roses into her studio and laid them on her desk.

Sissy said, 'Let's see what happens now. If they *stay* cut, then we'll know that we can have an actual physical effect on things that are painted, even if they're not really real.'

'Like Red Mask, you mean?'

'Let's hope so.'

That afternoon, while Molly was making a vegetable pot pie for supper, Sissy went over the DeVane cards again and again, trying to decode the symbolism of the roses.

Now and again she glanced across at the flowers that were still lying on Molly's desk, but so far they were showing no sign of changing back into paintings. They reminded her of the day she had married Frank. He had heaped their honeymoon bed with dozens and dozens of roses, crimson and white.

Molly had borrowed four library books on roses, which she was using for reference for her *Fairy Fifi* story. 'Roses are a symbol of beauty and love,' declared *The Illustrated Rose*, 'but at the same time they are a sad reminder that beauty and love always fade away and die.

'Roses are also a symbol of great secrecy. There is a myth that Cupid offered a rose to Harpocrates, the god of silence, to bribe him not to disclose the sexual indiscretions of the goddess Venus.

'In ancient Rome and Greece, a host who suspended an

upside-down rose over a table would expect the guests who were gathered underneath it to keep their discussions confidential – hence the term "sub rosa."'

Sissy frowned. *An upside-down rose, suspended over a table?* She shuffled through the DeVane cards until she found *Les Amis de la Table*, the first card she had turned up after Molly had painted the roses and they had come to life. Here they sat, four people eating a lavish dinner together, two young people and an older woman, and a mysterious man whose face was hidden under a gray hood. And there it was, hanging above their heads: an upside-down rose, tied to the candelabrum with a ribbon.

Unlike some of the other cards, there was no writing on *Les Amis de la Table* apart from its title, so the presence of the rose could mean only one thing. The picture itself must hold a secret. But what?

She tucked the card back into the deck, and shuffled them. But when she tried to pick out another card, it was the same one, *Les Amis de la Table*. She tried again, shuffling even more thoroughly this time. But again, when she drew out a card, there it was, *Les Amis de la Table*. She did it again, and again, and every time *Les Amis de la Table* reappeared.

She took the card into the kitchen, where Molly was cutting up carrots. 'You see this card? The first time I picked it, I thought it meant that I was welcome to stay here another week.'

'Well, you are,' said Molly.

'Yes, but now the same damn card has come up four times in a row. I shuffle the deck, I pick a card, and it's always the same one. The cards only repeat themselves when they're trying to tell you that you've missed the point. It's like they're saying, *Hallo, stupid!*'

'So what *is* the point?'

'I'm not sure. But this upside-down rose means that the card has a secret hidden in it someplace.'

Molly looked at the card and shrugged. 'I don't see any secret. Except . . . well, you can't see this hooded guy's face, can you? So you can't tell why this old woman is looking so worried about him.'

'Maybe that's it. Maybe he's somebody famous. Or somebody who *was* famous, back in the eighteenth century. An artist, you know? Or a politician. Or maybe he's a saint. Maybe, if we knew who he was, we could begin to understand how to turn murderers back into drawings of murderers.'

Molly examined the card more intently. 'Look . . . you can see his face reflected in that dish cover, can't you?'

'Yes. But it's so distorted. He's all nose.'

'That's easily fixed. Here.' Molly took down a ladle from the rack above the hob, and held it up close to the card. Inside the concave bowl of the ladle, the image of the hooded man's face was turned upside down, but his features appeared almost normal.

She turned the card around, and now they could clearly see who the hooded man was.

'My God,' said Sissy. She felt as if the floor had dropped away beneath her feet. She stared at the hooded man's face in disbelief and then she stared at Molly. 'It can't be.'

Molly shook her head. 'It *is* him, isn't it? But how could it be?'

The hooded man's forehead was slightly too prominent, and his chin was too small, but Sissy had recognized him at once. The face reflected in the dish cover in *Les Amis de la Table*, a card which had been devised and drawn nearly 250 years ago, was her late husband Frank.

Drawn From Memory

They tried it again, this time using a shiny silver bowl that Trevor had won last August at the Blue Ash Golf Tournament, so that the image of the hooded man's face was much larger.

'It's Frank, isn't it?' said Sissy. Her heart was beating so fast that it actually hurt. 'It doesn't just *look* like him. It *is* him. He even has that diamond-shaped scar on his cheek. He got that when some punk threw a screwdriver at him.'

'I totally can't understand how it *could* be him,' said Molly.

'How do people's faces appear on windows, or slices of bread? How did the image of Christ appear on a ten-dollar bill, instead of Alexander Hamilton?'

Molly put her arm around Sissy, and gave her a comforting squeeze. 'You're not upset, are you?'

'Yes. I am a little. I am a *lot*. I feel like crying, but I don't think I can.'

'How about another drink?'

'No, I'm fine. I think I need to sit down, is all.'

'At least the cards are starting to give you some answers.'

'Yes, I think they are. But I'm not so sure I like what they're telling me.'

'What do you think they *are* telling you?'

Sissy sat on the end of the couch, and took out her Marlboros, although she didn't light one. 'The real police can find the *real* Red Mask, can't they? He has to have an address that they can trace, and DNA that they can check up on. But when you think about it – what kind of cop is going to be able to hunt down a couple of *painted* Red Masks?'

'You're not suggesting what I think you're suggesting? You can't be serious!'

'Oh, no? What else do you think this card is showing us? There are four people sitting at this table. The young man represents Trevor. The girl represents you. The older woman, that's me. But look at the older woman's face. I thought she was worried at first, or frightened, but she's not. She's asking the hooded man for help. *Please*, she's saying. Look at the way her left hand is pressed flat against her chest. *Please, I'm begging you. Help me*.'

'Sissy, I can't!'

'Why not? You can do it with roses, and police composites. I have plenty of photographs you can use for reference.'

'Sissy, how old was Frank when he got killed?'

'Forty-seven. Why?'

'Forty-seven. So what's going to happen if I draw him and he comes to life and he's only forty-seven and you're seventy-one? I mean, how are you going to deal with *that*? How are you going to deal with seeing him at all, talking to him, even though he's dead? How is Trevor going to deal with it? And Victoria?'

Sissy took a deep breath. She knew that what she was thinking was deeply unnatural, and probably wrong. These days, she wasn't religious. After Frank had been killed, she had stopped attending church. But she did believe in greater powers, and a moral order, and to bring Frank back to life did seem like flying in the face of God. She thought of all of those stories like 'The Monkey's Paw,' in which a grieving father resurrects his horribly-injured son. Deals with the devil always carried a price that was far too great to pay. In fiction they did, anyway. She didn't know whether the same was true of real life.

'I don't honestly know *how* I'm going to deal with it,' she admitted. 'How do you think he's going to deal with seeing *me*? But we're not even sure that you can do it yet, are we?'

'Sissy—'

'We have to try, Molly. If there's one thing the cards are quite certain about, there's going to be a massacre. How are we going to live with ourselves if we don't try everything we can to stop it?'

'It's too scary.'

Sissy reached out and took hold of her hand. 'Come on, Molly, Frank was never scary. He was tough, yes, and a very good cop. But he was always fair, and he was always kind, and he always had a terrific sense of humor.'

'Yes, but he's *dead*, Sissy. He died over twenty years ago, and we're talking about bringing him back to life. That's what frightens me.'

Sissy said nothing for a while, but looked down at Molly's hand as if it held the answer to everything. Then she said, 'Would you at least try?'

'I have to ask Trevor. Frank was Trevor's father, after all. He may want him left in peace.'

'You can't let any more innocent people get killed, Molly. I know you didn't bring those drawings to life on purpose. Those murders weren't your fault. But you have to face the fact that you're the only person who has the ability to turn them back into drawings again, and destroy them.'

Molly stood up and went to the window. 'I think I need to find out more about this necklace first. I don't want to start bringing any more drawings to life until I'm sure of what the consequences are going to be. I'm sorry, Sissy, but this really creeps me out.'

'Can you remember who sold you the necklace?'

'She gave me her card. She said she had a small antiques store, out near the country club.'

Molly went through to her studio to find her purse. She was only gone for a moment before she called out, 'Sissy! Come here, quick!'

Sissy followed her. 'What's wrong?'

'Nothing. Nothing at all. But *look*.'

She pointed toward her desk. The roses had gone. The 'real' roses, anyway. But on the sheets of paper on which she had rested them, they had reappeared as paintings.

'Well, I'll be damned.'

Sissy picked up the painting of the red Mr Lincoln rose, and sniffed it. It had no fragrance at all, only the smell of cartridge paper. 'We can do it,' she said. 'I'm sure we can do it.'

Molly said, 'I'm still frightened, Sissy.'

'All right. I know you are. So let's find out more about your necklace.'

Molly reached into her embroidered bag and took out her purse. 'Here it is . . . Dorothy Carven, Persimmon Antiques, Madison Road. Why don't I give her a call?'

At that moment, they heard the front door open, and Trevor call out, 'Hi, Molly! Hi, Mom! We're home!'

Persimmon Antiques turned out to be a fussy, high-class antiques store with a single Sheraton chair in the window, and thick brown carpeting inside. A little bell jingled as Sissy and Molly walked in through the front door.

'Classy,' said Sissy. There were fewer than a dozen pieces of furniture in the store – two chaise longues, a pair of handed armchairs, two bureaux and a gilded desk. On one of the tables stood some eighteenth-century figurines of shepherds and shepherdesses, as well as a Meissen dinner service. The walls were hung with oil paintings, mostly landscapes, and views of the Ohio River.

A woman appeared from the back of the store, with her mouth full. She was tall, fiftyish, with rimless half-glasses and a wing of white hair. She was wearing a purple silk pants suit and at least twenty gold bracelets.

'May I help you, ladies?' she asked, and immediately pressed her fingers to her lips. 'Do forgive me! I have just picked up some strawberry cheesecake from the Bonbonnerie and I couldn't wait until I got home. Have you tried their cherry trifle? To die for, I promise.'

Molly said, 'Ms Carven? You may not remember but I bought this necklace from you at the Peddler's Flea Market.'

The woman peered at the necklace over her glasses, and then

took hold of it and lifted it up. 'Yes, of *course* I remember. It's very unusual, isn't it? I mean, it's only glass, but I don't think I've ever seen another one quite like it.'

'Do you know anything about its provenance?' asked Sissy.

'Provenance? I don't think it has any kind of provenance. It's just a costume piece, that's all. I pick up quite a few interesting bits and bobs when I'm clearing houses. I wouldn't sell them here, so now and again I take them down to the flea market to see what I can get for them.'

'So you don't know anything about it? Where it came from, or who collected all of these mascots?'

'Well, I bought it from an elderly woman in Hyde Park. Her husband had died and she wanted to get rid of everything. He had one or two very fine paintings, as I remember, and a wonderful long-case clock. But he also had an awful lot of junk. Boxes and boxes of newspapers and old theater programs and buttons and coins. I think he was one of these people who never throw anything away.'

'You don't have the woman's name?'

'May I ask why you want to know?'

'Oh, I'm writing a book about jewelry and superstition,' Sissy lied. 'You know, charm bracelets and birthstones and things like that. And, as you say, this necklace is very unusual, isn't it? I'm sure it must have a story.'

Ms Carven went over to the gilded desk, opened the top drawer and took out a leather-bound book. She licked her thumb and leafed through it, until she came to the page she wanted. 'Here you are . . . Mrs Edwina Branson, 1556 Observatory Road. There's a telephone number, too, if you want it.'

Mrs Edwina Branson was well into her eighties. She was white-haired, small and stooped, although she was dressed in a smart cream blouse with a pearl pin at the collar, and a green plaid skirt, and she obviously took good care of herself.

She lived in a ground-floor apartment overlooking a small courtyard. Her ginger cat was sleeping on the bricks outside her window. The apartment was furnished entirely with modern furniture – a beige couch, two beige chairs, and an oak-topped coffee table. The only pictures on the walls were photographs of her children and grandchildren.

'I have some iced tea if you'd care for some,' she told them.

'Thanks all the same,' said Sissy. 'We don't want to take up too much of your time.'

'But I *enjoy* having visitors. When you get to my age, most of your friends are dead and your children are all too busy.'

She turned toward Molly and said, 'It suits you, dear – the necklace. I think I only wore it once. I never liked it. Too *flamboyant* for me.'

'So it wasn't yours, originally?' Sissy asked her.

Edwina Branson shook her head. 'My late husband Felix gave it to me. He brought it back from France after World War Two. I used to teach European history, you see, at Miami University in Oxford, and Felix thought that I would find it interesting.'

'Do you know anything about it? Who it used to belong to?'

'He said that some woman in Paris gave it to him, in exchange for chocolate. Well, I hope it was in exchange for chocolate. She said that it was called a "necklace of fortune." None of the charms on it are worth very much, but every one of them is supposed to have belonged to somebody famous.'

'Such as?'

'The woman didn't know who all of them were. But the little crocodile allegedly came from Alexandre Dumas, who wrote *The Three Musketeers*. He used to wear it on his watch chain. And those earrings were brought back from Devil's Island by Alfred Dreyfus, after he was pardoned. This ring here, with the small red stone, *that* used to belong to Vincent van Gogh.'

'Surely this is worth a *fortune*,' said Molly.

'Not really. None of the charms are particularly valuable, and there's no proof at all that any of them are genuine. Felix and I did quite a lot of research into them, but we couldn't find any way to authenticate them. No certificates, no letters. No bills of sale. All we had was the word of a French woman who wanted chocolate.'

She was silent for a moment, and then she said, 'These days, I don't take much of an interest in history, not like I used to. History does nothing but take away the ones you love.'

'You say this ring was supposed to have belonged to Vincent van Gogh?'

Edwina Branson lifted up the ring between finger and thumb. 'It's only brass, and the stone is only a garnet. But if it really *is* van Gogh's ring, there's quite an interesting story behind it. You know that van Gogh shot himself, don't you?'

Molly nodded. 'I learned all about him at art college.'

'I'm afraid I only saw the Kirk Douglas movie,' Sissy confessed.

'Well, van Gogh went out into the countryside one day and shot himself in the chest with a revolver. But he didn't die straight away. He managed to walk back to the inn where he was staying and it was two more days before he finally passed away. I looked all this up on the Internet and I came across a letter from van Gogh's brother, Theo. Apparently – because he had no money – Vincent gave his ring to the serving girl at the inn who took care of him while he was dying.

'Vincent told the girl that, whatever she did, she must never give the ring to another artist, because it had madness in it. He said something like, "*Je suis deux personnes*," – "there are two of me, the good and the evil, and this ring can separate us, and allow my evil self to walk where it will." He had a split personality, didn't he? I guess that this was his way of describing how he felt.

'Funny thing, though. According to Theo, a local farmer saw Vincent propping up his easel before he went around to the back of this château where he shot himself. But only a few seconds afterward, he saw Vincent for a second time, with his pistol in his hand "almost as if there was another Vincent, following the first, intent on shooting him."'

Sissy gave Molly a meaningful look, but raised her fingertip to her lips, to indicate that Molly should say nothing.

Edwina Branson picked up another charm, a tiny citrine brooch with a single pearl dangling from it. 'I can tell you the story behind this one, too. This used to belong to Marie Curie. It was given to her by her first boyfriend, just before she left Warsaw to go to Paris. He hoped that she would be persuaded to stay in Poland and marry him. Think what a different world it might have been if she had! No radioactivity! But then – no X-rays, either.'

Sissy said, 'Even if this necklace isn't genuine, it's a fantastic conversation piece. I'm surprised you didn't want to keep it.'

Edwina Branson let the citrine brooch drop. 'No,' she said. 'I don't want to put you off it or anything, but I never liked it. That's why I only wore it once. I felt as if I had dead people hanging around my neck.'

Trevor Says No

'No,' said Trevor. 'Absolutely not. You're nuts even to *think* it.'

'But it could be the only way,' Sissy told him.

'Have you heard yourself? You want to bring Dad back to life? Not that I believe for a single second that you actually can.'

'We showed you the roses.'

'All right, you showed me the roses. But what kind of proof is that? You could have thrown the real roses away and painted some more.'

'But we didn't. They're the same roses.'

Trevor clamped his hands over his ears, to show that he didn't want to listen to any more of this lunacy. 'I don't *care* if they are the same roses. You expect me to believe that Molly's two sketches came to life, and murdered all of those people? Drawings can't hurt people, Momma. Only people can.'

'Those drawings *are* people. But they're drawings, too, which is why we need your father to hunt them down.'

'You're *nuts*,' Trevor repeated, in total exasperation. 'I mean, where's your respect? Where's your morality?'

'What difference does it make, if we can't actually do it?'

'It makes all the difference in the world, Momma. Look.'

Trevor took a silver-framed photograph of his father from the bookshelf. Thin-faced, serious, with that same diamond-shaped scar on his cheek.

'This is Dad we're talking about. My father and your husband. This is the man who loved us and looked after us and who died in the line of duty. This is not some – some superhero out of a comic book.'

'I know that, Trevor. But think of all the innocent people who have been killed already. Do you think your father would have allowed that to happen, if he thought that he could stop it?'

'Momma, read my lips. Dad is dead. Dad doesn't know anything about this Red Mask character, and never will. He's in the

Morningside Cemetery in Squash Hollow Road and that's where he's going to stay. At peace. Undisturbed. Not chasing homicidal drawings all around Cincinnati.'

Sissy took a deep breath. Victoria had gone to her bedroom, supposedly to finish her homework, but they could hear her chatting and laughing on the phone to her friend Alyson.

Molly finished wiping the dishes. She said nothing. Trevor was her husband and Trevor was Frank Sawyer's only son, so if he was adamant that he didn't want his father to be resurrected, there was nothing she could do.

Sissy said, 'These Red Masks, they're going to kill many more people, you know that, don't you?'

'So your cards say.'

'Yes, they do. And so far they've been absolutely right.'

'So far they've been totally confusing. And if you think I'm going to allow you to bring Dad back to life simply because you imagine that you can see his face reflected in some goddamned dish—'

'But you don't believe that it's possible.'

'It isn't! How the hell can it be? But it's sacrilegious enough, just *thinking* of doing it.'

Sissy sat down on the end of the couch. 'That's your last word, then, is it?'

The television was on, even though the sound was mute. WKRC's 11 p.m. news was on, showing downtown Cincinnati, and anxious shoppers being interviewed. Sissy picked up the remote in time to hear Kit Andrews saying, '—avoiding the elevators in almost all office buildings and major department stores.'

Colonel Thomas H. Streicher, Cincinnati's chief of police, appeared on the screen. 'I cannot deny that there has been a wave of panic throughout downtown Cincinnati. This afternoon, it was virtually a ghost town, with office workers leaving early and shoppers staying well away.

'But at the same time I cannot emphasize strongly enough that my officers are hunting for these murderers round the clock, and I am satisfied that we can not only apprehend them, but that we can protect the good people of Cincinnati before we do.

'So – please. Be vigilant. Be careful out there. But go about your daily business as usual. These Red Mask individuals want to cause as much fear and disruption as possible, and we should not allow them to succeed.'

'There you are,' said Sissy. 'Do your bit for the city's morale. Go out and get yourself stabbed to death by red-faced maniacs.'

'You're a cynic, Momma. You always were.'

'I'm not a cynic, Trevor. I'm a realist.'

'A realist? That's pretty rich, coming from a woman who wants to bring her dead husband back to life by having his picture painted.'

Sissy reached for the Cherry Mashes on the table, unwrapped one and popped it into her mouth. She didn't trust herself to say anything polite, so she thought it better if she said nothing at all.

That night, she dreamed that she was somewhere in the South of France, on a very hot afternoon. The sky was intensely blue and the fields were stacked with bright yellow corn. All she could hear was the sewing-machine sound of crickets in the hedgerows, and the cawing of crows as they circled overhead.

She was walking along a dry, rutted road, beside a long stone wall. At the far end of the stone wall there was a gateway, with two dilapidated oak gates. A man was standing in the gateway, with his back to her. He had a shock of gingery hair, and he was wearing a red checkered shirt. He seemed to be having trouble with a complicated wooden structure, like a deckchair frame without any canvas.

'*Monsieur*,' she said, 'do you need any help?'

The man finished folding up the deckchair, and propped it up against the gate. He turned around to face her and he was Red Mask. His eyes shone like silver ball bearings and his forehead was shiny with sweat.

'What's done is done,' he challenged her. 'What's painted is painted.'

'You can't escape,' she replied. 'It doesn't matter where you go, somebody will find you. I can promise you that.'

Red Mask seemed to be amused. 'Even if you find me, child, what can you do? *Je suis deux personnes*.'

With that, he turned and walked away, through the archway behind the gates and into the orchard beyond. He reached the corner of a sagging stone barn, and disappeared. Sissy waited, but she was reluctant to go after him. She was only seven years old, after all.

She was just about to continue on her way when the same man appeared, walking very briskly. In each hand he was carrying a large triangular butcher's knife. Sissy stepped back, frightened, to let him pass.

When he reached the gateway he stopped and stared at her as if he had never seen her before. 'What are you waiting for, child? It's no use waiting. What's done is done, and all we can do is more of the same. No rest for the wicked. No justice for the innocent. *Je suis un fou qui crois qu'il est moi-même.* I am a madman who believes that he is me.'

With that, he stalked through the gateway toward the orchard, and disappeared behind the old stone barn. Sissy felt a cold tingle of fear, and she began to run away from the gateway as fast as she could.

Up ahead of her, however, the sky began to grow black, and she saw flickers of lightning. The poplar trees along the side of the road began to rustle uncomfortably and sway. Then, on the horizon, she saw the silhouette of a giant. He was standing beside the road, as if he were waiting for her.

She stopped, panting. She didn't know what to do. She didn't want to go back to the gateway, in case she met the gingery-haired man with the knives. But she was too frightened of the giant to carry on. Perhaps she should run across the fields.

The sky grew darker and darker, and the wind began to whistle. In the field to her left, she saw several gravestones, some of them tilted at odd angles.

Frank, she thought. *Frank can save me. He may be dead, but he can save me.*

Molly set a glass of freshly-squeezed grapefruit juice on the nightstand beside Sissy, and went across the room to pull up the blinds. It was a gloomy morning, with heavy gray cloud. Scores of cicadas were still crawling around the window frame.

'Looks like rain,' said Molly.

Sissy sat up. 'Did you talk to Trevor any more?'

'I tried, Sissy, honestly, but there was no point. He never really believed in any of your psychic stuff, did he? And when Trevor makes his mind up, that's it. Stubborn is his middle name.'

Sissy said, 'I had another bad dream about Red Mask. Actually, it was a dream about van Gogh. *Two* van Goghs. One was chasing after the other, with knives.'

'It *is* that necklace that does it, isn't it?'

Sissy sipped her grapefruit juice and wiped her mouth. 'More specifically, sweetheart, I think it's that ring. Van Gogh painted so many self-portraits, and I'll bet you that whenever he was wearing that ring, his self-portrait came to life.'

Molly shrugged. 'It doesn't matter any more, anyhow. I'm not going to paint any more pictures while *I'm* wearing it.'

Sissy didn't say anything. All she could think of were the tilted gravestones, in the field, with the storm clouds gathering overhead. All she could think of was Frank, lying in the absolute darkness of his casket, and how much she needed him.

'Am I being selfish?' she asked Molly.

'I don't know what you mean.'

'Do I want to do this to save people's lives, or do I want to do it for me?'

'It's academic, Sissy. It's not going to happen. Big Chief Trevor has spoken.'

'Even if I beg you?'

'Sissy, no. We never lie to each other, Trevor and me. We never do anything behind each other's back. And I can understand how he feels. Even if I paint Frank and he *doesn't* come to life, that's just as bad as if he does.'

Sissy thought of Mary, the cleaner, dying in the darkness of the elevator. She still felt so guilty about that. If only Mary could have seen daylight, before she died. She knew what Frank would have thought about Mary, too. Frank had always been so selfless. On the afternoon that he had been killed, Frank had been acting without any regard for his own personal safety.

But of course, that had been *his* decision, not hers. Maybe Trevor was right. How could she resurrect Frank without knowing if he would be resentful at being resurrected, or angry, even? Maybe the dead preferred to be dead, sleeping their way through all eternity, resting in peace.

'How about you and me going for lunch together today?' Molly suggested.

'What about Trevor and Victoria?'

'Trevor promised to take Victoria downtown to buy her some designer jeans.'

'Designer jeans? She's nine years old!'

'You think that makes her any less fashion conscious? And she's getting an iPod, too, for doing so well in her spelling bee.'

'Hmm, OK. But I'm not so sure he should take her downtown.'

'I didn't think it was such a good idea, either. But he said that he and Victoria weren't going to be using any elevators, and besides, he doesn't believe that Red Mask will try to attack any more people, not with so many cops around.'

'Maybe not the real Red Mask . . . but how about the other two?'

'That's what I said. But he doesn't believe in them. I mean, he *believes* in them, but he thinks they're just two guys with their faces painted red. He doesn't think that they're my drawings, come to life.'

She paused, and then she said, 'He loves you, Sissy. You know that. But he thinks you're losing it, and there's not much I can do to persuade him otherwise.'

'He thinks I'm going senile?'

'He didn't exactly put it like that.'

'Oh – so how did he put it, exactly?'

'I think he used the word "bananas."'

'I'll give him bananas. I'll give him bananas where you don't need Ray-Bans.'

'Come on, Sissy. You know what he's like. Pragmatic.'

'I guess so. I just hope that he's careful. Pragmatic or not, he's still precious to me. And so is Victoria.'

'So you're OK for lunch, then?'

'Sure, I guess so. What do you have in mind?'

'A huge chicken stir-fry at Through The Garden, with Jamaican glaze.'

Sissy couldn't help smiling. 'Have you ever heard of the phrase "seriously tempted?"'

Blood on the Skywalk

'OK,' said Trevor, 'how do you spell "embarrass?"'

'Oh, Dad! You're not going to make me spell all day, are you? I did enough spelling at school!'

'Just one more word. Impress me.'

Trevor and Victoria were walking along the second-story

skywalk that overlooked Fountain Square. On the opposite side of the square stood the Tyler Davidson fountain, on top of which stood the nine-foot-high figure of a woman, with water cascading from her outstretched hands. Even though it had been raining, the square would normally have been crowded on a Saturday morning. Today, however, it was almost deserted, with shoppers hurrying across the glistening wet bricks as if they would rather be anyplace else but here.

White squad cars were parked on all four corners, and uniformed officers were gathered in almost every store doorway. Trevor had seen on the news this morning that a twenty-one-strong team from the FBI had been called in to help the CPD, including experts in serial killings, terrorist activities, and profilers.

'Two "r"s and two "s"s,' said Victoria.

'That's right!' said Trevor. Then he frowned. 'At least I *think* that's right.'

'It's easy. You just have to remember "she was *rosy red* with *severe shame*." Two "r"s and two "s"s.'

'Hey, that's excellent! And just for that, we can go to Hathaway's after we've bought your jeans, and I'll buy you a hand-dipped chocolate shake. They're really good for the waistline, so they tell me.'

They crossed over 5th Street and followed the skywalk past Tower Place Mall. The bridge that crossed over Race Street into Saks Fifth Avenue was all glassed in, and the windows were still beaded with raindrops. They had to go to Saks because Saks was the only store in Cincinnati that carried pre-worn, pre-washed Seven for all Mankind jeans for pre-teens, and that was what Victoria insisted on having.

'Look at the state of these jeans,' Trevor complained, as they rummaged through the denim department. 'They're all worn out. They're *rags*. This is more like a thrift store.'

'Daddy, that's the *whole point*. What do you think of these? Aren't they the neatest of the neat?'

'My angel, they have a huge triangular hole in the seat. They're also ninety bucks.'

'I can sew up the hole. Please, Daddy. I love them.'

Trevor turned toward the assistant, a white-faced girl in a Marc Jacobs blouse and a pair of Rock jeans with rips in the knees. He smiled conspiratorially, as if to say, Kids, what can you do? But the assistant gave him a wintry look, as if to say, You're an almost-middle-aged man, wearing a brown sport coat, what do you know?

'Cash or charge?' she asked him.

'How about a discount for the hole?'

'You want a discount for the hole?'

'I can ask, can't I?' Trevor poked his finger through it, and waggled it. 'I can't have my nine-year-old daughter displaying her tush to all and sundry.'

'*Daddy!*' Victoria protested.

'I'll ask my supervisor,' said the assistant. She left the word 'asshole' unspoken.

Ten minutes later they left the designer denim department. Victoria said, 'Daddy – sometimes you can be so-o-o embarrassing.'

'Two "r"s and two "s"s – right? But I got us a seven fifty discount, didn't I?'

They had almost reached the Race Street bridge leading back to Tower Mall when Trevor heard someone hurrying up behind them. Without warning, a heavily-built man pushed between them, almost knocking Victoria sideways.

Trevor shouted, 'Hey! Watch where you're going!' But the man kept on storming toward the bridge – at least until he reached it, when he suddenly stopped.

There were at least twenty people crossing the bridge – including six or seven children, of various ages. Trevor witnessed what happened next, but he could hardly believe it was real.

Another heavily-built man had appeared at the opposite end of the bridge. Trevor saw that he was wearing a black suit and a red shirt, and he had close-cropped, brush-like hair. But it was his face that alarmed Trevor the most. It was practically scarlet, with narrow black eyes, and a thin black gash for a mouth.

The second man crossed his arms, and then uncrossed them, pulling two enormous triangular knives out of his coat. The first man did the same. The knives made a sliding, metallic sound, and they flashed brightly as the men held them up over their heads. A woman shopper screamed, twice, and a man shouted, 'What the hell? *What?*'

The two men started to walk toward each other, making stabbing gestures in the air. The bridge was only a hundred feet long, if that, and the shoppers and their children were caught in between them. Some of them rushed to the windows and started to bang on the glass, trying to attract the attention of the car-drivers who were passing beneath them. Others started crying out, and huddling together.

They stood no chance at all. The two men bore down on them from either end of the bridge, chopping at them with such ferocity that Trevor saw fingers flying through the air. There was blood everywhere, a blizzard of blood. It spattered the windows and splashed across the skywalk in long arterial loops. The shoppers dropped to their knees, their hands covering their heads to protect themselves, but the two men continued to stab them, piercing their hands and their arms and their shoulders and their backs.

Nobody shouted or screamed. Instead, they whimpered, like animals. And all the time the knives flashed up and the knives flashed down, and there was the *chih! chih! chih!* sound of constant stabbing.

Trevor seized Victoria's sleeve and yanked her close to him. He dragged her backward into a rail of summer coats, so that they toppled over, and were buried. Victoria was gasping, 'They're killing them, Daddy! All those poor people! They're killing them!'

Trevor was rummaging through his pockets for his cell. 'Ssh!' he told her. 'Don't you move! Don't you make a sound!'

'But they're killing them!' she protested. She tried to sit up but Trevor pulled her back down again, under the coats.

'What are we going to do?' said Victoria. 'Supposing they come looking for *us*?'

Trevor punched out 911. 'Police? There's another stabbing attack in progress. Right now, yes! The skywalk bridge over Race Street, between Saks and Tower Mall. Send somebody as fast as you can!'

'*May I have your name, sir?*' asked the police operator.

Trevor snapped his cell phone shut, and then climbed up on to his hands and knees. 'You ready to make a run for it?' he asked Victoria.

Victoria, half-hidden under a pink flowery coat, gave him a nod. 'OK, then, let's make a run for it.'

The Summoning

Molly gave Victoria half a Versed tablet to calm her down, and put her to bed. Trevor chose a double Jack Daniel's instead of a sedative, and Sissy joined him.

'I couldn't believe my eyes,' he said, as he hunched in his armchair in the living room. 'It was like a horror movie. There was so much – *blood*.'

They had already seen on the news that seventeen men, women and children had been fatally injured on the Race Street skywalk. The attack had lasted a little less than three and a half minutes, but between them, the victims had been stabbed 324 times.

The two men who had perpetrated the attacks fitted the descriptions of Red Mask – or at least two out of the three Red Masks. Witnesses at both ends of the bridge had seen them rushing toward the skywalk before the attack took place, but nobody had seen where they had gone afterward.

'We are urgently appealing to anybody who might have seen these men leaving the scene of the stabbings,' said Lieutenant Kenneth Moynihan, of the homicide unit. 'So far, we have no idea how they managed to make their escape without a single person noticing them. We don't know if they went through the mall, or out through one of the department stores, or made their way along the skywalk. They could have had a getaway vehicle parked in the Fountain Square Garage, but none of the attendants there saw anybody who matches their description.'

Trevor switched the sound off. 'Do *you* have any idea?' he asked Sissy.

'I do. But do you really want me to tell you?'

'Momma, for better or for worse I saw those two Red Masks today. I saw them with my own eyes, and I saw what they can do. My God, if I hadn't had a run-in with the girl in the denim department, Victoria and I could easily have been on that skywalk, too.'

'Well, I thank whatever fates there are for that.'

'So? How do you think they got away?'

Sissy sipped her whiskey. 'You saw those roses yesterday evening. One minute they were three-dimensional, and real. The next, they were only two-dimensional – nothing but drawings.'

'And what does that tell me?'

'Roses are roses. Roses don't have intelligence, or choice. Roses can't make decisions. But men can. I'm beginning to think that those two Red Masks have the ability to choose when they want to be real, and when they want to be drawings. A man can be traced, but a drawing can hide anywhere – on a wall, on a sheet of paper, just waiting for the time when he wants to turn himself back into a man again.'

Trevor said, 'I find it so goddamned hard to get my head around all of this. Surely there must be some other explanation?'

'Like what, for instance?'

'Maybe it's some kind of a conjuring trick. You know, like Harry Houdini. *He* could make himself disappear, couldn't he? And *he* wasn't a drawing.'

Sissy laid a hand on his shoulder. 'It's all in the cards, Trevor. The cards show an image that comes to life. It's just like those killings that happened this morning. The cards predicted them, but I didn't understand what they were trying to say to me.'

She took out *L'Avertissement* and handed it to him. 'Look here. A bridge, with a man warning people not to walk across it. Red roses, entwined on the railings . . . but they're not red roses at all, they're hands, covered in blood. Seventeen of them, if you count. Adult hands, children's hands. One for every person who was killed today.'

Trevor said, 'That could be a coincidence.'

'It could be, yes. Except for the five magpies, which stand for the month of May, and for the two crosses on the hill. Diagonal crosses, two Xs. And what's the date today? May twentieth. Roman numerals, XX for twenty. Not only that . . . look at the two men nailed to the crosses. They both have red hair and red faces.'

Trevor finished his whiskey and put down his glass.

'Do you want another?' Molly asked him.

'I'd like to, but I need a clear head for this.'

Molly said, 'Whatever decision you make, honey, you know that I'll respect it.'

'I know. But I don't have a choice, do I? Not after seeing all those people butchered.'

'So you agree we should do it?' Sissy asked him.

'On one condition. That Dad really *wants* to help us. If it distresses him too much – or if anything else goes wrong – then we send him back to wherever he came from and that's an end to it. We leave him in peace.'

'Of course,' said Sissy.

Now that Trevor had actually agreed to them resurrecting Frank, she herself was less than sure that she wanted to go through with it. It had been one thing to fantasize about it, but to do it for real . . .

'I think I need a cigarette,' she said.

'Dad's not going to like it when he finds out that you're still smoking.'

'No, you're right. I don't need a cigarette.' She hesitated, and then she said, 'Goddamn it. Yes, I do.'

She went out into the yard, where the cicadas were chirping more raucously than ever. She lit a cigarette and inhaled deeply.

It had been nearly twenty-five years since two young troopers had come to her door with their hats in their hands, telling her that Frank had been killed. She had said, softly, 'Oh, dear God,' but she hadn't cried. She hadn't even cried at his funeral.

The first time she had sobbed, it had come upon her quite unexpectedly, when she was sitting with her friend in Aurora's Café drinking coffee and they had played *Oh, Pretty Woman* on the jukebox. Frank had always sung it to her – not that Frank could sing in key – but he had always found it difficult to pay her compliments, and so he let Roy Orbison do it for him.

She sang it now, under her breath. '*Pretty woman . . . walking down the street . . .*'

Molly came out, carrying a leather-bound photo album. 'I found plenty of reference,' she said. 'That's if you still want to go ahead with it.'

'I can't believe I didn't see the warning in the cards,' said Sissy. 'The twentieth of May, at a quarter after ten, on a bridge. It was all there, if only I could have read it. I could have saved all of those people's lives.'

'Sissy, you tell fortunes. You talk to dead people in mirrors. You're the most amazing, sensitive person I've ever known. But you're not infallible. Nobody is.'

Sissy turned around to face her. 'I used to be. I used to be infallible. But – well – maybe Trevor's right. Maybe I *am* losing it. Maybe I am going bananas.'

Molly had bookmarked the album and now she opened it. Inside was a large color photograph of Frank, standing on the shore at Hyannis. Sissy had taken it herself, only about two weeks before he was killed. His hair was ruffled by the ocean breeze and he was grinning at her. She had forgotten how blue his eyes were.

'That's good, that's a good one. I like that.'

'I won't draw him at the beach, though. I'll draw him here.'

'OK. Under the vine trellis, how about that?'

'I could draw him anyplace. In the living room, if you like.'

'I know. But when he materializes – if he does – it seems like something he should do without us all staring at him. Something private.'

Molly nodded. She understood what Sissy meant. She couldn't guess what it would feel like for Frank, being resurrected through a drawing of himself, but she imagined that it would be momentous, both physically and emotionally.

'What are you going to say to Victoria?' asked Sissy, as they went back inside.

'I don't know. We haven't done it yet, have we? But if we do – I guess I'll simply tell her the truth.'

'"Victoria, this is your grandpa, who died long before you were born. Come and say hi!"'

'Sissy, you're such a cynic.'

'No, I'm not. I'm a jelly, if you must know. I'm just trying to protect my feelings.'

Molly sat at her desk, while Sissy sat close beside her. Trevor stayed on the opposite side of the study, pacing up and down. Every now and then, he nervously cleared his throat, as if he were waiting for a job interview.

With the photograph of Frank at Hyannis propped up in front of her, and three smaller photographs showing his right and left profiles, and a three-quarters view, Molly began to sketch. She had never met Frank, of course, but Trevor had told her so much about him that she felt she knew him well. His matter-of-fact attitude to life, his dry sense of humor. But she also knew that he had been dedicated to helping other people, particularly those who were helpless and down on their luck, and that didn't always mean those who were victims of crime, but the criminals themselves.

Frank Sawyer had done everything he could to help a nineteen-year-old drug addict called Laurence Stepney to turn his life around. One morning he had seen Stepney and another youth trying to break into a car in the parking lot of the Big Bear Supermart near Norfolk. He had walked up to Stepney and asked him what the hell he thought he was doing. Without hesitation Stepney had pulled out a .38 revolver and shot him in the face.

'That's it,' said Sissy, as Molly started to shade in Frank's cheekbones. 'You've really got him, you know? When you come to the eyes, though . . . I always thought that Frank looked a little long-sighted . . . like he was focused on something way behind you. My friend said that he always made her feel *transparent*, as if he could see right through her.'

Trevor came halfway across the room, leaned over to peer at

Molly's sketchpad, and then went back to his pacing. 'This is not going to work, is it? I can't see how this is possibly going to work.'

Sissy said, 'Trevor . . . even if it doesn't work, we'll still end up with a very fine portrait of your father, and I can't complain about that.'

'The whole thing's nuts. *I'm* nuts for going along with it.'

'Trevor, I *like* you when you're acting nuts. You've been so serious all your life. You were even serious when you were potty-training.'

'For Christ's sake, Momma.'

'Do you know why your father married me? He told me once. He said, "Sissy – you are the most irrational person I ever met. You're completely crazy, and that's just what I need in my life. A little bit of crazy."'

'I'm sorry if I didn't inherit any of that.'

'You don't think so? I think you did. I think you're more like me than you care to admit.'

Now Molly was filling in the shadows under Frank's cheekbones, and the lines around his mouth. She really was a remarkable artist, thought Sissy. Her portraits weren't at all like photographs. In a way, they were much more real than photographs. They breathed life, and character. As she highlighted his lips, Sissy almost expected Frank to start talking to her. And as the drawing came nearer and nearer to completion, Trevor came back across the room, and stood right behind her, staring at his dead father in fascination, but also in deeply-suppressed pain.

'OK,' said Molly, at last. She held the portrait up so that they could see it better. 'All we can do now is wait and see if anything happens.'

'Well, I suggest we leave it for a while,' said Sissy. 'Let's sit down and have a drink, and say a prayer to whatever gods we happen to believe in.'

Molly washed her paintbrush and put it back into its jelly jar. Before she stood up, she sorted through her necklace until she found the brass-and-garnet ring, and squeezed it tight between finger and thumb.

'Saying a prayer to Vincent van Gogh?' Sissy asked her.

'Asking for his blessing,' said Molly. 'If anybody knew what madness and fear and disappointment were all about, *he* did.'

They left the study and went back into the living room. Trevor filled up their glasses and they sat down and looked at each other, almost as if they had done something for which they should all feel guilty.

'Do you want to smoke, Momma?' Trevor asked her.

Sissy blinked at him in surprise. 'You don't mean that, do you?'

'What the hell. What difference is it going to make?'

'Well, thank you for your consideration,' said Sissy. 'But your father's coming back, and you know what *he* felt about my smoking.'

They sat in silence for five minutes longer. Then the phone warbled, making Sissy jump. Molly picked it up and said, 'Sawyer residence. Oh, Mike. How are you? . . . I know, terrible. Victoria's really upset. Well, and Trevor is, too. I know.'

She covered the receiver with her hand and said, 'Mike Kunzel. He wants to know if I can draw him another composite.'

'Not if you're wearing that necklace, you can't.'

'Of course I won't. And I don't have to go downtown. Trevor saw the perpetrators as clear as anybody. I can do it here.'

She took her hand away from the receiver. 'For sure, Mike. I can do that. Give me an hour, and I'll e-mail it to you.'

She said, 'Yes,' and then, 'yes,' and then she held out the receiver for Sissy. 'He'd like a word with you, too.'

'Me?'

Detective Kunzel said, 'Hi, Mrs Sawyer. How's it going?'

'Well, we're all very upset, naturally.'

'Last time that Red Mask called me on my cell phone, you said that he had given us a clue. But I never had the chance to ask you what it was.'

'No, you didn't, and I have to say that I was kind of relieved. I didn't think that you'd believe me, even if I told you.'

'Try me, Mrs Sawyer. You never know. I'm supposed to be the most skeptical guy in the unit, but there are times when even us skeptical guys find ourselves clutching at straws. We've raided three addresses this afternoon, looking for red-faced men – one in Betts-Longworth and two in Over-the-Rhine. But the only red faces were ours.'

Sissy tried to choose her words with care. 'Let me put it this way, Detective. You've heard about people having doppelgängers, exact doubles of themselves?'

'Go on.'

'I think that the two Red Masks who killed those people at the

Giley Building and the Four Days Mall, and the two Red Masks who killed those people on the skywalk this morning – I think they could be doppelgängers, of a kind.'

'I don't get it. You mean, like identical twins?'

'In a way. But identical twins are two separate people. These are the same person, twice. Like two copies of the same picture.'

There was a very long pause. Then Detective Kunzel said, 'I'm sorry, Mrs Sawyer. You got me there. I don't really understand what you're saying.'

'It doesn't really matter if you understand it or not, Detective. The most important thing is to be aware of it. When you send your men out looking for these Red Masks, tell them to watch their backs. My cards have given me a very strong warning: the hunters could end up becoming the hunted.'

'Well . . . I'm a whole lot more confused than I was a minute ago,' said Detective Kunzel. 'But I'll take your word for it. I'll tell my men to look out for one guy who could be two guys.'

'He may be no guys at all,' Sissy told him.

Another pause. 'Let's just stick to your doppelgängers for now,' said Detective Kunzel. 'But if you do have any more theories—'

Sissy hung up and handed the phone back to Molly. 'I have a very bad feeling about this,' she said.

Mr Boots, who had been sleeping on the carpet next to the couch, suddenly lifted his head and let out a *Whuff!*

'See? Mr Boots can feel it, too.'

A Painting of Frank

Eleven o'clock chimed. Molly felt too tired to stay up any longer, and so she went to bed – 'although if anything happens, you have to wake me!'

After another twenty minutes, Trevor followed her, and then there were only Sissy and Mr Boots in the living room, with the cicadas busy singing outside, and the weary ticking of the wall clock.

Sissy went into Molly's study to see if the painting of Frank was still there. She looked down at it sadly, and touched his lips with her fingertips, as if she expected to feel him kissing her. One fall day, when they were kicking their way through the leaves, he had said to her, 'You were so easy to fall in love with. And so easy to *stay* in love with.'

'Frank,' she whispered. Then she went back into the living room and sat on the couch so that she could stroke Mr Boots's ears while he dreamed of whatever he dreamed of. Not giants, that was for sure. Nor red-faced men with butchers' knives and slits instead of eyes.

Sissy slept, and snored, without realizing that she was snoring. She dreamed that she was walking through an underground parking lot, all echoes and shouts and squealing tires, and that she didn't know which way to get out of it.

'*Watch your backs!*' she called out, but her voice was thin and strangulated, and she wasn't sure if anybody could hear her. '*There are two of them! Watch your backs!*'

She woke up with a jolt. The living room was dark, but the desk lamp in the study was still shining. Mr Boots stirred in his sleep but didn't wake up. The wall clock told her that it was ten after two in the morning.

She eased herself up from the couch and went through to the kitchen. She poured herself a glass of iced water from the fridge and drank it all in one, so that she gasped. Outside, the yard was in shadow, although the sky was stained with orange from the city lights. She opened the back door and stood there for a while, listening to the sounds of the night.

As her eyes became accustomed to the darkness, she saw somebody underneath the vine trellis. A man, sitting quite still. She slowly lifted her hand to her mouth and bit her knuckle, partly out of fear and partly to make sure that she was really awake. She had never felt a sensation like this before: such a mixture of elation and terror. She didn't know whether to call out for Trevor and Molly, or to go back into the kitchen and lock the door behind her, or to challenge the man to his face.

But it was the man who spoke first. 'Excuse me,' he asked her, 'where *is* this?' – as if he had fallen asleep on a train journey, and just woken up.

Sissy approached him. His face was hidden in the shadows, but she recognized the wave of gray hair.

'Frank?' she said. 'Frank – is that you?'

'Where am I? I don't know how the hell I got here. Is this a dream?'

She sat down beside him. Now she could see that he really was Frank. That lean, angular face. That diamond-shaped scar. He even *smelled* like Frank, of Boss aftershave, which she had given him for Christmas, twenty-four years ago.

'This isn't a dream, Frank. We've called you back.'

'Called me back? Called me back from where?'

'It isn't easy to explain. But this is Trevor's house, in Cincinnati.'

'Trevor's house? What do you mean? You mean Trevor doesn't live at home any more? Why?'

'Trevor's all grown up now, Frank. He's married, and he has a nine-year-old daughter.'

'Trevor? How can that be? Trevor's only eleven.'

'You've been away, Frank. It's been twenty-four years.'

'What are you talking about? What do you mean, I've been away? Where?'

Sissy laid her hand on top of his, but almost immediately he drew his hand back.

'You've heard about people in a coma,' said Sissy. 'What happened to you, it's kind of like that.'

'I've been unconscious? For twenty-four years? You don't expect me to believe that?'

'It's true, Frank. I'll take you inside to see Trevor, then you'll believe me.'

Frank didn't say anything for almost half a minute. The cicadas chirruped on and on, and somewhere in the night, a police siren wailed.

'So who are you?' Frank asked her, at last. 'I'm sure I recognize your voice.'

'Lots of things have changed, including me.'

'*Sissy?*'

'Yes,' she said. She was very close to tears. 'Not quite the Sissy you remember, but still the same Sissy.'

Frank stood up, so that the light from the kitchen window shone on his face. Sissy couldn't believe how young he looked. When he was forty-seven and she was forty-five, she had always thought that both of them were beginning to show the signs of encroaching age.

'Here,' he said, and held out his hand. Sissy took it, and he helped her on to her feet.

'Your hair,' he said. 'What's happened to your hair, darling?'

She turned toward the light. 'Not only my hair, Frank.'

He touched her cheek, very gently. There were tears sparkling in his eyes. 'I don't understand,' he told her. 'Have I really been unconscious for so long?'

She held his wrist and kissed his fingertips. 'I'm so sorry. I shouldn't have called you back, should I?'

'I still don't understand. How did I lose consciousness? How come I'm not in a hospital or anything? Twenty-four *years*, did you say?'

He looked around the yard, at the clusters of chirruping cicadas. 'This *is* a dream, isn't it? This can't be real. But it feels so damn real.'

'Why don't you come inside?' said Sissy. 'Then I can explain.'

Frank stared at her. 'Oh my God,' he said. 'This *isn't* a dream, is it?'

Bad Memories

Frank followed Sissy into the kitchen as if he were concussed. He looked around, taking in the flowery red-and-yellow drapes and the hutch with its decorative pottery plates and jugs. He peered closely at the family photographs on the wall beside the fridge.

'Is this—?' he asked, pointing at a picture of Trevor.

Sissy nodded. 'That's right. Looks so much like you, don't you think?'

'And this is his wife? And his daughter?'

'Molly and Victoria. Molly's an artist. Well – you can see by all of these flower paintings. They're all hers. This landscape, too. Do you recognize it? New Milford Green. She painted it when she and Trevor came to visit last fall.'

Frank pulled out a chair and sat down at the kitchen table. 'I'm finding this real hard to take in, Sissy. The way you look, everything. You're still just as pretty as you ever were. But I've missed out on so many years, haven't I? How could that happen?'

Sissy sat down opposite him and took hold of his hands. 'It's so wonderful you came back. You don't have any idea how much I've missed you.'

'Is Trevor here? Aren't you going to tell him I'm back?'

'Of course I am. But there's something you need to know. It's going to be very difficult for you to understand, and if it makes you angry with me, then I won't be at all surprised.'

'You've found somebody else. Is that it? After twenty-four years, darling, I can't say that I blame you.'

Sissy said, 'I have had plenty of men friends, yes. Good ones, some of them. But nobody serious. And nobody who could ever replace you.'

'So why am I going to be angry?'

Sissy stood up again and went over to the sink. She took down a small mirror with a frame made of ceramic daisies. She handed it to Frank and said, 'Take a look at yourself, Frank. Tell me what you see.'

Frank frowned into the mirror. Then he touched his forehead and prodded his cheeks. 'I don't *look* old, do I?' he said. 'I mean, I don't look as old as you do. How come?'

'The last twenty-four years, Frank – well, let's put it this way, they just passed you by.'

'They passed me by? How in God's name did that happen?'

'Do you remember a kid called Laurence Stepney?'

'Sure I do. A real tearaway, that boy, but if I can straighten him out, I reckon that he could go far. Heck – listen to me. If twenty-four years have gone by, then Laurence Stepney must be nearly forty by now.'

'Do you remember him trying to steal a car from the Big Bear Supermart?'

Frank thought for a while. Then he slowly nodded. 'Kind of . . . him and some other kid called Thomas Cusack.'

'You tried to stop him, Frank. Can you remember that?'

Frank's eyes, which always looked as if he were longsighted, seemed to focus even further away, into the past. He reached out his hand as if he were trying to take hold of somebody's shoulder.

'Yes – yes, I do remember. I said, "You're not letting *me* down, Laurence. Only yourself, and your parents."'

'Then what happened?'

Frank lowered his hand and looked up at Sissy in bewilderment. 'I don't know. I honestly don't know. What *did* happen?'

'Laurence Stepney shot you, Frank. He shot you without any warning at point-blank range.'

Frank looked down at his chest, almost as if he expected to see his shirt soaked in blood. 'Is that what put me into a coma?'

'No, Frank.' Sissy had to stop for a moment, because she was so choked up. 'That's what killed you.'

Frank sat in complete silence while Sissy explained about the roses, and the ring, and Red Mask, and what the DeVane cards had predicted.

'That's why we called you back, Frank. It's the only way I could think of to save scores more people from being murdered. But Trevor and I agreed that if you didn't want to help us, if you wanted to rest in peace, then we'd honor your wishes, and let you go back to sleep.'

Frank lifted his left hand, and stared at it. 'So what you're telling me is that I'm dead, and this is a dead man's hand?'

'The Frank Sawyer I was married to, the actual Frank Sawyer, he's dead, yes, and his remains are lying in the Morningside Cemetery in New Milford. But you are Frank Sawyer's likeness. You have Frank Sawyer's memories, and Frank Sawyer's character, and hopefully you have Frank Sawyer's talent for hunting down criminals.'

'I'm a *painting*?'

'You were recreated as a painting, yes. We don't know for sure how it happens, but we think that the ring on Molly's necklace has the power to bring her paintings to life.'

Frank stood up. He touched Sissy's hair, and wound one of her silver curls around his finger. 'Wild as ever,' he told her. 'Never known a woman whose hair was always so flyaway.'

'I loved you, Frank. I loved you so much. When you were killed, it was like I was killed, too.'

'How can I be a painting?' Frank asked her. He traced her eyebrow with his fingertip, and touched her cheek, and then her lips. 'How can a painting walk, and talk, and wind your hair around his finger?'

'I don't know. I just don't know. But there are so many stories about paintings and drawings that come to life.'

'Crazy,' said Frank, and shook his head. 'I always said you were crazy, didn't I? That's why I love you so much.'

Sissy said, 'Do you think you want to stay and help us, my darling? Or do you want to go back?'

'I was dead. Now I'm alive again. Maybe I'm only a painting, but I still *feel* like me. So what do you think?'

'Let me wake up Trevor and Molly.'

She turned toward the corridor that led to their bedroom, but she didn't have to go to rouse them. Trevor and Molly were standing in the doorway, staring at Frank as if they were two children who had surprised Santa putting out their presents.

'Dad,' said Trevor, with a catch in his throat. 'Dad, I don't believe it!'

He came forward. The two of them looked at each other for a moment, long-lost father and grown-up son. Then they embraced each other tightly, as if they never wanted to let go, ever again.

'It *is* a miracle,' said Trevor. 'It really works. It *is* a miracle.'

Sissy turned to Molly and smiled. Molly was wiping her eyes on the sleeve of her stripy nightshirt. 'You did wonderful work tonight, Molly. He's just like the Frank that I remember.'

Molly was holding her necklace in her hand, and she held it up. 'Look,' she said. 'I could see it glowing on my dressing table and I knew that something must be happening.'

The stone in van Gogh's ring was shining so brightly that it looked as if it had a red light in it.

Molly said, 'It must be like *your* ring, Sissy – except that your ring goes dark to show that people are telling lies.'

'Yes,' said Sissy. She took the necklace and held it up in front of Frank's face, so that the ring was reflected in his eyes, like twin red sparks. 'It can sense that you're alive,' she told him. 'And – look – the closer it gets to you, the brighter it shines.'

'How about a drink to celebrate?' Trevor suggested.

'Trevor, it's three o'clock in the morning.'

'So what? I have a bottle of cuvée Napa in the fridge if anybody fancies some. This is something that's really worth celebrating, don't you think?' He hesitated, and then he said, 'Dad? You do drink, don't you? What I mean is, you *can* drink?'

Frank shrugged. 'So far as I know. I feel real enough, don't I? I expect I can eat, too. You still make that corned-beef hash, Sissy?'

They sat in the living room talking until it began to grow light outside. Even though Sissy knew that 'Frank' wasn't the real Frank that she had buried, the experience of seeing him again and sitting next to him again made her feel so young and happy that she couldn't stop herself from smiling.

It was only when she caught sight of the two of them in the mirror that she grew quieter, because he was so much younger than her. Twenty-four years had etched their marks around her eyes, and around her mouth, and these days she usually wore a silk scarf or a large enameled necklace to hide her neck.

'So what happens next?' asked Frank. 'How do I locate these two Red Mask characters?'

'I think the best place to start is the Giley Building,' said Sissy. 'That was where Red Mask first attacked George Woods and Jane Becker. Like I told you, I couldn't sense him at all, and the police tracker dogs couldn't pick up any kind of scent. But that was where Molly first drew him, and I think there's a very strong possibility that he's hiding out there.'

'And if we find them? What do we do then?'

'Summary justice,' said Sissy. 'There's no point in trying to arrest them, and put them in jail. They would simply disappear. When we find them, we have to destroy them. It's as simple as that.'

Frank finished his glass of sparkling wine. 'That was good,' he said. 'Never tasted nothing like that before. Who would have thought twenty-four years ago that young Trevor would be educating his own daddy in sophisticated tastes?'

Sissy said, 'I'm going to start by seeing if *you* can sense where the Red Masks are hiding. After all, you're the same as they are, a painting, and you can follow them into places that nobody else can.'

'I'm not psychic like you, Sissy. I never could understand how you knew there was somebody coming to pay us a visit, about an hour before they showed up, or how you could tell when something bad was going to happen.'

'I know, darling. But you always had an intuition for hunting down the bad guys, didn't you? And I think you'll find that you have new abilities now.'

Frank turned his head around. 'I can *hear* something,' he said. 'I've been hearing it ever since I got here.'

He stood up, and approached Molly's painting of New Milford Green, with its colonial houses and its bandstand and its scattering of leaves on the grass. He lifted his hand toward it, and said, 'I can feel the wind, Sissy. I can hear the cars going by, and the people talking.'

He turned back toward her, but as he did so he staggered, and his knees gave way. He seized the back of one of the kitchen chairs, but he collapsed on to the floor, with the chair on top of him.

'Frank!' said Sissy, kneeling down beside him. 'Frank, are you OK?'

Frank looked up at her. The pupils of his eyes were very small, as if he had been staring into an intensely bright light.

'I'm OK, I think. Funny turn, that's all. For one second . . . I didn't know where I was.'

Sissy took hold of his hand, lifted it toward her lips, and kissed his wedding band. 'Wherever you are, Frank, you'll always be with me. Always.'

Hide-and-Go-Seek

Detective Kunzel was sitting at the counter in Hathaway's, the 1950s-style diner with the pink Formica tabletops, forking up a breakfast of scrapple and fried eggs. The waitress had just come up to ask him if he wanted more apple butter when his cell phone played *Hang On, Sloopy.*

'Kunzel,' he answered.

'*Enjoying your breakfast, Detective?*' whispered the harsh voice of Red Mask. '*Could be your last, if you're not careful. The condemned detective's last meal.*'

'What do you want, you murdering piece of shit?' Detective Kunzel demanded, and the elderly man sitting next to him turned and stared at him in alarm.

'*It's not what* I *want, is it? I'm getting what* I *want. I'm getting my revenge, in spades. No, Detective, I'm talking about what* you *want.*'

'Go on,' said Detective Kunzel, putting down his fork. Suddenly he didn't have an appetite any more.

'*You want* me, *don't you? You want to see me handcuffed, and locked up in a cell, and then hauled up in front of a court and sentenced to death. You want to see me in Mansfield, don't you, with a needle in my arm?*'

'Well, you got that right. But I'm not going to assume that you're going to give yourself up.'

'I'm not. You think I'm a fool? But justice is justice, Detective. Justice should be fair, and I'm giving you the chance to come after me.'

'Why would you do that?' he asked Red Mask. He waved the waitress away, and said, 'No, thanks.'

'Maybe I'm bored. Maybe I feel like some sport, along with my revenge. Maybe killing all of these poor innocent folks is getting to be as easy as shooting fish in a barrel.'

'So this *is* about what you want?'

'You don't have to take me up on this, Detective. But it's a one-time offer. After this, it's back to the massacres. No rest for the wicked, remember. No mercy for the innocent, neither.'

'All right, then, Mr Mask,' said Detective Kunzel. 'What exactly do you propose?'

'You can find me at noon exactly, in the parking structure next to the Giley Building. Bring plenty of back-up. You're going to need it.'

With that, Red Mask cut off the connection. Detective Kunzel immediately punched out Lieutenant Booker's number at headquarters.

They parked across the street from the Giley Building and climbed out of their car. Although it was nearly noon the street was in shadow, and unnaturally chilly.

'He couldn't have picked anyplace grimmer, could he?' said Detective Bellman, looking up at the eight-story parking structure. It had been built in the late 1950s, and it was due for demolition as soon as the Giley Building itself was vacated. It was made of grimy concrete, with black streaks down the walls. The sides of each floor were open, but they were all covered with rusty steel mesh.

Three squad cars had already parked on Race Street, and twelve more would arrive in the next few minutes, without sirens or lights. The CPD had cordoned off a six-block area between Elm and Vine Streets, from 7th Street as far south as 3rd Street.

'Here come the cavalry,' said Detective Kunzel, as two black SWAT vans appeared around the corner, followed closely by three silver-metallic cars carrying FBI agents. Off to the north-east, they could hear the *flacker-flacker-flacker* of a police helicopter. There were two police sharpshooters on board, but the helicopter crew had been instructed to stay well away unless Red Mask ventured out on to the parking structure's flat roof.

Two FBI agents came over. One of them was tall and wide-shouldered, with a jutting chin and black slicked-back hair like a young Jack Lord from the early series of *Hawaii Five-O*. The other was black, with a shaved head, and he had the steel-sprung walk of a man who gets up at 5 a.m. every morning for a punishing workout.

'Agent Morrison, Agent Greene,' Detective Kunzel acknowledged them.

Special Agent Morrison looked up at the parking structure. 'So what's going down, Detective? Lieutenant Booker said that the unsub challenged you to meet him here.'

'That's right. He pretty much told me that he was bored with killing defenseless people, and wanted a little sport.'

'You say "he" like he's only one person.'

'I know. But I'm pretty sure it's the same guy who calls me up every time. And he's adamant that he has no accomplice.'

Special Agent Morrison turned to Special Agent Greene. 'Can you believe this? I've had to deal with so many schizos over the years, who seriously believe that they're two different people. But this is the first time I have ever come across two different people making out like there's only one of them.'

'Could be twins,' Special Agent Greene suggested. 'Sometimes they have this really highly-developed synchronicity. You know – one of them bangs his thumb with a hammer and the other one says, "Shit!"'

Detective Kunzel blew his nose. 'Whatever the truth of it is, these guys are illogical, apparently motiveless, and it seems like they're killing people just for the kicks. But remember what I told you when I first briefed you: however many Red Masks there are, they seem to be able to come and go without being seen, and they have no moral compunction about who they attack.'

'OK, Detective. Thanks for that. Let's hope we can wrap this one up for you.'

Two SWAT teams of ten officers each had climbed out of their vans and were gathering around the front of the parking structure. The entrance was low, with a huge concrete beam over it, bearing the letters G LEY BUI D G PAR ING. Immediately inside stood a red-and-white sentry box in which an attendant usually sat to collect parking fees. Then a concrete ramp curved up to the left, its surface shiny from years of use.

'Why do I have such a bad feeling about this?' asked Detective Bellman, as one of the SWAT teams started to jog up the ramp, their rubber-soled boots squeaking on the concrete. The other team split up and headed to the right – four toward the elevator and six toward the stairs.

'You're beginning to sound like Mrs Sawyer,' said Detective Kunzel. 'Double, double, toil and trouble. There's a logical explanation for this Red Mask character, believe me, whether he's one perpetrator or two.' All the same, he couldn't help thinking of Sissy's last words to him. *Be careful: the hunters could end up becoming the hunted.*

The SWAT team had reached the first parking level. One of them appeared behind the rusty mesh and shouted out, 'First level clear!' Immediately, the two FBI agents took out their guns and followed them into the building and up the ramp.

'Are *we* going in?' asked Detective Bellman.

'No need. Not yet, anyhow. These guys know what they're doing.'

'*Level two clear!*' they heard, over Detective Bellman's radio.

They waited two or three minutes. Then they heard, '*Level three clear!*'

'I don't think Red Mask is even here,' said Detective Bellman. 'He's probably watching us from some office building across the street, laughing his goddamned nuts off.'

'*Elevator – elevator has malfunctioned,*' said a different voice, over the radio. Then, '*We're immobilized halfway between the sixth and seventh floors.*'

Detective Kunzel said, 'Shit.'

A minute-long pause, then, '*We need a technician to get us out of here. We've tried everything but the emergency switch has been disconnected. All the goddamned wires have been cut.*'

Another pause, and then, '*The hatch is jammed. We can't open it. We're pretty much trapped.*'

Detective Kunzel snapped, 'He's in there, Freddie! Red Mask is in there! Come on!'

They hurried across the street toward the parking structure. Before they could enter the building, though, Detective Kunzel's cell phone rang.

'Kunzel. Is that you?'

'I'm waiting for you, Detective. I thought this was going to be our showdown.'

'I'll meet you face to face any time you like. Just tell me where you are.'

'Sorry, Detective. You'll have to come find me. High Noon. That's the name of this story, isn't it?'

Detectives Kunzel and Bellman entered the parking structure. It smelled of oil and dust and diseased concrete. Inhuman smells. But what surprised them was how silent it was. Only the dripping of a sprinkler pipe, and the soft flapping of a discarded newspaper.

'Which way?' asked Detective Bellman, crouching down low with his SIG-Sauer automatic held in both hands.

'I don't know. Let's go up to level two and check it out.'

They climbed cautiously up the ramp until they reached the second level. There were no cars parked here except for a thirteen-year-old Buick station wagon covered in thick, sandy-colored dust.

'Maybe we should try the stairs instead.'

'I don't know, man. I don't like this one little bit. Why is it so quiet? There are twenty SWAT guys in this building, and it's like a fricking church.'

Detective Kunzel sniffed. 'It could be they have Red Mask cornered, and they don't want to make any sound in case they reveal their position.'

'You really believe that?'

'I don't know what to believe. But we won't find out unless we go up and take a look, will we?'

They walked across to the door that led to the stairwell. But as Detective Kunzel opened it, they heard scuffling and shouting from one of the levels up above them. Then a scream. They looked upward, between the dark concrete pillars, and then at each other.

'Jesus H. Christ!' said Detective Kunzel. He had heard men scream before, when they were shot, or stabbed, or had their arms broken, or when they were doused in blazing gasoline. But he had never heard a scream like this before. It had started off as a piercing, panicky falsetto, like somebody begging, *Please don't hurt me, please don't hurt me*, but now it descended into a wide, agonized howl.

There was a last shout of utter despair, and then it stopped.

Detective Kunzel unclipped his radio. 'Control? This is Kunzel. What the hell's going on? We're inside the building and we can hear screaming from one the upper floors.'

His radio made a blurting noise, and then he heard, '*—signal, can't – have to pull back—*'

'Control? I can't hear you! What's happening up there?'

'*—see who's—*'

The radio crackled and went dead. He shook it, and slapped it furiously in the palm of his hand, but it still didn't work. 'Goddamned piece of Chinese crap. Try yours.'

Detective Bellman tried his radio, too. He listened intently, but after a few moments he had to shake his head. 'I think I can hear somebody shouting, but they're much too faint.'

Detective Kunzel said, 'Something's gone shit-shaped. We need to get up there, fast.'

'Hey – do you seriously think that's a good idea? There are ten SWAT guys up there, and two FBI agents. You think they can't handle a psycho like Red Mask? Or even two psychos like Red Mask?'

'Maybe it's *three* psychos like Red Mask,' said Detective Kunzel. 'But the point is, we won't find out unless we go up there.'

All the same, he felt suddenly afraid. The Cincinnati SWAT teams were highly trained, and some of the best in the country. They were armed with Colt carbines and Glock automatic pistols and shotguns that fired tear-gas, as well as flashbangs to deafen and blind any adversary, and 50,000-volt Tasers. But so far he had heard no radio reports of any arrests. No shots fired, no CQC. Only that long-drawn-out scream, and then silence.

'We should call for more back-up,' said Detective Bellman.

Detective Kunzel tried his radio again. Like Detective Bellman, he thought he could hear some tiny, faraway voices, as faint as flies, but it was impossible to make out what they were saying.

'Control,' he repeated. 'Can you hear me, control?'

There was no response. Detective Bellman said, 'Come on, man. We just can't get a signal in here, that's all. These walls – they must be six feet thick.'

'Maybe you're right,' said Detective Kunzel. He glanced upward again. 'Let's get back outside.'

They were less than halfway down the ramp, however, when they heard another scream, just as agonized as the first, but even higher, like the climactic note in some hideous opera. It echoed and echoed down through the tiers, until it abruptly ended with a loud bang, which sounded more like a huge door slamming than a gunshot.

Detective Kunzel dragged out his gun again and started to run back upward, his belly joggling under his brown checkered shirt. Detective Bellman reluctantly ran after him.

When he reached the crest of the ramp, Detective Kunzel roared out, 'CPD detectives! CPD detectives! What in the name of God is happening up there, you guys? SWAT commander! Can you hear me? Sergeant Rookwood! Kenneth! Special Agent Morrison!'

There was no answer, only a strange scraping noise, and then nothing.

Detective Kunzel said, 'Jesus,' and hurried over to the stairs.

'Mike!' said Detective Bellman. 'This is not a good idea!'

Detective Kunzel opened the door to the stairwell. He was panting and sweating. 'People are being hurt up there, Freddie. What do you expect me to do?'

'Be serious, Mike. If the Red Masks have killed all of those SWAT guys, and those two FBI agents, what do you think they're going to do to us two mooks?'

'It's our job to save people in danger, Freddie. To protect and serve.'

'Sure. But it's not our job to commit suicide, is it? Who was the first person to tell me that you never rush headlong into any situation where you might get killed?'

'So what are we going to do, Freddie? Mosey back down to the street to round up some more back-up, while even more of our people are being killed?'

'For Christ's sake, Mike. You don't *know* they're being killed. You don't have any idea what's happening, do you?'

'What did it *sound* like, Freddie? People don't scream like that unless they're sure that they're going to die. Don't tell me you don't remember that young guy on Walnut Street – the one who got crushed by that Metro bus? Now – I'm going up there, OK, and there's nothing that you can do or say to stop me.'

With that, he seized hold of the handrail and started to heave himself up the staircase.

Detective Bellman hesitated, then he shouted, 'I'm going for back-up! OK?'

'OK! OK! Do whatever you damn well like!'

Carrion

Detective Kunzel reached the next level and kicked open the door. He listened and waited for a moment. Nothing. No sound at all, except for dripping, and the faintest soughing of a draft down the stairwell, as if the parking structure was an elderly cancer victim who was breathing his last.

He stuck his head out, looking quickly to the left and then to the right. He kept his gun held tight in both hands, the slide cocked back ready.

'*Red Mask!*' he shouted, in a phlegmy voice.

Still nothing.

'Special Agent Morrison! Special Agent Greene!'

He waited and waited but there was no response. He started to climb up to the next level, panting. His shoes made a chuffing sound of the concrete steps, like a train. He wished to God that he had gone easy on the scrapple and goetta breakfasts. His chest felt tight and the blood was thumping in his ears.

He had one more flight of steps to go when he heard another agonized scream. He stopped, gasping for breath, and listened. Although the hollow structure of the building made it very hard to decide exactly where the scream was coming from, he could tell that it was close.

God save whoever that is, and please save me too. He knew that he had to go on. He could have stayed here in the stairwell and waited for Detective Bellman to bring more back-up. But if he did, and he later discovered that he could prevented more officers from being killed, how was he going to live with himself for the rest of his life?

He continued to climb.

'I'm coming, you bastard,' he repeated. 'I'm coming, you bastard. I'm coming. You. Bastard.'

He reached the next landing. He dragged out his big red handkerchief and wiped the sweat from his face, and wiped his hands, too, and the butt of his automatic. He crossed himself, even though he wasn't a Catholic. He thought that he might as well hedge his bets. Then he pushed open the door and stepped out of it, moving across the floor as nimbly as a waltz instructor, swinging his gun from left to right, and back again.

At first he thought that this floor was deserted, too. There were no vehicles next to the stairwell, and all the parking spaces on the right-hand side were taken up with broken cardboard boxes and rolls of worn-out green stair carpet.

He waited for a few seconds, and then he edged his way around the stairwell to the main parking area, still treading lightly, still swinging his gun. But as he came around the corner, he stopped dead, and his stomach seemed to drop, as if he had stepped off the edge of a building.

Hanging from the sprinkler pipes which ran across the ceiling were the mutilated bodies of the SWAT team, all ten of them, and the two FBI agents, too. Somehow their heads had been forced into the gap between the pipes and the concrete ceiling, and then their bodies had been reduced to rags, as if each of them had been stabbed more than a hundred times.

Detective Kunzel tried his radio again, but it still produced nothing but a crackle. He advanced slowly across the concrete floor, half-crouching, keeping his gun held high. He glanced at each of the bodies he passed, but he didn't want to look too closely. Some of them had been so severely cut up that their insides had dropped out, and were hanging between their thighs in glistening loops. Most of them were still dripping blood.

He felt that he was making his way through the larder of some terrible flesh-hungry monster. He crossed himself again, but this time it was less for his own protection than a gesture of respect for the dead.

'*Red Mask!*' he shouted. He tried to sound stern but his voice came out as more of a scream. '*Red Mask! Where are you hiding yourself, you sadistic bastard?*'

He had to sidestep to make his way around the suspended bodies of Special Agents Morrison and Greene. Special Agent Morrison's face had been so comprehensively sliced open that Detective Kunzel recognized him only from his dark suit and his highly-polished black Oxfords.

'Red Mask! Come out and show yourself! Or are you too goddamned chickenshit?'

He crossed the parking area toward the elevator.

'Red Mask! You wanted to see me? Well, here I am!'

As he turned the corner, he jerked in shock, and almost let off a shot. On the whitewashed brick wall directly in front of him was a life-sized painting of Red Mask, with two bloodstained butchers' knives, one in each hand. His face was scarlet and he was grinning triumphantly.

Detective Kunzel span around, expecting the real Red Mask to come up behind him, but there was nobody there. He approached the painting with a mixture of bewilderment and dread. Who the hell had painted it, and why? It was so detailed that it almost looked alive.

'Red Mask!' he shouted, yet again.

'*Looking for me?*' said a hoarse voice, close behind him.

He swung around again. Red Mask was standing only a few feet away from him, in a red shirt and a black suit. His face was even redder than Detective Kunzel had imagined it would be, and shinier, and his eyes and his mouth were thin black slits, as if they had been cut into his face with a sharp knife.

Although Red Mask was so close, his image appeared to be wavering slightly, as if Detective Kunzel were looking at him through a haze of rising heat.

Detective Kunzel cleared his throat. Then he said, 'Take your knives out real slow and toss them out of reach.'

Red Mask held up both of his hands, palms outward, like a conjuror. '*I don't have any knives, Detective. See?*'

'Open your coat. Do it real easy.'

Red Mask opened the front of his coat. There were no knives there, either.

'OK . . . now I need you to get down on the floor. Flat on your face. Arms and legs spread wide.'

'*Oh, I don't think so, Detective. I came here today to talk to you, not to give myself up. Look around you. My work isn't finished yet. Not by a long chalk.*'

'I'm giving you a count of three to kiss the concrete, Mr Mask. If you haven't done it by then, I'm going to drop you, and that's a promise.'

'*If you do that, how are you going to find out how I managed to make such mincemeat out of all of your fellow officers? I mean, look at them, Detective. Twelve good men and true. Courageous fellows, all of them. Heroic, even. And armed to the eyeballs. How can one man hang them all up like so many sides of beef? One man, all on his ownsome? If you know the answer to that, Detective, then by all means go ahead and drop me. But otherwise, you just listen to what I have to say to you, and you listen good.*'

'One,' Detective Kunzel warned him. 'Two.'

'*You're not going to shoot me, Detective, and the reason you're not going to shoot me is because you believe there's two of me, or even more. I've sworn to you that there ain't, but you can't work that out, either, can you? And suppose I'm lying to you, and there is two of me, or three, or even five? If you shoot me now, how are you going to find out if they truly exist, and where they are, and what they're bent on doing next?*'

'Three,' said Detective Kunzel. 'That's it.'

Red Mask raised both his hands, not so much in surrender, but in exasperation.

'*You don't have any idea what you're up against, do you, Detective? You don't have any idea at all. But let me tell you this: whatever you do now, whether you squeeze that trigger or not, the streets of Cincinnati are going to run ankle-deep in blood, and there's nothing that you can do to stop it. Abso-damn-lutely nothing.*'

Detective Kunzel hesitated. He knew that Red Mask was right. If he shot him here and now, too many critical questions would remain unanswered, and it was possible that even more innocent people would be killed.

'So what did you want to say to me?' he asked.

'*I'm trying to do you a favor here, Detective. You will never find me and you will never catch me, no matter how hard you try. So stop wasting your time and your valuable resources. Stop putting your men in harm's way. Do you know how much it costs to train a police officer? And look at them! Dead meat, every one!*'

Red Mask took a step closer, and then another. His voice dropped to a whisper. '*One day, I may feel that justice has been served and that my thirst for vengeance has been slaked. Good word, that, isn't it – "slaked?" But that day isn't today, I regret to tell you, and it won't be tomorrow.*'

Drop him! said a voice in Detective Kunzel's head. But it was then that he heard an extraordinary noise right behind him, a noise like a huge sheet of drawing paper being torn in half. He twisted around, almost losing his balance – just in time to see the painting of Red Mask step right out of the wall, as if it had entered the parking level through some kind of invisible door.

Both of his arms were raised high, and Detective Kunzel glimpsed the rusty-colored glint of a bloodstained blade.

He fired. Inside the parking level, the sound of his gun was deafening. Chips of shattered brick flew off the side of the wall, and the bullet ricocheted across the parking area with a mournful whine.

He fired again, at point-blank range, and this time he hit Red Mask full in the chest. He turned back toward the first Red Mask, shouting, '*Hit the deck! Now!*' But the first Red Mask simply smiled at him, and stayed where he was, and without any hesitation the second Red Mask came right up to him and stabbed him in the shoulder and the side of his head, right behind his ear. He felt the point of the knife dig right into his skull.

He raised his arm to protect himself, but the second Red Mask stabbed him in the elbow with one knife, and the back of his gun hand with the other. Detective Kunzel felt warm wet blood spraying against his face.

He tried to fire again, but the knife that had gone through his elbow and cut his tendons. His fingers opened and the gun clattered on to the floor.

He was stabbed again and again, but he ignored the knives, even when they cut into his hands, and he pushed the second Red Mask away from him. The first Red Mask dodged from side to side, trying to block his way.

'*Leaving us, Detective? So soon? And we were just beginning to enjoy ourselves!*'

Detective Kunzel was stabbed in the back – once in the shoulder and once in the ribs. He dropped forward, on to his knees, but before the second Red Mask could stab him again, he hunched his shoulders and lowered his head, and reared up from the floor with a bellow of rage and pain.

He collided with the first Red Mask, knocking him aside. Then he started to run across the parking level, in between the hanging bodies and the concrete pillars. He hadn't run as fast as this for years, but he was damned if he was going to be stabbed to death and hung up from one of the sprinkler pipes.

He could hear himself panting, as if he were listening to somebody else who was running close behind him, and he could see droplets of blood flying in front of him with every step that he took.

My mother didn't give birth to me to die like this. My father didn't take me to baseball games to die like this. I didn't go to the Police Academy to die like this. I'm going to die in my bed with my family all around me and the evening sun shining through the window.

He reached the door that led to the stairwell, and pulled it open. Looking back, he could see that the second Red Mask had stopped trying to chase him now, and was standing in between the suspended bodies of two SWAT officers, thirty yards away, both knives lowered, staring at him. His face shone in the midday sunlight like a red warning lamp.

Detective Kunzel went through the door and the first Red Mask was standing there waiting for him, and he was holding a knife in each hand, too. Without any hesitation, he plunged them with a sharp chopping noise into Detective Kunzel's stomach, cutting first one deep diagonal, upper left to lower right, and then another, upper right to lower left.

Detective Kunzel felt pain so intense that his whole body began to quake. Nothing could hurt this much. It just wasn't possible. He stared at Red Mask, and tried to speak, but all that came out of his lips was a bubble of blood.

'*Now* that *was the kind of sport I was looking for*,' Red Mask whispered. '*Entertainment and revenge, all in one. And a mystery, too. Am I one? Am I two? Maybe I'm neither. Maybe I'm both. So sad that you'll never get to find out, Detective*.'

He stepped away, sliding his knives back into his coat. Detective Kunzel staggered back against the wall. He stood there for a moment, his chest heaving. Then he tilted sideways and tumbled down the stairs, twenty of them, and lay in a bloodied heap on the landing below.

He wasn't quite dead. He could see the light fitting on the ceiling above him. He could hear voices and the sound of people running. He thought of his mother, standing by the kitchen window. She was smiling at him and saying something that he couldn't hear very distinctly.

It sounded like '*Liebling*.'

'Mom?' he croaked. 'Mom, is that you?'

He heard a loud, resonating bang, somewhere in the parking structure, but he had no way of knowing that it was the elevator, dropping from the top floor down to the basement, with the remaining SWAT officers inside it.

Bad Day Dawning

Sissy opened her eyes. She was lying on top of her pink-and-green comforter, fully dressed except for her shoes. Frank was lying next to her, with the covers over him, still sleeping.

She reached over and touched his hair, just to make sure that he was real. It was such a miracle to see him again that her eyes filled up with tears, and she lay there for almost five minutes, stroking his shoulder, touching his ear.

She lifted her head a little and looked across at her bedside clock. It was nearly half after eleven. After Frank's collapse, Sissy had insisted that he go to bed for a rest. He may not be the real Frank, only a likeness of Frank, but she still loved him and she still wanted to take care of him.

There was a soft knock and then the bedroom door opened. It was Trevor, with Molly close behind him.

'How is he?' Trevor asked.

'He seems to be fine. He's been sleeping.'

'We told Victoria.'

'How did she take it?'

'Pretty good, so far as we can tell. But you know what kids are like. As far as they're concerned, anything's possible until you can prove beyond doubt that it isn't. I think she still believes in fairies. And remember what she said about giants.'

'Well, she may be right,' said Sissy, easing herself off the bed. 'I'm seriously beginning to believe in giants myself. I can't stop dreaming about them. Or at least this one particular giant.'

'Do you think that means anything, that dream?' Molly asked her.

Sissy looked down at Frank and couldn't help smiling at him. 'I don't know. Probably not. Maybe I just need to believe in magic, too.'

Frank stirred, and opened his eyes, and frowned at her.

'Frank? Good morning! How are you feeling?'

He blinked, and sat up. 'OK, I think. How long have I been asleep?'

'Are you hungry?' asked Molly.

'Sure. Yes. You don't have any pancakes, do you?'

At that moment, Victoria came shyly into the bedroom, wearing jeans and a white embroidered blouse, and took hold of her mother's hand. She stood staring at Frank with a solemn expression on her face.

'Victoria,' said Trevor, 'this is your grandpa. Are you going to say hi?'

Frank smiled at her. 'Hi, Victoria. It's a pleasure to meet you. You're a very pretty girl, just like your momma.'

'Mommy says she painted you.'

'Yes, she did. And that's why I'm here. I guess you could call it a kind of a miracle.'

'You're not as old as Grandma.'

'No, I'm not, because this is what I looked like, the last time that anybody saw me.'

Victoria approached a little closer. 'You *look* real.'

'I *feel* real. I even feel hungry.'

He held out his hand. Victoria hesitated, and then she held it. She stared directly into his eyes, as if she were searching for some kind of sign that he was a trick, or an optical illusion.

'Do you think *God* made you real?' she asked him.

'God? I don't know, honey. All I can say is, that I'm deeply grateful. Even if I can't stay for very long, at least I've had the chance to see my granddaughter, and my son, and your momma, too. And most of all I've had the chance to see my wife again.'

Sissy sat next to him at the kitchen table as he ate pancakes and syrup and two fried eggs, and drank three mugs of black coffee. Victoria sat opposite, staring at him in obvious fascination.

'Don't *stare*, Victoria!' Molly scolded her.

'She can stare all she wants,' said Frank. 'It's not every day your momma brings your late grandpa back to life, now is it? I'll bet all of those people in Bethany had a darn good stare, when Jesus resurrected Lazarus.'

He put down his knife and fork. 'If you ask me, what we really are and the way we picture ourselves, they must be pretty much the same thing. I've heard of statues that cry and turn their heads around, and what's a statue made of? Stone, or bronze, or plaster, sure, but that isn't all, is it? It's made out of human imagination, too. What it looks like, that's what it *is* – just like me.'

'Well, I'm glad you've come back to life,' said Victoria. Frank reached across the table and ruffled her hair.

After Frank had finished eating, they went out into the yard. It was humid outside. The sky was hazy and the cicadas creaked even louder than ever, as if Frank's presence had somehow unsettled them.

'Homely little critters, ain't they?' said Frank, picking one off his sleeve.

Mr Boots seemed to be perplexed by Frank, too. When Frank tried to pat him, he shied away, but he couldn't take his eyes off him. He stood at the far end of the yard with his head cocked on one side, making a mewling noise in the back of his throat.

Molly used a rolled-up copy of the *Enquirer* to sweep cicadas off the seat under the vine trellis. Sissy took out her cigarettes. 'We need to decide how we're going to go after Red Mask.'

'You're not still smoking, are you?' Frank asked her.

'I'm sorry. I was going to give it up after—' she nearly said 'your funeral' but she stopped herself. 'Well, I've tried a few times but it isn't easy, especially since I live on my own. It gives me comfort.'

'Well, I don't think I'm in any position to tell you what to do,' said Frank. 'But try to think of your health, OK? The longer you live, the more time Victoria can spend with her grandma.'

Sissy said, 'We should go downtown to the Giley Building this afternoon and search it all over again. Maybe I can't find Red Mask, Frank, but I'll bet anything you like that you can.'

'Do you think the police will let us do that?' said Trevor. 'The building was evacuated after the last attack, and so far as I know they haven't allowed anybody back in.'

'I'll call Mike Kunzel. I'm pretty sure that I'm beginning to win him over to the dark side. I'll tell him that I need to check for any new psychic resonance.'

'Psychic resonance?'

'That's when somebody leaves a building, but they leave a kind of an echo behind them. It can be their actual voice. Most times, though, it's their emotions – especially if they've been angry, or frightened, or very upset. Occasionally, the resonance can last for days, or even weeks, or even longer. Does the word "ghost" mean anything to you?'

Trevor pressed his hand against his forehead as if he were developing a migraine, but said nothing.

'There's one more thing that's been nagging at the back of my mind,' Frank put in. 'You said that George Woods appeared to be lying about something, although you don't know what. George Woods was killed first, right? The girl was stabbed, too, wasn't she – what was her name?'

'Jane Becker.'

'That's it, Jane Becker. But it doesn't seem to me that Red Mask intended to hurt her at all, and that her injuries were simply the result of her trying to stop him from killing George Woods. They weren't too severe, anyhow. No – I think it was George Woods that Red Mask was after, to begin with, and George Woods alone. I also think that Red Mask had a very strong motive for killing him, although we don't know what it was. Revenge, sure. But revenge for what?'

Trevor said, 'Maybe it was revenge for whatever it was that he kept trying to tell his wife that he was sorry for.'

Sissy took out one of her hairpins, and prodded it more securely into her bun. 'I really don't know what his motive could have been. The trouble is, George Woods wouldn't say, and I'm not so sure that I could raise his spirit a second time – not willingly, anyhow. I guess I could read his cards. That might tell us something. I was going to read them anyhow, to see if they would give me clues about how we find Red Mask.'

'You and those darned cards, Sissy.'

'I know you never believed in them, Frank. But even if they speak in riddles, they always turn out to be telling the truth, one way or another. And they've been a comfort to me, too, just like smoking. At least I always have some idea of what's coming down the line.'

Frank said, 'I've come across perpetrators like Red Mask a few times before. The first time they kill, they're doing it for a very specific reason – mostly because they're angry, or because they feel that they've been wronged, or insulted, or not given the respect they think they deserve. They're seriously looking for justice. But when they find out how exciting it is to kill another human being, and what a feeling of *power* it gives them—'

Sissy quickly dealt out the cards, with a cigarette dangling from one side of her mouth and one eye closed against the rising smoke.

'Hmm,' she said, when she was finished. 'Not a whole lot of

change. A few cards haven't reappeared, though. *L'Avertissement* has gone, the Warning – that's because that attack on the skywalk is yesterday's news now, not tomorrow's. The *Cache-Cache* card has gone, too – the Game of Hide-and-Go-Seek.'

'Is that good or bad?'

'I'm hoping it's good. It predicted that any police who went looking for Red Mask would be massacred, and *that* doesn't seem to have happened, thank God.'

She turned over the second to last card. It was the blood card again, totally scarlet.

'What does that mean?'

'There's still some more killing to come, I'm afraid. But it isn't the ultimate card, which means that there might be a way of stopping it.'

She turned over the very last card. She had turned it up only once before in the whole of her fortune-telling career, when a four-year-old girl had gone missing in the Litchfield Hills close to the Massachusetts border. At Sissy's suggestion, troopers with tracker dogs went searching for her deep in the furthest recesses of the legendary Colebrook Cavern. After three days she was found hungry and shivering, but alive.

The card was called *Le Flambeau de la Vertu*, the Torch of Righteousness. It showed a man in a dark blue cloak walking through a shadowy place that could have been a cavern or a forest or a tunnel. He was holding up a fiery torch so that he could see where he was going, but he was also being led by a large black bloodhound, or St Hubert hound, as the French called them.

Around its neck, the bloodhound wore a collar of wilted roses.

'This is it,' said Sissy. 'This is what we have to do to find those Red Masks.'

'We have to take a dog for a walk?'

'This is a tracker dog We need a tracker dog to find them, and a torch to set fire to them.'

'Set fire to them?'

'Of course. They're paintings. They're inflammable. They can burn.'

'Just like me,' said Frank.

'I guess so, my darling. Just like you. But I'm still so happy that you're here.'

'So where are we going to find ourselves a bloodhound?' demanded Trevor. 'Mr Boots isn't much of a tracker. I threw a stick for him the other day and he came back with somebody's bicycle pump.'

'I wasn't thinking of Mr Boots. We need a scenting dog. Molly can paint us one.'

Trevor said, 'For God's sake, Momma. Where is this going to stop?'

'We have to! Red Mask doesn't have a scent that a real dog can follow. But a painted dog could. Think of what happened this morning, when your daddy looked at that painting of Litchfield Green. He could hear it and feel it and smell it, and a painted dog should be able to do the same.'

'My God,' said Trevor.

Sissy crushed out her cigarette. 'Molly?' she said. 'Do you think you can do it?'

Molly looked up at Trevor and took hold of his hand. 'Come on, sweetheart. We've come this far. And it's only a dog.'

'For Christ's sake. Why don't you paint some horses, too, while you're at it? Then you'll be able to ride downtown.'

'Trevor,' said Sissy, and her voice was stern, 'over forty people have already been killed, and if we don't do something about it, a whole lot more are going to die, too.'

Trevor was about to answer when his cell warbled. He fished it out of his shirt pocket and said, 'Trevor Sawyer?'

He listened, and nodded, and then he passed it over to Sissy. 'It's for you, Momma. Detective Bellman. Something really bad has happened.'

Mask Hunt

A huge black traffic cop waved them through the police barrier on 7th Street and told them to take a left on Vine and then a right on 6th. They drew into the curb outside the Giley Building and found Detective Bellman waiting for them on the steps outside.

Although it was still warm and humid, the sky was slate-gray, and there were snakes' tongues of lightning across the river to the south-west. Further up Race Street, at least ten ambulances were parked in a line, with their emergency lights flashing, as well as cars and vans from the coroner's office.

Detective Bellman opened the passenger door for them and helped Sissy to climb down.

'I was so shocked when you told me about Detective Kunzel,' she said. 'That was one death I didn't see coming.'

'We're all shocked,' said Detective Bellman. 'Mike Kunzel – it was like he was invulnerable, you know? Bulletproof, knife-proof. Death-proof.'

'No witnesses?'

Detective Bellman shook his head. 'Like I told you on the phone, he said he had a call from Red Mask, inviting him to meet him here. Red Mask even challenged him to bring as much back-up as he wanted.'

'How many casualties?' asked Molly.

'Twenty-three, all told, including Mike. Twelve stabbed to death on the third parking level, six stabbed to death on the stairs between the fifth- and the sixth-level landings – that was a really frenzied attack, believe me. Another four fatally injured when the elevator dropped to the basement.'

Frank came around the SUV, and nodded to Detective Bellman.

Sissy said, 'Detective Bellman, this is my younger brother Frank.'

'Good to meet you,' said Detective Bellman. 'Connecticut State Police, yes?'

Frank held up the eagle-crested badge that Molly had painted for him. 'That's right, Detective. Glad I've got the opportunity to help you out.'

Detective Bellman pointed up to the parking structure. 'We've had more than seventy officers searching the parking levels, roof to basement, and they found absolutely no sign of the perpetrators nowhere. Not even a footprint.'

'Anybody see them leave the parking structure after it was all over?'

'Nope. There's an alley at the rear but that was covered, and there's no direct access from the parking structure to the Giley Building itself. There used to be a third-story walkway between the two of them but they demolished it about three years ago for security and safety reasons.'

'How about the Giley Building itself? Have you searched that again?'

Detective Bellman shook his head. 'It's been locked and guarded ever since the last attack, so there's no way that the perpetrators could have gotten back in there.'

'What did your lieutenant say when I asked you if *I* could search it?' asked Sissy.

'He said that you were welcome to look for any additional forensics. Provided, of course, you don't tell anybody what kind of forensics we're talking about. Especially the media.'

'Don't worry,' said Sissy. 'The words "psychic resonance" won't even pass my lips.'

Detective Bellman said, 'You pretty much convinced Mike that something psychic was going on, did you know that? I think it was when you heard that cleaner, calling out to you from the elevator.'

'How about you?'

'Me – I'm a total non-believer. But I don't believe in not trying out something just because *I* don't believe in it. I'm not God, am I, so what do I know? Besides, I think that Lieutenant Booker is pretty keen to give it a try. He used a medium when he was stationed out at Shaker Heights, to look for some missing kid. The woman found the kid in two hours flat. Well, she found his remains.'

Trevor went to the back of his SUV and opened the hatch. 'Come on, boy,' he said, and out bounded a large German Shepherd, with pricked-up ears. Trevor clipped a leash on him.

'OK if we take Deputy with us?' asked Sissy. 'He's a first-class scenting dog.'

Detective Bellman said, 'Whatever. Sure. Good idea.'

They climbed the steps to the entrance of the Giley Building where two uniformed officers with shotguns were standing guard. One of them untied the yellow police tape for them, and unlocked the revolving doors.

'Officer Gillow here, he'll come with you, just in case you run into any trouble. If you see or hear anything suspicious, no matter what it is, don't try to be heroes, OK? Get the hell out of there, quick.'

Molly said, gently, 'Did you speak to Betty yet?'

Detective Bellman nodded. 'I went around to see her a couple of hours ago, to tell her that Mike was gone. She didn't say a whole lot. I think she's like the rest of us, we can't believe that Mike won't be coming trundling back through the door, whistling that goddamned *Goin' Courtin'*.'

'It's so sad. He was such a great guy. Do you know what he used to call me? "Crayola," like it was my name.'

'I *told* him,' said Detective Bellman. 'I *told* him he shouldn't go up there on his own. We needed serious back-up. Mike was always the first person to say don't rush into things until you've checked them out first. But he wouldn't listen. He went charging up those stairs like a bull, and that was the last time I saw him alive.'

As if he were offering his sympathy, Deputy came up to Molly and Detective Bellman and gave them a single sharp bark. He was a handsome dog, with intelligent brown eyes and a long black-and-tan coat. He should have been good-looking: as reference for her painting of him, Molly had used three color photographs of the Cincinnati scenting dog champion Fritz.

It had taken her an hour to paint him, and a further two hours before his image had eventually faded from her cartridge paper. As a precaution, they had shut Mr Boots in the utility room while they waited for Deputy to make his appearance, in case the new arrival made him jealous. The last thing they had wanted was a dogfight.

Even so, when Deputy had materialized in the yard, and started sniffing at the cicadas, Mr Boots had started to make that mewling sound in the back of his throat. Something strange was happening, and he knew it.

Detective Bellman patted Deputy's head. 'Good dog. You go sniff out those scumbags who killed my partner, OK? Then I'll give you all the bones you can eat, I promise you. For ever.'

Officer Gillow pushed his way through the revolving doors first. He was a short, chunky young man with cropped ginger hair and bulging blue eyes. His expression was permanently pugnacious, as if he were bursting for somebody to challenge him or talk back to him or step out of line. Sissy tore open a roll of LifeSavers Cryst O Mints because she didn't want to confuse Deputy's scenting with cigarette smoke. She gave one to Frank and then and she held the roll out to Officer Gillow. He stared at her as if she were offering him a hit of her bong.

They walked across to the center of the lobby. It was gloomy and silent, and the only sound was their footsteps on the polished marble floor, and the clicking of Deputy's claws.

'Where do you want to start, sir?' asked Officer Gillow.

Sissy opened her purse and drew out a length of red cotton. It was Red Mask's shirt-sleeve – or, more accurately, a *replica* of Red Mask's shirtsleeve. Molly had painted it at the same time as Frank's Connecticut State Police badge, based on the description that Mr Kraussman had given her. 'Red shirt, like he was soaked in blood already.'

She bent down and held the sleeve under Deputy's nose. Deputy sniffed, and growled, and shook his head.

'He sure doesn't like *that*,' said Frank.

But, quietly, Sissy said, 'The most important thing is, he can actually smell it. If he was a real dog, he couldn't.'

Deputy barked, and barked again, and then he started to pull at his leash, trying to head toward the elevator.

'Seems like he wants to go up,' said Frank. 'All right with you, Officer?'

Officer Gillow unhooked his radio and said, 'Charlie, we're taking the elevator. I'll check back with you as soon as I know which floor we're on.'

He pushed the button for the center elevator. The doors shuddered open and they stepped inside. Sissy looked at herself in the mirror. She thought she looked surprisingly unperturbed, considering what they were doing. But as Officer Gillow pushed the button to close the doors, and the elevator began to rise, she thought she could see shadows in the mirror, standing around her. The shadows of Mary Clay, the cleaner who had died in the dark in this elevator, and her two companions.

We're here. Please help us. We're here. Don't let us die in the dark.

They went past floor after floor, and at each floor Office Gillow opened the doors so that Deputy could sniff at the air.

'I'm beginning to feel that this mutt just likes riding on elevators,' said Trevor, as they stopped at the sixteenth floor. The doors opened, Deputy sniffed at the reception area, but stayed where he was.

'Onward and upward,' said Sissy.

But as they rose toward the seventeenth floor, Deputy began to grow increasingly agitated, and to circle around the interior of the elevator, lashing his tail against the walls.

'What is it, boy?' Frank asked him. 'Do you smell something? Red Masks, maybe?'

They reached the seventeenth floor. Deputy was jumping up and down now, scrabbling his claws against the elevator doors.

Officer Gillow unholstered his gun before he pressed the button to open them.

'I want you all to stay way back,' he instructed them. 'Any sign of trouble, and we're out of here.'

With a series of squeaks, the elevator doors juddered apart. If Frank hadn't had him on a leash, Deputy would have gone tearing off into the reception area and along the corridor before he could have stopped him. As it was, he reared up, panting and whining, half-choked by his collar, and it took all of Frank's strength to hold him back.

'Come on, boy, what can you smell?'

Deputy dragged Frank along the corridor into the main office, with all of its half-abandoned cubicles and worn-out carpets.

'Come on, boy, take it easy, boy.'

'What do you think he's picked up?' asked Trevor.

'A trail, most likely,' said Sissy. 'This must have been where Red Mask was hiding out before – except real police bloodhounds couldn't scent him, and *I* couldn't sense him, either.'

She lifted her head, and closed her eyes for a moment. She had no sense of Red Mask having been here, even now. Nothing at all, except the barely audible echoes of all the people who used to work in this office, before it had closed down. Faint baby voices, from the family photographs. Fainter sounds of laughter from the vacation pictures. The *plink-plink-plink* of a glossy red beach ball, bouncing along a concrete pathway, someplace long ago and very far away.

'Here – I think there's something in here!' Frank called out. Deputy had reached a stationery cupboard and was growling and scratching at the paintwork.

Officer Gillow came forward, with his revolver held up high in his right hand. 'OK, sir, let's take it real easy, shall we?'

Sissy said, 'He's right, Frank. Please be careful. It's probably nothing – just a scent that's gotten him all excited – but you don't know for sure.'

Frank reached cautiously across the door and rattled the handle. It was locked. But still Deputy kept clawing at it, and keening, and it was obvious that he wasn't going to stop until they opened it up.

Officer Gillow took a letter opener from one of the office desks. He holstered his gun and hunkered down in front of the doorway, poking the letter opener into the lock. 'There's no key on the other side. Unless the perp has taken it out, there's nobody in here.'

With that, he stood up again, and gave the door a devastating kick. Even Deputy jumped back, on all fours.

The side of the doorframe was splintered, but the door was still hanging on. Officer Gillow gave it another kick and it collapsed inward, bouncing sideways on top of a stack of stationery boxes.

Deputy hurtled forward, so violently that Frank lost his grip on his leash. He threw himself into the darkness of the stationery cupboard, furiously barking.

'*Deputy!*' Frank shouted at him, but none of them was prepared for what happened next. They heard more boxes falling, and a heavy crash like a fax machine falling over. Then a hoarse, unintelligible roar, more like a beast than a human being.

Officer Gillow immediately yanked out his handgun again, and yelled in his radio for back-up.

'Seventeenth floor! Seventeenth floor! Newman! Bitzer! Get your asses up here right now, you guys! We got the bastards cornered!'

There was another shout, and then Red Mask almost exploded out of the stationery cupboard door, in a snowstorm of copy paper. He was clutching Deputy by the neck, holding him up in the air so that his hind legs were barely touching the floor. His fingers were digging so deeply in to Deputy's neck that the dog's eyes were protruding, and his breath came in high-pitched shrieks.

Red Mask was scarlet-faced, huge, and bursting with rage. He was stabbing at Deputy with a large triangular kitchen knife, so that the fur on Deputy's chest and belly was matted with blood, and blood was splattering on to the floor.

'Drop the dog, or I shoot!' shouted Officer Gillow. 'I said *drop*—!'

Frank tried to step forward, but Red Mask brandished his knife at him, and he couldn't get close.

'This is your last warning!' warned Officer Gillow, and fired.

Red Mask shuddered, the way that a reflection shudders when you throw a stone into a darkened pool, but apart from that the shot didn't appear to affect him at all. He let out another roar, and swung Deputy wildly from side to side. Deputy screamed in pain, until Red Mask swung him sideways and hurled him clear across the office, so that he collided with a thump with the side of one of the cubicles, and left streaks of blood down the side of it.

'Hold it right there!' Officer Gillow demanded. 'Put your hands on top of your head and kneel down on the floor!'

Red Mask held up the knife in his right hand, and then slowly and defiantly drew a second knife out of his coat. His eyes were black slits. His mouth was a gash, like a lizard's.

'Thought you'd be clever, did you?' he said. He turned his head around and looked at each of them in turn.

'I said kneel on the fucking floor, scumbag!' Officer Gillow yelled at him. 'Are you deaf, or what?'

'Oh, I can hear you sure enough,' said Red Mask. 'I can hear you clear as those cicadas. You're loud, and irritating, and twice as ugly.'

'You got three,' said Office Gillow, cocking his revolver again, and pointing it directly at Red Mask's chest.

Red Mask slowly approached them. Frank said, 'I'd stay back, friend, if I were you.'

'Friend? I'm not your friend. But I do know one person here.' He turned to Molly, and said, 'I know *you*, don't I, my darling? You and your brushes.'

'What the hell is he raving about?' said Officer Gillow.

'Your brushes, my dear . . . your soft, sable brushes . . . licking my skin like the tip of your tongue, coaxing out my colors. And your pencils . . . the way they shade my face and my body so intensely, giving me shape, giving me strength. You have a wonderful gift. You can make life rise up from nothing but whiteness.'

They could hear the elevators whining. Any minute, back-up would arrive.

Red Mask slowly sank to his knees, although he was still holding the two knives over his head. Officer Gillow stepped up closer to him, pointing his revolver directly at his face.

Red Mask was still staring at Molly. 'You gave me personality. You gave me everything. I should be grateful to you, shouldn't I? Except, you know, that I'm not. The only reason you painted me was so that I could be caught, and tried, and sentenced to death. No wonder I have no faith in human kindness.'

'Drop the knives!' Officer Gillow demanded. He was almost as red in the face as Red Mask now, and he was sweating.

Red Mask didn't take his eyes off Molly. 'But the way you brought me to life . . . that was so sensual. As soon as you painted my eyes I could see you. But I knew that I wanted revenge. That was all I was born for.'

Without warning, he snapped his head around so that he was

facing Officer Gillow. Officer Gillow shouted, 'Hold it right there!' But Red Mask reared to his feet as if he were a red-and-black volcano erupting, both of his knives held up high.

Officer Gillow fired two shots. Sissy ducked and covered her ears with her hands. She was sure that Officer Gillow must have hit Red Mask, but the shots didn't seem to have any effect on him at all, except that black tatters flew from the back of his suit.

Trevor came bounding across and tried to jump on Red Mask's back. Molly cried out, '*Trevor*! *Don't!*' But Red Mask swung his left elbow behind him, and then his right, and sent Trevor sprawling back on to the floor.

Then, without any hesitation, he brought both knives down into Officer Gillow's shoulders, and into his chest, and into his neck. Officer Gillow staggered backward, with both arms held up in front of him to protect his face, but Red Mask's attack was so furious that he couldn't fend him off. He fell backward over a chair and then Red Mask was on top of him, his knives flashing like some terrible harvesting machine, chopping him apart.

But Frank was on him now. He grabbed Red Mask around the neck in an armlock, and forced his knee into the small of his back.

Red Mask roared, '*Get off me! Get off me! I'll cut you to pieces!*'

'Oh, yeah, you son-of-a-bitch? Just try it!'

Frank pulled Red Mask's head up even more, and gripped his right wrist, and began to slam it against the side of one of the desks, again and again.

'*Get off me! I'm going to cut your guts out for this! Do you want to see your own intestines? I can show you, you maggot, in glorious Technicolor!* Get off me!'

Frank slammed Red Mask's wrist right against the edge of the desk, and the knife went flying. Then he twisted him around, and made a grab for his left wrist, too, pinning him down.

For almost ten seconds, Red Mask strained against him, glaring directly into his face. And it was then that he let out a bark of triumph. '*You're the same as me, goddammit!* I can see it in your eyes! I can see it in your face! You piece of shit! You're *painted*, too!'

Sissy cried out, 'Frank!' – frightened for him, terrified that Red Mask was going to hurt him – but at the same time pleading for his forgiveness, for bringing him back to life.

As Frank and Red Mask continued to struggle, Trevor and Molly pulled Officer Gillow well away from them. Officer Gillow was decorated in stab wounds, and his uniform was soaked in blood.

He was quivering from head to foot, but he was still conscious. He held up his blood-slippery radio and said to Trevor, 'Call them. Find out what the fuck is holding them up.'

Trevor took the radio and clicked the switch.

'Hallo? Hallo? This is Trevor Sawyer with Officer Gillow, on the seventeenth floor. We have serious trouble here. Officer Gillow's badly hurt. Hurry!'

'*—goddamned elevators are stuck – have to use the stairs—*'

'For Christ's sake, hurry! And send paramedics, too!'

Frank and Red Mask struggled and grunted and punched at each other. They rolled over and over across the office floor, colliding with desks and chairs. Red Mask still had one knife left, and he repeatedly jabbed it at Frank's face, trying to put out his eyes.

He succeeded in nicking Frank three or four times on the forehead, and once on the bridge of his nose, but Frank had his wrist in too tight a grip for him to succeed in blinding him.

Sissy said to Trevor, 'Here – hit him with a chair.' But even though Trevor picked up a stacking chair and circled around the two wrestling men, there were rolling over too much for him to be sure that he would hit Red Mask, and not stun Frank instead.

Red Mask grunted, and tried to jab at Frank's face again. But Frank managed to pin his wrist to the carpet, and punch him on the side of the head. He pulled himself upward so that he could press his right knee on Red Mask's wrist, with all of his weight, and at the same time he punched him again and again until Red Mask roared at him in frustration.

'Sissy!' he shouted. 'Sissy, your lighter!'

'What?'

'Your lighter! Throw me your lighter!'

Sissy fumbled her lighter out of her purse. Trevor took it from her and tossed it to him. Frank caught it one-handed.

'Frank!' said Sissy.

Frank was sitting astride Red Mask now, but Red Mask was much heavier than Frank, and very strong, and he was gradually forcing Frank to tilt to the right, where his knife was still in his hand, and sticking upward. One powerful push, and he could force Frank sideways on to the floor, and the point of the knife would be driven straight into his ear.

'No rest for the wicked!' gasped Red Mask. 'No mercy for the innocent!'

'Why don't you save your—'

'No mercy for you, either! Nothing for you but blood! And more blood!'

There was a moment of supreme struggle, in which both men were pushing against each other to the very limits of their strength. Frank's teeth were clenched, but Red Mask's mouth remained a black, soulless slit. All the same, he was uttering this high, continuous hiss, like steam-pressure building up to danger level.

Red Mask was gripping his left wrist, but Frank gradually managed to lift the cigarette lighter up toward Red Mask's face.

Red Mask's voice dropped an octave. 'You wouldn't dare,' he said, hoarsely.

'Oh? You don't think so?'

'What are you, some kind of a martyr? I burn, you burn. You think any of these people are worth it?'

'You value *your* life.'

'I was created. I came out of the whiteness. The same way you did. We were like Arctic explorers, lost in the snow, and then one day we just appeared.'

Red Mask coughed. It was the first sign of how much physical strain he was under. 'You wouldn't throw your life away, would you? Just to punish me?'

Frank flicked the lighter and a long blue flame curved out of it.

Molly called, 'Frank! Be careful! Frank – remember that you're only—'

But Frank gradually forced his hand around until the flame was playing directly on Red Mask's cheek. Red Mask screamed, and thrashed, and kicked his legs, but Frank kept the flame concentrated on his face. His red skin crinkled like cellophane, and Sissy could hear it crackle.

'Get that off me! *Get that off me!*'

Red Mask managed to yank his left arm free, and immediately started to stab at Frank's shoulder and sides, screaming all the time. But it was then that his face burst into flame, and then his shoulders, and then his arms.

'*Frank!*' screamed Sissy. 'Oh my God! Frank!'

Frank had caught alight, too. His hair was burning and within seconds the fire had spread down his back, as if he were wearing a cloak made of waving flames.

Frank and Red Mask screamed at each other in a terrible chorus of hatred. Then they both exploded. A huge orange fireball rolled across the office, and it was them, rolling over and over. They collided with a central pillar and then they stopped, still blazing so fiercely that Sissy had to raise her hand in front of her face to prevent her cheek from being scorched.

There was a second explosion, and then the whole office was filled with a whirlwind of white ash, which spun around and around and filled the air from floor to ceiling. The whirlwind was furious, but almost silent, and after less than a minute it gradually began to die down.

Sissy, Molly and Trevor stood amongst the softly settling ash. It reminded Sissy of the first Christmas she had spent alone after Frank had been killed, and she had walked out into the yard and the snow was falling.

'You did it to me again, Frank,' she whispered. She couldn't stop her eyes from filling up with tears.

Roses Are Red

Trevor knelt down beside Officer Gillow. The policeman was groaning and coughing but he was still alive. Sissy knelt down beside him, too, and took hold of his hand, sticky-fingered with blood.

'What's your name, Officer?'

'Herbert, ma'am, but everybody calls me Duke.'

'Well, you're going to be OK, Duke. I'm a psychic and I can feel it. You're going to recover, I promise you.'

'You don't have to lie to me, ma'am.'

'I wouldn't, and I'm not. But after you've gotten yourself well, you're going to retire from the police department so that you can run your own business. A bakery, maybe, or a restaurant. You're going to get married and you're going to have at least five children, all girls.'

Officer Gillow blinked up at her, his face speckled with ash. '*Five girls?*' he asked her, and a bubble of blood popped between his lips. 'Why don't you just let me die?'

Molly came back from the other side of the office.

'Poor Deputy's dead.'

Sissy stood up and took hold of her hand and squeezed it. 'Deputy did us proud. And remember, he was only made of paint and paper.'

She didn't have to add that Red Mask and Frank were only made of paint and paper, too. Their ashes were still tumbling across the carpet.

'Only Deputy could have picked up Red Mask's scent,' Sissy said. 'And only Frank could have burned him. Look how many times Red Mask was shot, and it didn't affect him one bit.'

'We still have another Red Mask to find,' Molly reminded her. 'And the police still don't have any leads at all on the *real* Red Mask.'

'Well – finding the real one, that's up to them,' said Sissy. 'We can only find the painted ones.'

They heard pattering footsteps and clattering noises from the stairwell, and somebody shouting, 'Breaching ram! Bring up that breaching ram!'

'Do you hear that, Duke?' Sissy told Officer Gillow. 'Your buddies are coming to get you. You'll soon be fixed up.'

A loud banging came from the stairwell doors, and then they heard the locks broken open. Trevor came up to Sissy and laid his hand on her shoulder. 'How are we going to explain this, Momma?'

'All we can do is tell the truth. Whether they believe us or not, that's up to them.'

'I just want to say that – everything I used to say about your psychic stuff—'

Sissy reached up and patted his hand. 'You don't have to say a word. Even *I* find this hard to believe, and me – I've had conversations with real live dead people. It's like a dream, isn't it? Your father, and everything. I keep thinking I'm going to wake up and I'll be back in my bed in Connecticut.'

Half a dozen police officers and two young paramedics came weaving their way between the cubicles. The paramedics immediately started work on Officer Gillow, cutting off his shirt, while two of the police officers came up to Sissy and Molly and Trevor. One of the officers was big-bellied, with a yard-brush moustache. The other was round-faced with flaming red cheeks and looked far too young to be a cop.

'What the hell happened here?' asked Yard-brush Moustache.

Before anybody else could answer, Sissy said, 'We were looking for forensic evidence.'

'*You* were looking for forensic evidence?'

'That's right. We were checking this office for latent scents when the suspect appeared without any warning and attacked Officer Gillow.'

'*You* were looking for forensic evidence?' Yard-brush Moustache repeated. '*You?*'

'Well, not *just* me. Me and my son and my daughter-in-law.'

'It was authorized by Lieutenant Booker and Detective Bellman,' Molly put in. 'I'm an accredited CPD sketch artist, and my mother-in-law . . . she has special forensic expertise.'

The officer turned to Molly, in her flowery blue gypsy blouse and her tight designer jeans. Then he looked Sissy up and down – a seventy-one-year-old woman with wild hair and silver bangles and a black-and-silver dress with moons and stars on it.

'Special forensic expertise?' he said. 'I'll bet.'

'We had a scenting dog with us,' Trevor explained. 'He tracked Red Mask to that cupboard. Officer Gillow kicked down the door and all hell broke loose.'

'That the dog there?'

Trevor nodded. 'Red Mask stabbed him to death and then he went for Officer Gillow. He was like a crazy person. A lunatic.'

The officers looked around the ash-strewn office. 'So where is he now? This Red Mask character?'

'He *disappeared*,' said Sissy, promptly.

'OK – which way did he go?'

'I couldn't exactly say. There was so much confusion, you know. Stabbing, shouting. It was like he vanished into thin air.'

'Did *you* see which way he went?' Yard-brush Moustache asked Trevor, as if Trevor was his last hope of getting a sane answer.

'I, um. No. Not really.'

'So what's all this fire damage, all this ash?'

'Some paper caught light, that's all. It got a little out of hand.'

'Some paper caught light? I see. How did that happen?'

'Listen,' said Sissy, 'is Detective Bellman with you?'

'Detective Bellman took the elevator, so he's trapped between floors. The engineers reckon at least a half-hour before they can get it working again.'

'I really need to talk to Detective Bellman. He'll understand what happened here.'

Yard-brush Moustache jammed his notebook into his breast pocket. 'OK, ma'am. That's fine by me, so long as you don't mind sticking around to make a statement. But you *will* stick around, won't you? You won't leave the building?'

'Of course not. I'll wait in the lobby.'

Yard-brush Moustache and his red-cheeked partner went across to examine the black scorch marks on the office carpet. One of the burns distinctly resembled the outline of a man, with one arm outstretched.

Trevor said, 'Are you going to be OK with the stairs, Momma? It's seventeen flights down to ground level.'

Sissy picked up her purse. As she did so, she lifted her head and frowned.

'Momma? We can always wait till they fix the elevators.'

'Actually, sweetheart, I think I'm going to go *up* first.'

'*Up?* What the hell for?'

'If I remember rightly, George Woods used to work on the nineteenth floor, didn't he, Molly?'

'Yes,' said Molly. 'He was a realtor for Ohio Relocations.'

'I'd like to go up and take a look-see.'

'I don't understand.'

'I'm not so sure that *I* understand, either. I have one of my tingles, that's all. George Woods told a deliberate lie, during my séance.'

'So?'

'It's very rare for gone-beyonders to tell lies, even to spare the feelings of the loved ones they've left behind. I told Frank about it, and he was interested to know what George Woods was lying about, too.'

As Sissy and Molly and Trevor walked across to the stairwell, Yard-brush Moustache called out, 'Can you manage all those stairs, ma'am?'

'I'm not an invalid, Officer. I walk ten miles a day, as a rule, and I smoke forty cigarettes down to the filter.'

'Nothing like a healthy lifestyle, ma'am.'

As they went through the door, Trevor said, 'Listen, I need to go to the office to pick up some paperwork. Why don't I catch you later? I can take a cab home.'

'In other words, you don't want to be involved in what I'm

going to do now?' Sissy asked him. 'OK . . . if you feel like you have to.'

Trevor lifted both hands. 'Momma . . . psychic investigation I can put up with. But when it comes to real serial killers . . . I don't think I really want to know. Especially when you're going to go poking around in somebody's private office. I have my job to think of here.'

Sissy tapped her forehead so that the little bell on her index finger jingled. 'Sorry, Trevor. There's a little voice inside of me someplace, and it's telling me to go upstairs.'

'Yes, Momma. I believe you, Momma. But all I can say is, don't do anything stupid. I don't want you ending up in the women's reformatory, at your age. Molly – make sure she doesn't do anything stupid.'

Trevor kissed Sissy on both cheeks, and kissed Molly, too. Then he took the left-hand staircase, and went down. Sissy and Molly took a quick look around to make sure that nobody was watching them, and took the right-hand staircase, and went up.

'Christ on a bicycle.' Sissy found it much harder to climb up two flights of stairs than she had imagined. On the landing of the eighteenth floor, she stopped to take a rest, tilting against the railings, trying to get her breath back.

'What's happened to me, Molly? I used to bound up stairs like a mountain goat.'

'I hate to say this, Sissy, but forty years and forty Marlboro a day can take their toll on you.'

'I don't believe it. They're just building stairs steeper than they used to, when I was a girl.'

'The Giley Building was completed in 1931. You weren't even *born* in 1931.'

'Don't split hairs.'

They carried on slowly climbing until they reached the nineteenth floor. Sissy tried the door to Ohio Relocations and to her surprise it was unlocked.

'This is very handy indeed,' said Sissy, as she opened it up and peered into the offices. 'I thought I would have to use my lock-picking skills.'

'You can pick locks?'

'A very smooth conjuror taught me – amongst other things. All you need is the right kind of hairpin.'

'The staff probably left in a panic, after that last attack. Forgot to lock it.'

They ventured into the offices. They were laid out in cubicles, in much the same way as the office on the seventeenth floor, except that these cubicles had higher sides to them, and the chairs and desks were very much smarter and more modern. The carpets were deep purple, and there was purple lettering across the wall – *Ohio Relocations – Moving Ohio* – and a picture of a circus strong man with an uprooted buckeye tree over his shoulder.

'Sissy,' said Molly, 'are you OK?'

'I'm out of breath. Otherwise, I'm hunky-dory.'

'You know what I'm talking about. Frank.'

Sissy looked away. 'That wasn't the real Frank, and you know it.'

'He was real enough to make you happy.'

'Yes. But I knew that it couldn't last. Apart from anything else, look at the difference in age.'

'There's still Red Mask Number Two.'

'Meaning?'

'Meaning we're going to need another Frank. And another Deputy, too.'

Sissy pressed her hand over her mouth and kept it there for a long time. Eventually, she said, 'If that's what it takes.'

'But what about afterward?'

'Afterward?'

'What if Frank *survives* this time?'

'You have plenty of erasers, don't you?'

'I'm not so sure that you mean that.'

'No,' said Sissy, 'neither am I. But let's cross that bridge when we come to it, shall we?'

Molly looked into one of the cubicles. 'What exactly do you think we're going to find here?'

'I don't know. Let's try the secretary's office.'

'You really do have a feeling about this, don't you?'

'Yes, but I don't exactly know *what* I can feel. During that séance, I think that George Woods was desperately trying to cover something up – something he was ashamed of. Usually, when people die, they don't care what they confess to. They like to clear the air. But George Woods was hiding something and I'll bet that whatever it was, it had something to do with his life at the office. What other life did he have? He went to work, he came home.'

They walked along the corridor until they found a frosted glass door with gold lettering on it – Frances Delgado, personal assistant. Sissy went inside and looked around. A desk, a PC, a dried-up yucca plant. A bookshelf, with rows of files and framed photographs of Ms Delgado's family.

Sissy picked up one of the photographs and peered at it through her bifocals. 'God almighty. They look like orang-utans.'

Molly went across to the gray filing cabinet marked *O.R. Personnel* and tugged the handle, but it was locked. Sissy opened the drawers in Ms Delgado's desk, but Ms Delgado was plainly a neat freak, because it contained nothing but magic markers in order of color and paperclips in order of size and dictation CDs arranged A–Z.

As she closed the drawers, however, Sissy noticed a cardboard box under the side table, the one on which the dried-up yucca stood. She maneuvered the box out with her foot, so that she wouldn't have to bend too far, and then she lifted it up on to Ms Delgado's desk. On the lid was scrawled *G. Woods, desk* in felt-tip marker.

Inside, Sissy found mostly trash. Unused matchbooks from Jeff Ruby's Steakhouse and Neon's. A dog-eared copy of *How To Win At Horse Racing*. A blue flashlight with no batteries in it. The instruction booklet for an HP Desktop Printer. Nail-clippers. Six or seven ball-pens, all with their ends gnawed. A wooden Indian's head, roughly-carved, with the name *Quamus* on it.

She found heaps of old receipts, too. Receipts for gas, receipts for pharmaceuticals, receipts for drinks at Japp's and the Crowne Plaza bar. And five receipts for a dozen roses.

Sissy lifted the florist's receipts out of the box. She could sense at once that these were what had alerted her psychic sensitivity. They almost prickled her, like real roses. *Roses*. Just like the roses that had appeared in every DeVane card that she had turned up recently.

Each delivery had come from Jones the Florists, on Fountain Square. They had been delivered every Tuesday for five weeks to Ms Jane Becker, at Taft, Clecamp & Evans, attorneys-at-law, #21, Giley Building, Cincinnati.

'You see this?' said Sissy. 'I thought Jane Becker told you that she didn't know George Woods.'

'That's right, she did. She called him "that poor man."'

'Did she? Well, "that poor man" was sending her a dozen roses every week. Fifty-three dollars' worth, including delivery. That was from the second week in March to the third week in April.'

'Do you think they were having an affair?' asked Molly, peering at the receipts over Sissy's shoulder. 'That would account for George Woods wanting to say sorry to his wife, wouldn't it?'

'Yes. But I don't understand why Jane Becker should give everybody the impression that she didn't know George Woods at all. If some man sent *me* a dozen red roses every week for five weeks, I'd sure want to find out who he was, wouldn't you?'

'Every order had the same message on it,' Molly pointed out. '"*Remember the Vernon Manor . . . when our dreams came true*." So she *must* have known who he was.'

'I think we need to go talk to her,' said Sissy. 'I'm pretty sure she's only told us half of the story. If she was having an affair with George Woods, that would have given Red Mask a motive to attack her, too, wouldn't it? Red Mask didn't stab her at random, just because she happened to be in the elevator at the wrong time. It was premeditated. He *meant* to hurt her. He might even have intended to kill her.'

Sissy tucked the florist's receipts into her purse and they left Frances Delgado's office. As they began the long, careful climb down the stairs, Molly said, 'Red Mask could be one of Jane Becker's boyfriends . . . or maybe some guy who was obsessed with her, a stalker, who didn't like to see her getting too friendly with anybody else.'

'Or a relative of Mrs Woods,' Sissy suggested. 'A brother or a cousin who wanted to punish them for cheating on her. So there's a high probability that Jane Becker knows who he is.'

'So why lie about it?'

'That's what we have to find out, don't we?'

Sissy paused on the fourteenth landing, and pressed her hand to her chest.

'Whoever said exercise was good for you was lying through their teeth.'

'Do you want to stop and rest for a while?'

'No . . . I think I want to get out of this building as soon as I can. There's still a second Red Mask on the prowl, remember?'

They carried on down. As they reached the ninth floor, Sissy said, 'Remember . . . even if we do find out who Red Mask is, it's not going to stop him from murdering more people. We have to track him down – the same way we tracked down this Red Mask today.'

'So you *do* want me to bring Frank back?'

Sissy looked down at Molly and her eyes were glistening. 'What do you think?'

Talking to Detective Bellman

Detective Bellman was hot and exhausted after nearly an hour in the elevator. He sat astride one of the office chairs with his necktie loosened, drinking from a bottle of mineral water. His white shirt was sticking to his back.

Sissy had explained to him exactly what had happened on the seventeenth floor. She had told him the truth about Frank, and who Frank really was, and how Molly had created Deputy. She described how Red Mask had come bursting out of the cupboard and stabbed Officer Gillow.

She told him how Frank and Red Mask had burned into ashes, right in front of their eyes.

Detective Bellman listened to all of this wearily, without making notes. When Sissy had finished, he said, 'How am I supposed to file a report on this?'

'I don't know. It depends if you believe it or not.'

'No, it doesn't. It depends if my lieutenant takes me off the case and sends me for a psych evaluation. It's madness. It's like something out of *Alice's Adventures in Wonderland*. Playing cards, coming to life.'

'Where do you think Lewis Carroll got the idea from? It's been recorded in so many cultures . . . pictures that step out of their frames and sculptures that move.'

Detective Bellman took another swig of water and wiped his mouth with the back of his hand. 'Well, it's not going to be recorded in the Cincinnati Police Department culture. It's going to stay our little secret, *capiche*?'

Facing the Giant

They ate a subdued supper that night. Molly was too tired and distracted to cook so Trevor went to Blue Ash Chili and brought home three four-ways and one five-way for Sissy, who didn't believe that a chili was a chili without beans. She didn't really believe that chili should be eaten with spaghetti, either.

'Who eats chili with spaghetti?' she said. 'It's against God's law.'

'You'll get used to it,' Trevor told her. 'One day, when you're back in New Milford, you'll think to yourself, I just *got* to have myself a Cincinnati five-way – chili, cheddar, onions and beans, all on top of a big pile of spaghetti – and I got to have it *now*!'

Victoria said, 'Isn't Grandpa coming for supper?'

Sissy glanced at Molly. If they were going to recreate Frank to go after the second Red Mask, then she didn't want to say that Grandpa had to go away – not yet.

'Grandpa had some business he needed to attend to,' she said. 'Maybe he'll be back tomorrow.'

'Is Grandpa going to come live with us, like Grandma?'

'You understand that he isn't your real grandpa? He's just like a picture of your grandpa, except that he can walk and talk?'

'I know,' said Victoria. 'But that doesn't matter. He's still my grandpa, isn't he? And he can come to my school and everything and see my play?'

'Victoria, sweetheart,' said Sissy, taking hold of her hand, 'I'm really not sure how long Grandpa will be able to stay with us.'

'I'll tell him he has to stay for ever.'

Sissy thought about that, and then she said, 'OK. That sounds like a plan. When a granddaughter has asked for something – anything – what grandpa in recorded history has ever been able to say no?'

Sissy could eat only a few spoonfuls of chili. She was trying hard not to show it, but seeing Frank burn up today had shocked her badly. She couldn't stop herself from shivering, even though the evening was so warm, and she felt the same iron-cold hopelessness in her heart that she had felt twenty-four years ago, when the state troopers had knocked on her door.

She must have been mad to suggest that Molly bring Frank back. But she had been so worried about how Frank would feel that she had forgotten her own emotions – especially her grief.

'Not hungry, Momma?' Trevor asked her. 'Don't worry about it, Mr Boots loves five-way chili.'

'You're not going to give it to Mr Boots, are you?' asked Victoria. 'He always makes such horrible smells.'

'Actually, I think that's Daddy,' said Molly. 'He just blames it on Mr Boots, that's all, and poor Mr Boots can't say, "Hey – it wasn't me!" can he?'

She started to collect up the plates but then the phone rang. She answered it, and said, 'Sawyer residence.'

Somebody must have answered, because she frowned, and said, 'Who is this?'

Trevor stood up. 'What is it, honey? Give it to me.'

Molly covered the mouthpiece with her hand and stared at them wide-eyed. 'I think it's Red Mask.'

Trevor said, 'Give it to me!'

But Sissy said, 'No! This could be important! Switch on the speaker and let's hear what he has to say! Victoria – can you do something for me? I want you to take Mr Boots outside and give him this chili, OK?'

'But—'

'Victoria, this is something you don't need to hear, OK? Now be a good girl and feed Mr Boots for me.'

Molly said, 'How did you get my number?'

She listened, and said, 'I see.' But she waited until Victoria had left the kitchen before she switched on the speaker.

'*You're trying to track me down, aren't you, Molly?*' said Red Mask. '*You created me, so you think you have the divine right to hunt me down and destroy me.*'

'You're a mass-murderer,' Molly retorted. 'What do you expect me to do?'

'*I expect you to take the responsibility for your own creation, Molly. Is it* my *fault if I'm so driven by revenge? I have to have justice, Molly, it's in my blood, or what passes for blood when you're nothing but paper and pencils and paints.*'

'Don't you think you've had enough justice? Why don't you stop, and show some mercy?'

'I can't, Molly. It's not the way I was painted. I thought I might be able to stop, but now I know that I can't. You killed me today, burned me. But I didn't feel nothing. It wasn't cathartic. I didn't feel purged. What I felt was even more vengeful. I felt like killing even more people, scores of people, hundreds of people! I wanted to see their blood spraying like warm summer rain!'

'You have to stop,' Molly told him. 'If you don't stop yourself, then *I'll* stop you, and that's a promise.'

There was a long pause, during which they could hear Red Mask breathing, almost like a single cicada clicking. Eventually he said, '*Making a promise like that, Molly, that was a serious error of judgment. If you make a promise to come after me, then by God I'll make you a promise to come after you.*'

'Hang up!' hissed Trevor. But Sissy raised her hand. She wanted to hear everything that Red Mask had to say.

'*You'd better keep looking behind you,*' he breathed. '*You'd better watch out for every shadow on every wall. And you'd better keep your loved ones close to you, too. Yours was the very first face I saw when I was created, Molly. Make sure that the very last face you see in your life isn't mine.*'

Trevor snatched the phone, and snapped, 'You listen to me, you s-o-b—!' But there was a clattering sound, and Red Mask hung up.

Trevor said, 'That's it! That's it! I'm not having my family threatened! We're going to go after this psycho first thing tomorrow! We're going to find him and we're going to burn him, the same as we did today!'

Sissy said, 'I need a drink. Not only that, I need a cigarette.'

She went outside into the backyard. Victoria was sitting on the kitchen steps, watching Mr Boots as he wolfed down his five-way chili.

'Mr Boots likes spaghetti, doesn't he?'

Sissy lit her Marlboro. 'Mr Boots likes everything, except for tuna.'

She sat down next to Victoria and blew smoke into the warm evening air.

'Why do you do that, Grandma? It's really, really dangerous.'

'I know. I'm a fool. I've tried to give it up more times than I can count. But, you know, every time I light a cigarette, I hear your grandpa's voice saying, "When are you going to stop smoking, Sissy?" And I guess that hearing him say that is better than not hearing him at all.'

'I love him,' said Victoria.

'Yes. Me too.'

At that moment, however, Mr Boots finished his chili and came trotting up to them, messily licking his lips. He tried to nuzzle Victoria, but she screamed out, 'Get away! Get away! These jeans are clean on today!'

Trevor poked his head out of the kitchen window. 'Something wrong?'

Sissy smiled. 'Nothing that a wet cloth can't fix.'

Trevor said, 'Something's been puzzling me . . .'

'Oh, yes?'

'Red Mask . . . he *knows* he's just a painting, doesn't he? But Dad didn't realize that *he* was, when we brought him back to life.'

'I don't know the answer to that, Trevor. Maybe some people are more aware of what they really are than others. Maybe all of us are figments of somebody's imagination, but we live our whole lives through without ever knowing it.'

Sissy opened her eyes. It was daylight. Her cheek was sticky where she had been lying against the leather seat of her uncle Henry's Hudson Hornet. She lay there for a while, listening to the monotonous whine of the automobile's transmission, and feeling the bumping and jiggling of the Hornet's suspension.

She couldn't think what she was doing here. It had been so long since she had visited Uncle Henry and Aunt Mattie that she wasn't even sure that they were still alive. Yet they must be, if this was Uncle Henry's car and Uncle Henry was driving it.

After a while she sat up. Sure enough, that was the back of Uncle Henry's head in the driver's seat, with his sunburned, prickly neck. That was Uncle Henry's straw hat, with the red snakeskin band around it, and those were Uncle Henry's red suspenders.

She looked out of the window. The prairie was gloomy and seemed to stretch for ever. In the far distance, she could see a farmhouse, and a white-painted Dutch barn. The sky was overcast, and heavy with smudgy brown clouds. Or maybe they weren't clouds at all. Maybe they were swarms of cicadas.

A strange song was playing on the car radio. It had an odd, irregular rhythm, as if it were being played backward. '*I saw you in the garden . . . I saw you turn away . . . I saw you smile and asked you why . . . but while you smiled I knew you lied . . .*'

'Where are we, Uncle Henry?' Her voice sounded as if she were speaking into a cardboard tube.

'West of the east and east of the west.'

'Yes but where are we going?'

'Don't you remember? It's the stormy season. We have to run ahead of the storm, don't we?'

She knelt up on her seat and looked up ahead, through the windshield. The sky was growing darker and darker, even though the clock on the instrument panel told her that it was only two in the afternoon. She could smell rain in the air.

They passed a sign that read 'Entering Borrowsville, pop. 789,' and at the same time, she caught sight of the huge figure of a man, standing by the side of the road. He was still over a half-mile away, so he must have been at least thirty feet tall.

She gave an involuntary jerk, like she did when she was falling asleep, but this was a jerk of sheer terror.

'Can we turn round? I don't like giants.'

'Not this time, Sissy.'

'What do you mean?'

'You know what I mean. This time we have to take a closer look at him. You can't put it off any longer, no matter how frightened you are.'

'But it's a giant and I don't like giants. Please can we turn around, *please*.'

'Not this time, Sissy.'

They drove nearer and nearer to the giant. Sissy was so frightened that she was breathing in little gasps. As they approached it, Uncle Henry drove slower and slower. He shifted the Hornet into neutral, so that it was rolling along on nothing but its own momentum. Gradually, it crept to a stop, about thirty feet away from the giant's huge black feet.

'Come on, Sissy. Let's take a closer look.'

'Please, Uncle Henry. I'm so scared.'

'You have to do this. There's no other way. You're here for a very good reason, Sissy Sawyer, and you know it. So you have to overcome your fear, young lady, and do what's necessary.'

Uncle Henry tugged on the parking brake and climbed out of the car. He came around to Sissy's door and opened it. There was a warm wind blowing from the south-west and his baggy pants were rippling.

'Come on, Sissy. He's not going to hurt you.'

Reluctantly, Sissy took hold of Uncle Henry's hand and stepped down on to the road. Some grit flew into her eye and she had to blink furiously to get it out. Uncle Henry led her along by the side of the road, where blazing star and purple prairie clover were nodding in the wind.

They reached the giant's feet. At first Sissy didn't want to look up at him. His feet were black and his pants were black, all painted in shiny varnish.

'Lift up your eyes, Sissy. You have to. Look him in the face.'

'Please, Uncle Henry, I'm too frightened. What if he recognizes me, and comes chasing after me in my dreams?'

'He's made of wood, Sissy. He can't chase you anywhere.'

'Are you sure?'

'Surer than rabbits. Surer than all fall down.'

Very slowly, Sissy raised her head. The giant was wearing a black coat, with a dark red shirt underneath it. His arms were crossed over his chest, and in each of his hands he held a large triangular butcher's knife, painted metallic silver.

It was when she saw his face that she really froze. It was painted bright red, with two narrow chisel-cuts for eyes, and a wider chisel-cut for a mouth.

'Red Mask,' she whispered. 'Oh God in heaven, it's Red Mask!'

But Uncle Henry was shaking his head and smiling and saying something to her, although the wind made his voice sound very blurry.

'I can't hear you. I don't understand.'

Uncle Henry took hold of her arm and pointed to a large aluminum-sided building not far away, with trucks and pick-ups parked outside it. A large sign on top of the roof said Borrowsville Meat Packing Co.

'It's an advertisement, that's all. It's never going to chase you.'

But a harsh voice said, '*Trust your uncle Henry, do you? Uncle Henry died years ago. What does* he *know about reality? You wait till the blood starts spraying like summer rain!*'

There was a deep rumble of thunder, and rain began to fall, only a few silvery spots at first, but then harder and harder.

Run, Sissy! Run!

The Face of Fear

Molly said, 'Wake up, Sissy. There's somebody to see you.'

She opened her eyes. It was morning and her bedroom was filled with sunshine. Molly was standing at the end of the bed with a large glass of fresh-squeezed grapefruit juice for her.

'What? Somebody to see me? Can't it wait until I'm decent?'

'I shouldn't worry about it. I think this particular somebody has seen you in your nightgown once or twice before.'

Sissy sat up, and reached across to the night table for her glasses. As she did so, Frank came in, wearing a blue striped shirt and khaki chinos. He came straight across to her and took hold of her hands and kissed her.

'Oh my God. Frank! I don't believe it.'

'I couldn't sleep,' Molly told her. 'Instead of tossing and turning, I thought I might as well do something useful, and – well, I brought him back to life again.'

'Oh, Frank.' Sissy pulled him closer and kissed him again, and for a few dreamlike moments she forgot that he was nothing but a likeness of Frank, and that she was twenty-four years older than he was. He felt like Frank and he smelled like Frank and she wanted him so much to be alive and real that her very bones ached.

'Sissy,' said Frank. 'You haven't changed, have you?'

'My hair is gray, Frank. I have crows' feet. Look at my hands.'

Frank gave her a sloping, rueful smile. 'I didn't mean that. But even that's better than being dead, any day.'

'Do you remember what happened yesterday?' she asked him.

'Sure I remember. I may be a painting, and nothing more than that, but there's nothing wrong with my short-term memory.'

'When you were burning – didn't it *hurt*?'

'Didn't feel a thing. I guess it might have been different if I was flesh and blood. But I've known guys catch alight, ninety percent burns, and *they* didn't feel nothing, either. Once the nerve endings are burned away, you might as well be made out of wood.'

Sissy said, 'I had a dream last night, about a man made out of wood. It was Red Mask, I'm sure of it.'

'I don't get it. Red Mask is made out of wood?'

She nodded. 'Didn't you ever see those giant roadside figures like Paul Bunyan and the Muffler Men? When I was a child, I used to go visit my uncle Henry and my aunt Mattie on their farm in Iowa, and on the way to Webster there was this huge man all dressed in black, with two huge butcher's knives.

'It used to scare me so much that I always used to close my eyes tight shut whenever we drove past it, and I wouldn't allow myself even to think about it. But I've been having dreams about it ever since I first saw one of Molly's sketches of Red Mask. I kept seeing it on the horizon, but I was always too frightened to take a look at its face. Until last night, anyhow.'

'What made you look?' Frank asked her.

'Losing you, Frank. That's what made me look. I don't want to lose you again.'

'And this giant figure? It *was* Red Mask?'

'No doubt about it. He's a roadside advertisement for some meat-packing company in Borrowsville.'

Molly said, 'Wait up a moment, Sissy. Why would anybody disguise themselves as a giant roadside figure from Iowa? Like, draw attention to yourself, or what? And it's so darned – I don't know. It's so darned *obscure*.'

'There are dozens of roadside giants,' Frank told her. 'Indian braves, cowboys, halfwits, girls in swimming costumes. Up near New Milford, we have a thirty-foot corn dolly.'

'I know. But why choose a meat-packer from Nowheresville, Iowa?'

Sissy pulled back her bedcovers. 'I think we need to talk to Jane Becker, urgently. I really have a bad feeling about this.'

Frank said, 'I'll come with you. And we can take Deputy, too.'

Sissy looked across at Molly. 'You didn't?'

'I surely did. I had a busy night last night, while you were dreaming about scary giants.'

Sissy climbed out of bed and went to the window. In the

backyard, Mr Boots and Deputy were jumping up and down together, snapping at cicadas.

'They made friends right away,' said Molly. 'I think that Mr Boots kind of understands that Deputy isn't going to try to take his place.'

'Oh, that's what you think?' said Sissy. 'I think that Mr Boots is intelligent enough not to get into a fight with a German Shepherd half his age.'

Frank said. 'I'll let you get dressed. My coffee's getting cold, and my chocolate pecan cookies are getting staler by the minute.'

When he had gone back through to the kitchen, Sissy said to Molly, 'Has Victoria seen him yet?'

'No. She left for school before he – you know – *rematerialized*, or whatever we're supposed to call it.'

'She'll be so delighted.'

'I know. But I'm not so sure this is something that I want her to get delighted about. It can't last, can it? He's a painting, an image, not a real person.'

'He *feels* real.'

Molly looked at her sharply. 'He's too young for you, Sissy. Don't start getting ideas.'

'For God's sake, Molly. He's my *husband*.'

They arrived outside the Becker home in Lakeside Park a few minutes before noon. The day was hot and brassy, with only a single cloud in the sky. The house was a large, colonial-style two-story in pinkish brick, with sloping grounds of at least three-quarters of an acre, most of them given over to very dry grass. The sawing of cicadas was even louder than ever.

'Let's hope she's at home,' said Frank.

There were two vehicles parked in the driveway: a black Jeep Cherokee and a red Honda Civic. The Civic had a sticker in the rear window saying *Glaring Anomalies*.

'Glaring Anomalies?' said Frank.

'It's a rock band,' Molly told him. 'A few years after your time, I'm afraid.'

'Don't worry about it, sweetheart. *Everything's* a few years after my time.'

They went up to the front door and Sissy pushed the bell. They waited for nearly half a minute before Jane Becker answered, wearing a baggy, oversized T-shirt with ketchup stains on the front of it. She looked very white-faced and her curly chestnut hair was tied up in a lime-green nylon scarf.

'Yes?' she blinked.

'Hi, Jane,' said Molly. 'Remember me?'

Jane Becker frowned at her, and then she said, 'Oh, yes. Oh, *sure*. The sketch artist lady. Erm – what are you doing here?'

'I just wanted to talk to you a little more, that's all. I guess you've seen on the news that they still haven't caught this Red Mask character. I was wondering if maybe there was something else that you can remember about him. Something that might have slipped your mind the first time. You know – what with the shock and everything.'

'Well . . . I don't think so.' Jane Becker peered around the front lawn as if she half-expected Red Mask to come bursting out of the bushes.

'Do you mind if we come in for a moment? Would that be OK? This is my mother-in-law, Sissy, by the way, and this is Detective Frank Sawyer.'

Frank flashed up his shield, without giving Jane Becker the time to see that it was Connecticut State Police, and not Cincinnati.

'I don't really know what else I can tell you,' she said. 'That picture you drew – that was so totally like him. Totally.'

All the same, without explicitly inviting them in, she opened the door wider so that they could step into the hallway, and then she led them through to the living room.

The house was cool and freshly decorated, with salmon-colored carpets and pale yellow couches and chairs. Over the fireplace hung an amateurish oil painting of a stone bridge, with an improbably blue stream flowing underneath it. There were shiny brass fire dogs in the fireplace, even though the logs were artificial and the fire itself was electric.

Frank said, 'You're absolutely sure that you'd never seen this Red Mask guy before he attacked you in the elevator?'

Jane Becker sat down next to the fireplace. 'Never. He was a total stranger.'

'And you have no idea why he wanted to kill Mr Woods?'

'None whatsoever.'

Sissy felt a prickling sensation in her fingers. She lifted her hand and saw that her mother's amethyst ring had turned several shades darker. So the probability was that Jane Becker was lying. But lying about what, exactly? That Red Mask was a stranger to her, or that she didn't know why he had murdered George Woods?

The prickling sensation was caused by more than her mother's ring, however. It was the kind of sensation she felt when some potent or meaningful artifact was very close. She felt it whenever one of her clients brought her a loved one's scarf, or a pair of gloves, in order to help her to communicate beyond the grave. She felt it whenever she walked into a room and saw a photograph of a gone-beyonder. She always knew they were dead, even without being told.

Molly was saying, '—anything about his hair, or his skin texture? How about scars? Did you notice any scars? Scars can be a real important clue, because they might have been caused by a sports injury, or an occupational accident.'

Sissy turned slowly around and around, trying to locate where the prickling sensation was coming from. Frank held her arm and said, 'Sissy? Are you OK?'

'Sure. I'm fine. It's just that—'

'I don't remember anything else about him, except what I told you,' said Jane Becker. 'He might have had a scar, but I really don't recall. I was fighting for my life, remember.'

Sissy said, 'May I use your bathroom, please?'

'Oh, sure. Along the hallway, second door on the right.'

'Thank you.'

Sissy left the living room. She walked slowly along the hallway, her ring hand raised, her eyes narrowed in concentration. *It's here, Sissy. The answer is right here. It's in one of these rooms.*

She passed the dining room. There was nothing in there but a highly polished oak table and eight oak chairs, and it smelled airless, as if it wasn't used very often. She reached the bathroom, which had a ceramic plaque on it with the legend 'The Littlest Room.' But as she turned the door handle, she felt the prickling on her back. There was another room opposite the bathroom, with its door ajar.

She hesitated for a moment, listening. She could still hear Molly and Jane Becker talking, and so she pushed the door open a little further. The room was a study, with a desk and a personal computer and shelves crowded with books. Whoever used this study, they weren't particularly tidy, because there was an empty coffee mug on the desk, as well as a scattering of pens and CDs and torn open credit-card bills. The computer's monitor screen was surrounded by yellow Post-it notes. 'Hairdrsr 8!!!' 'Call Ken B. re ins. claim!!!'

On the wall to the left of the desk there was a cork notice-board, crammed with postcards and Hudepohl beer mats and take-out menus and family photographs. Sissy slowly approached it, and now she could almost *hear* the prickling sensation, as well as feel it, like the effervescence on top of a glass of soda.

Close to the center of the notice-board, overlapped by a 'thank you' letter from a local children's charity, was a postcard of a giant red-faced figure, holding a triangular butcher's knife in each hand. The caption read, 'Butcher Buck, Borrowsville, IA.'

Sissy took out the thumbtack, and turned the postcard over. 'Butcher Buck used to advertise the Borrowsville Meat Packing Co., Inc., in Borrowsville, IA. Unusually for a giant roadside figure, he was made not of fiberglass but a single red crown oak tree, carved in 1957 by local artist Dean S. Ferndale II. Butcher Buck stood 32 ft 7 ins tall and was estimated to weigh 6.3 tons. He was severely damaged by lightning in 1974 and removed.'

There was a message scribbled in ball-pen, too. 'Hi, Rick & Family! Greetings from darkest Iowa! Lonnie says this looks like me when I've been lying in the sun too long! See you on the 15th! All best, Dave M.'

The card was dated May 12, 1993, so Jane Becker would have first seen it when she was very young. Young enough for it to frighten her.

Sissy went back into the living room. Jane Becker was saying to Molly and Frank, 'I'm so sorry I can't remember any more. All of those murders – they're just terrible. I wish I could think of something that would help you to catch this guy.'

Sissy dropped the postcard on to the table beside her. 'Who does this remind you of?' she asked her.

'Hey – you took that out of my dad's den!' Jane Becker protested.

'Where I found it, my dear, isn't important. What *is* important is who it reminds you of.'

Frank picked up the postcard and read the caption on the back. 'Butcher Buck. *That's* who attacked you?'

'He had a red face, just like that. Or maybe he had blood on his face. I don't know. I must have gotten confused.'

Molly looked at the postcard, too. 'But – Jane – the description you gave me, this is him, right down to the last detail. No wonder you said his eyes and his mouth looked like slits. They *are* slits, like they've been cut with a chisel.'

Sissy sat down beside her. 'Jane, what did he really look like, the man who attacked you?'

Jane Becker's eyes filled up with tears. 'I don't know! I don't remember! I didn't see him at all!'

Molly said, 'What? But you were so sure!'

'I know. But when you asked me to tell you what he looked like – I didn't want to let you down, that's all! I just described the most frightening man I could think of.'

'So you gave Molly a description of a man who doesn't exist?'

Jane Becker sobbed, and nodded. 'I figured, where's the harm? He's not real, so the police won't be able to find him, so it doesn't matter.'

'But – Jane – if Red Mask doesn't exist, who do you think has been committing all of these other attacks?'

'I don't know. I really don't. I guess some crazy guys have been making themselves up to look like him. I mean, you hear about these copycat killings, don't you? It's terrible. It's really terrible. But it's not my fault, is it?'

'Not entirely,' said Sissy. 'But something very strange happened when Molly drew that picture of Red Mask. Something you might call miraculous.'

'What? What are you talking about?'

'You may not believe me, Jane. That's up to you. But the sketch of Red Mask which Molly drew from your description came to life. Red Mask didn't exist before you accused him of attacking you in the elevator, but he sure did afterward.'

Jane Becker stared at her. 'He *what*? He came to life? Oh, come *on*! This is some kind of a joke, isn't it?' She turned to Molly, both hands held out, as if she were appealing for sanity.

Sissy stood up. 'Like I said, you don't have to believe me. But your description of Red Mask came to life and it was *that* Red Mask who committed the second attack. And when one of the witnesses described who had done it, Molly drew a second sketch, and *that* came to life, too. So we had *two* Red Masks . . . and it was those two Red Masks who committed both of the next two attacks.'

Molly said, 'It's true, Jane. I know it sounds completely unbelievable, but I saw it happen with my own eyes. Yesterday we managed to destroy one of the Red Masks – set fire to him and burn him up – but there's still one more left.'

'At least we know that there never was a *real* Red Mask,' Sissy put in. 'The real Red Mask was Butcher Buck, and he was probably burned for firewood, thirty-five years ago, after they chopped him down.'

Jane Becker pulled a crumpled tissue out of her sleeve and blew her nose. 'I don't believe any of this. I think you're all insane.'

'I'm sorry, Jane,' said Sissy, 'but it's true. And we need your help to finish Red Mask for good and all.'

'What can *I* do?'

'You can face him, that's what you can do. You can face him and you can show him this postcard and you can tell him that you made him up. He's alive because he believes he's alive. He's alive because he's convinced that he's the image of a real person. He needs to be told that he was never real – that he was only a wooden statue, nothing more, and that even that wooden statue doesn't exist any longer.'

'What?' said Jane Becker. 'You seriously think I'm going to go right up to some homicidal nutjob and tell him that I invented him? You're even crazier than I thought you were!'

'You're the only person who can do it,' said Sissy.

Jane Becker stood up. 'Listen,' she said, 'I think you'd better leave.'

Molly said, 'Jane! You have to come with us! You have to do this, or scores more people are going to be murdered!'

'If you don't leave right now, I'm going to call the cops.'

'I am the cops,' Frank reminded her.

'Well, I'll call your captain or whoever he is, and tell him that you've been harassing me.'

She came toward him but Frank raised his hand to stop her. 'We seriously need your help, Ms Becker. I know this all sounds pretty darn bizarre – sketches that come to life, paintings that murder people. But there is an explanation for it, and it's real. As real as I'm standing right here.'

'Are you going to leave or what?' Jane Becker demanded.

But Frank stayed where he was. 'Let me ask you something, Ms Becker. If Red Mask didn't kill George Woods, then who did?'

'I don't have to answer that. I've already answered that a hundred times.'

'No, you haven't. You said it was Red Mask, but now you've admitted that Red Mask doesn't exist. So who killed George Woods?'

'I don't know. It was a man, that's all. I can't describe him.'

'I get the picture. Average height, average build, no distinguishing features?'

'That's right. And he just started stabbing.'

'You said you didn't know George Woods, didn't you? Didn't know the poor man from Adam.'

'That's right. I never saw him before, ever.'

Sissy reached into her purse and took out one of the receipts from Jones the Florists.

'A dozen roses, every week for five weeks.'

Jane Becker tried to snatch it from her, but Sissy whipped it out of her reach.

'That's private, you bitch!' snapped Jane Becker. 'That has nothing to do with you!'

'Oh, I think it does,' said Frank. 'Especially when so many people have been murdered, because of you. What happened between you and George Woods, Ms Becker? You were having an affair, and the affair went sour? What?'

'An *affair*?' Jane Becker was quaking. When she had interviewed her in hospital, Molly had thought how forgiving she was, how docile, considering what had happened to her. But now her mouth was tight with rage, and her eyes seemed even further apart, like a flatfish. 'We weren't having an *affair*!'

'OK, then, maybe it was just a fling. "*Remember the Vernon Manor . . . when our dreams came true.*"'

'His dream. My nightmare.'

'What do you mean?'

Jane Becker had to take a deep breath to compose herself.

'It was a weekend seminar, OK? Realtors and lawyers, talking about property law and escrow and all that kind of stuff. George Woods hit on me from the moment I arrived, and he wouldn't let me alone.'

'So what did you do?'

'I told him to back off, but he wouldn't take any notice.'

She paused. Now her anger had given way to self-pity, and tears were sliding freely down her cheeks. 'I told him to back off but he must have put something in my drink. Rohypnol, maybe. He never admitted it. I don't remember him doing it but he took me up to my room and he raped me.'

She took a deep breath, and then she said, 'He raped me and he – *abused* me in every possible way you can think of. When I woke up the sheet was covered in blood. And he was still there, would you believe? He was still there, sitting on the end of my bed with a drink in his hand, smiling like the cat that got the cream.

'He had used a vodka bottle on me. Can you believe that?'

Sissy reached out and laid a hand on her shoulder. 'Sit down,' she said, gently. Jane Becker blinked at her for a moment, as if she couldn't understand what she was saying, but then she sat on the couch, and Sissy sat next to her.

'So there wasn't any Red Mask, and there wasn't any man of average height and average build?'

'No,' Jane Becker whispered.

'How did you do it? You managed to give yourself some pretty deep stab wounds in the back, didn't you?'

'I saw it on some TV program once. It probably wouldn't have worked with a really modern elevator, but the elevators in the Giley Building are so old and cranky.'

'So you stabbed George Woods and then you fixed the knife between the elevator doors and stabbed yourself in the back three or four times, and when the elevator got down to the lobby the knife fell out from between the doors and nobody realized it was you?'

Jane Becker nodded. 'I was so hyped up that it didn't even hurt. In a funny way, I almost enjoyed it, stabbing myself. It was like I was punishing myself. Not for killing George, I didn't deserve punishing for that. Killing George was justice. But I deserved to be punished for allowing George to do all those terrible things to me.'

'That wasn't your fault,' Sissy told her. 'How could you have stopped him? He drugged you!'

'No, I was stupid. I should have realized right from the very beginning what he was like. I allowed him to ruin my life. I allowed him to steal who I was. Look at me now! I'm nobody! I'm nothing!'

Sissy stood up again, and went over to Molly and Frank. 'Do you know who she sounds like? She sounds exactly like Red Mask. That's who Red Mask is. Jane Becker's need for revenge, made flesh.'

Jane Becker blew her nose again. 'What happens now?' she asked. 'Are you going to arrest me?'

'Well, not necessarily,' said Frank. 'Maybe we can come to some kind of arrangement. If you come along with us when we go hunting for Red Mask, we'll see if we can't suffer from collective amnesia as far as you and George Woods are concerned.'

'Are you for real? Can you actually *do* that?'

Frank rested a hand on her shoulder. 'Ms Becker, you'd be surprised. I can do anything and everything, and a couple of other things besides.'

At that moment, Molly's cell rang.

'Red Mask?' asked Sissy.

Molly shook her head. 'It's Yvonne, from next door.' She listened, and then she said, 'Oh, no! Oh my God. When?'

'What's wrong?' Sissy asked her.

'It's Victoria. Yvonne was bringing her home from school. She was getting out of the car and some guy grabbed her.

'She said it all happened so fast that she didn't get a very good look at him, but he was wearing a black suit and a red shirt, and he must have been strong, because he lifted her clear off the ground.'

'Oh, please,' said Sissy. 'Not Red Mask.'

'Sounds like him, doesn't it?' said Frank. 'Did your friend call the police?'

'First thing. Oh, please God don't let him harm her.'

'Call the police department yourself,' Frank told Molly. 'Tell them where you are and give them your cell number. Then call Trevor. Tell him we'll meet him outside the Giley Building.'

'The Giley Building? Why there?'

'Because that's Red Mask's home territory. That's his lair, if you like. And I'll bet you anything you like that he's taken Victoria there.'

'Then I should tell the police that.'

'No. It's too risky. Even if the cops can find him, what are they going to do? Shoot him? You know that they can't hurt him. But he might harm Victoria.'

'Oh God, Frank. No.'

Frank said, 'He's done this for a reason, Molly: to get his revenge on you. You created him, but now you're trying to destroy him, and you're the only person who can. You've betrayed him, so far as he's concerned.'

He turned to Jane Becker. 'Well, Ms Becker, it looks like you're going to be helping us sooner than we thought. How about getting yourself changed?'

'Are you serious?'

'Never more so,' Frank told her. 'Red Mask obviously wants us to come looking for him, on *his* terms, the way he did with Detective Kunzel and those two SWAT teams. He wants a showdown. So let's not disappoint him, shall we?'

The Falling Girl

As they drove back into the city over the Roebling Suspension Bridge, Sissy borrowed Molly's cell phone and called Detective Bellman. The bridge had a rumbling metal-grid floor so she had to shout to make herself heard.

'Freddie? It's Sissy Sawyer. We have a crisis.'

'Has Red Mask called you again?'

'Not since last night. But it looks like he's abducted Molly's little girl, Victoria.'

'What? Jesus! Have you called it in?'

'Molly's neighbor did, as soon as it happened. That was about twenty minutes ago, from her home in Blue Ash. Molly's called, too, and talked to a Sergeant Haskins.'

'Bella Haskins, yes, she's terrific. And the FBI will come in on this, too. They always do, when it's a child under twelve. Where do you think he might have taken her? Any ideas?'

'We believe he might be hiding her in the Giley Building. That's the only place where he really feels real.'

'OK, I'll get some units round there right now.'

'Freddie – I'm asking you a huge, huge favor. I know you were pretty skeptical about what happened in the Giley Building yesterday.'

There was a crackling silence. Then Detective Bellman said, 'In all honesty, Mrs Sawyer, I have to tell you that it did stretch my credibility to the universe and beyond. You know that I'm still trying to be open-minded here, and I saw for myself that *something* got burned on that office carpet – maybe even some*body*.'

'It was Red Mask, Freddie. I swear to you.'

'Well, maybe. But I didn't see no human remains and I didn't see no canine remains, neither. In fact, no material evidence to substantiate your story whatsoever.'

Sissy said, 'Listen, Freddie – that Red Mask was nothing but an image. So was Frank. So was the scenting dog, too. They vanished. When a living image dies, it fades away. It simply disappears, like it never was. Even the original sheet of paper that it was drawn on stays blank.'

'So, OK – what's this huge, huge favor?' asked Detective Bellman. It was obvious that he wasn't keen to get involved in any kind of existential argument.

'I want you to let us into the Giley Building, to look for Victoria. You can come with us if you want to, but I'd prefer it if it was just us. I think it's our only chance of finding Red Mask and getting Victoria back unharmed.'

'Who's "just us?"'

'Myself, and Molly, and Frank—'

'Frank? You mean your husband Frank? Am I missing something here? I thought you just told me that Frank had vanished?'

'He did, Freddie, but like I was telling you yesterday—'

'Go on, then. Who else?'

'Jane Becker. You remember her – she was one of Red Mask's first two victims, her and George Woods. We need her to confirm Red Mask's identity. And our scenting dog.'

'Don't tell me it's the same scenting dog come back to life?'

Sissy turned around in her seat. Deputy was right behind her, in the back of Molly's SUV, panting as if he had been running after rabbits.

'Let's put it this way. It's a *similar* scenting dog.'

Detective Bellman said nothing for a long time. Sissy could hear other officers talking in the background, and a siren whoop. At last he said, 'Mrs Sawyer, I don't have anything like the authority to do this. Apart from that, it's totally against CPD procedure. Civilians under no circumstances are to be put in harm's way during the course of any criminal investigation or arrest operation.'

'I see,' said Sissy.

There was another long pause, but then Detective Bellman said, 'On the other hand, you know and I know that we're talking about some decidedly weird shit here. We're talking about perps who can appear and disappear like they can walk through walls. We're talking about perps with nothing but kitchen knives who can wipe out two SWAT squads armed to the teeth with semi-automatic weapons. We're talking about people who can come to life even though they're supposed to be cremated.'

'I know, Freddie. I know. But let me just say that—'

'I have to admit that I'm bewildered, Mrs Sawyer, and I'm very skeptical. But there wasn't nobody more skeptical than Mike Kunzel, including me, and even Mike could see that these stabbings weren't your garden-variety massacres, not by a long way. He could see how goddamned weird they were. So just for Mike, I'm going to let you in to the Giley Building for thirty minutes if that's what you want – provided you never tell nobody what I allowed you to do, ever, and provided you don't get yourselves injured or, God forbid, killed. Where are you now?'

'We're just coming off the Roebling Suspension Bridge, by the ballpark.'

'OK, I'll meet you outside the Giley Building in five minutes.'

Sissy said, 'Thanks, Freddie. You won't regret this. They'll probably promote you to detective first-class.'

She switched off the cell phone and patted Frank on the shoulder. 'He's given us thirty minutes' grace. So let's step on it, shall we?'

Detective Bellman was waiting for them when they parked outside the Giley Building. The street was still crowded with vans and Hummers from the CPD forensic teams, who were painstakingly going over the parking structure next door, inch by inch and floor by floor. The media vans were still there, too, from Channel 5 and Channel 12 and WLW radio. After all, it had been the worst mass-murder in Cincinnati since 1987, when male nurse Donald Harvey had killed forty of his patients at the Drake Hospital.

'I feel like I'm dreaming this,' said Detective Bellman, as they gathered on the steps.

'Maybe that's the best way,' Sissy told him. 'After all, it *is* a dream, of sorts.'

'I'm coming in with you,' said Detective Bellman. 'I know what you said, that my weapon can't harm him. But this is my responsibility, this case, and I owe it to Mike Kunzel to see it through to the finish.'

One of the uniformed officers guarding the Giley Building unlocked the revolving door for them and they went inside. The lobby was gloomy and their footsteps echoed on the marble flooring.

Jane Becker said, 'I really don't want to do this.'

'I don't think any of us do, honey,' said Frank. 'But remember the roses, OK?'

Sissy went to the center of the lobby, under the chandelier, and closed her eyes. She breathed slowly and deeply to relax herself, and then she allowed herself slowly to rise up through the building, floor by floor. She passed by deserted offices, chairs tipped over, dead computer screens. She heard phones ringing, unanswered. But as she reached the twenty-third floor, she began to feel the faintest of tingling sensations, and her closed eyes were gradually suffused with opalescent light.

She rose higher, to the twenty-fourth floor. There was no question about it: Victoria was here, on the twenty-fifth floor, almost directly above her. She could sense her, almost as if she could actually reach out and stroke her hair. She could *see* her – a pale, flickering outline, with two dark smudges for eyes.

Victoria, it's Grandma. We're here. We're coming to find you.

Grandma? Where are you? I'm so scared, Grandma.

Don't say a word, sweetheart. Stay where you are. Don't let on that you can hear me.

He says he wants to kill us, Grandma. He says he wants to stab us and stab us and chop us into bits.

Don't you worry, Victoria. We won't let him hurt you, I promise. Just hold on.

She let herself sink back down again, down to the lobby. She opened her eyes. Molly was standing right beside her, biting her thumbnail with anxiety.

'Did you find her?' asked Molly. 'Is she here? Oh, please tell me you've found her!'

'Twenty-fifth floor,' said Sissy. 'It feels to me like he's shut her up someplace dark.'

'He hasn't hurt her, has he?'

'He's threatened her – but, no, he hasn't hurt her.'

All this time, Deputy had been snuffling around the lobby. When he arrived at the center elevator, he let out a single sharp bark.

'Are the elevators working now?' asked Sissy.

'I hope so,' said Detective Bellman. 'I don't want a repeat experience of yesterday. I get claustrophobia in the Tower Place mall, leave alone an elevator car with seven overweight cops in it.'

'Well . . . either we risk the elevator or we have to climb the stairs,' said Sissy. 'And I, for one, am not going to climb those stairs again. I don't have many breaths left in this life, and I don't want to use them all up in one day.'

The indicator light showed that the elevator was up on the seventeenth floor. Frank pressed the button, and the lights gradually began to descend – 13 – 11 – 9 – 7. Detective Bellman unholstered his gun and said, 'Let's stay well back, shall we, seeing as how this Red Mask character has a penchant for rushing out with his knives going like Edward Scissorhands.'

With an arthritic groan, the elevator arrived at lobby level and the doors shuddered open. Detective Bellman cocked his gun and jabbed it into the elevator car, but there was nobody in there.

'OK, folks. Let's do it.'

They stepped on to the elevator. Frank had his thumb on the button for the twenty-fifth floor when they heard an echoing shout of 'Wait!' It was Trevor, pushing his way through the revolving door. He jogged across the lobby and joined them, panting almost as hard as Deputy.

'Sorry – traffic. Is Victoria here?'

Sissy pointed straight upward. 'Top floor. Red Mask has her locked up someplace. That's what it feels like, anyhow. He hasn't hurt her.'

'I'm going to kill him,' said Trevor. 'I mean that. Painting or no painting, I'm going to rip his goddamned head off.'

Frank glanced across the elevator car at Sissy, and raised his eyebrows. Neither of them had ever heard Trevor talk so ferociously before. But then Trevor's family had never been threatened before, not like this.

The elevator rose painfully slowly, with its mechanism grinding and squeaking, and it hesitated at every floor, and lurched, even though its doors stayed shut. None of them spoke as they rose higher and higher, although Deputy was growing increasingly agitated, and kept jumping up on his hind legs and clawing at the doors.

At last they reached the 25th floor. The doors opened, and they cautiously stepped out. The offices were in darkness, and when Sissy saw the sign on the reception area she realized why: 'Hamilton Photo Processing, Inc.' All of the photographic equipment had been removed, but the windows were still blacked out, with only a few scratches to show that it was sunny outside.

There was a sour smell of developing fluids, and something else, too. Something rotten, like a dead animal.

Deputy wasn't put off by the gloom. He circled around the reception area, sniffing and wuffling, and then, suddenly, he began to pull Frank along the corridor off to their right.

Sissy followed close behind. She couldn't sense Red Mask at all, but she could feel Victoria. It was almost as if she could hear her singing, in another room.

'Left,' she said, although she didn't need to, because Deputy was already tugging Frank around to the left. He was straining even harder on his leash, so that he sounded as if he were strangling.

The corridor was lined with black-and-white framed photographs of thunderstorms and city skylines and women half-concealed in shadow. At the very end of it, there was a black door marked 'DARKROOM.' Deputy rushed straight up to it and barked, and wouldn't stop barking.

'Sissy?' said Frank.

'Victoria's in there,' said Sissy. 'She's right on the other side of that door.'

Frank wound Deputy's leash more tightly around his fist. 'Trouble is, so is Red Mask.'

'What do we do now?' asked Molly. 'We have to get her out of there! Victoria! Victoria! It's Mommy!'

Frank touched his finger to his lips to quieten her. 'All we can do is play it his way, for now.'

Trevor said, 'I think we should kick the goddamned door down and rush him. Come on, there are three of us, right, and only one of him.'

'There were ten SWAT officers, Trevor, and two FBI agents, and only two of him.'

'Dad – that's our daughter in there! And that's your granddaughter, too! We can't just leave her in there with that psycho!'

Abruptly, Deputy stopped barking, and backed away from the darkroom door. Detective Bellman unholstered his gun, and cocked it again.

'What is it, boy?' Frank asked him. 'What's wrong?'

They heard a key turning in the lock, and the darkroom door swung open. Deputy's fur bristled and he lowered his head and growled. Inside the darkroom, only a red lamp was shining, so that at first they could see nothing more than a silhouette. A bulky silhouette, with a squarish head. But in front of this silhouette, there was a smaller, paler figure.

'Well, well, well,' said Red Mask, thickly. 'So you came in force, Molly? You brought your own little army?'

'Give me back my daughter!' Molly screamed at him. She tried to lunge forward but Trevor took hold of her arm and held her back. 'Give me back my daughter, you monster!'

Detective Bellman said, 'Hands on your head, mister! Drop whatever weapons you're carrying, and down on your knees!'

'I don't think so,' said Red Mask. With that, he stepped out of the darkroom into the corridor, pushing Victoria out in front of him. He was gripping her left shoulder, and holding one of his butcher's knives across her throat.

'Always such a waste, don't you think, to spill a child's blood? Think of all the years they might have had. But revenge is revenge, Molly. And justice is blind. No rest for the wicked, don't you know. No mercy for the innocent, neither.'

'Let her go,' Molly whispered. 'Please let her go.'

Victoria looked very pale, and her eyelashes were stuck together with dried tears. But Red Mask was holding his knife so close to her throat that she couldn't lower her chin and she didn't dare to speak.

'You created me, Molly. You drew me in the image of a real man. So I am that man, and a man is an independent being, sacred unto God, no matter how he was created. So you have no right – you have no right – to come hunting for me, with this dog of yours, and these raggle-taggle friends of yours – seeking to destroy me.'

Red Mask was breathing deeply now, and working himself up into a righteous rage. 'What you are trying to do is kill your own creation! What you are trying to do is no less than abortion!'

Sissy said, gently, 'Let the little girl go. She hasn't done anything to you.'

'Oh, no? Why should she live, while I die? I'm one of God's children, too.'

'Ah, but you're not. You never were, and you never will be.'

'Get out of my way,' said Red Mask. He began to push Victoria toward them, so that they had to back off. 'Today, I get justice. Today, I get revenge. Today, I get the respect that I deserve.'

'You don't deserve any respect, you bastard,' Trevor told him. 'You're nothing but a butcher.'

Sissy said, 'That's truer than my son knows. You *are* a butcher. In fact, you're—'

'*Shut up*!' Red Mask roared at her. '*Shut the fuck up!* One more word from any of you and I'll cut this kid's throat right in front of you!'

He kept advancing along the corridor with Victoria in front of him, and they kept backing away, although Deputy kept snarling and pulling at his leash. Out of the side of his mouth, Detective Bellman murmured to Frank, 'I could get a head shot, Frank. Right between the eyes.'

But Frank said, 'No. No way. I don't think even that would kill him. And he would only have to fall wrong, and—' he made a slicing gesture across his Adam's apple.

They retreated all the way along the corridor until they reached the elevators.

Molly said, 'Please – if I promise not to come after you—'

'Oh, you won't be coming after me. I can guarantee that.'

'I'll do anything you want. Just let her go, I'm begging you.'

Red Mask pushed the button for the left-hand elevator. The doors opened, and they saw that there was no elevator car there, only an empty shaft, with greasy steel cables. A warm draft was blowing softly down it, whistling a sad, reflective tune.

'You want me to let your daughter go?' said Red Mask, hoarsely. 'Sure, I'll let your daughter go.'

Oh my God, thought Sissy. *The card. The girl falling down the well, like Alice in Wonderland. The card predicted it. He's going to drop her down the elevator shaft!*

'No!' screamed Molly, but Red Mask forced Victoria right to the very edge of the elevator shaft, still holding the knife against her throat.

'Let her go, you bastard!' Trevor yelled at him, but Red Mask slid the knife across Victoria's throat and drew a thin line of blood.

'I told you! Didn't I tell you? *Shut the fuck up!* One more word from any of you, and it's down she goes!'

Victoria made a pathetic squealing noise, but Red Mask snarled at her, 'That goes for you, too, my darling. Not a word.'

Then he said, 'Molly created me. Molly can destroy me. Now, I can't have somebody walking the world who has the power to destroy me, can I? But no creation has the power to destroy his creator, does he – even me. I can't destroy you, Molly, any more than you can destroy God. There's only one person who can destroy you, Molly, and that's you.

'So this is the choice. If you jump down this shaft here, Molly, your lovely young daughter will be spared. If you don't, then it's down she goes, and I won't spare the rest of you, either.'

'You're crazy!' Trevor screamed at him. 'You're completely and utterly crazy!'

Red Mask pushed Victoria until she was leaning even further over the elevator shaft. '*I warned you! One more word and it's down she goes!*'

Molly stepped forward, with her head held high and both fists tightly clenched.

Trevor said, 'No, Molly – no, you can't!'

But Molly walked right up to Red Mask and stood in front of him and said, 'If that's what it's going to take to save my daughter – all right, I'll do it.'

Red Mask stared at her with his slitted eyes. His expression was unreadable, like a painted wooden figure by a desolate highway, far from anyplace at all.

He took a step back from the open elevator shaft. 'There it is,' he told her. 'That's the way down. I have to tell you, this is almost like a religious experience. The fear. The ecstasy. The elation.'

Molly went right up to the edge of the elevator shaft. Her hair was ruffled by the updraft. Victoria was staring at her, appalled, but Red Mask was holding the knife so close to her throat that she couldn't cry out.

But it was then that Frank sprinted forward, dropping Deputy's leash as he did so. He collided with Molly, pushing her past the open elevator shaft, and straight into Victoria and Red Mask. At the same time, Deputy bounded up at Red Mask and sank his teeth into his arm.

Red Mask fell backward, dropping his knife. Frank shouted, '*Grab her!*' and Molly wrapped her arms around Victoria. Frank twisted himself sideways so that both of them could roll clear.

Red Mask picked up his knife and furiously stabbed at Deputy until Deputy released his grip on Red Mask's arm and limped off to the far side of the reception area, bloody and whining. Red Mask clambered to his feet.

'Do you think that's going to spare you?' he spat. 'Do you think that any of you are going to leave this building alive? You're going to be chopped liver, all of you.'

Frank ducked and feinted, but Red Mask kept advancing on him, lunging at him with his knife. He cut the back of Frank's right hand, and blood sprayed across the floor, and then he stabbed him in the left forearm, and the shoulder.

Red Mask raised his knife high above his head and was just about to plunge it into Frank's chest when Frank seized the lapels of Red Mask's coat and deliberately fell backward into the open elevator shaft. They both disappeared like a conjuring trick.

'Oh my *God*!' Sissy cried out. She hurried to the elevator shaft, with Detective Bellman and Trevor close behind her.

Both Red Mask and Frank were dangling from one of the steel cables in the center of the shaft. Red Mask must have snatched at the cable with his left hand, and then dropped his knife so that he could grip it with his right hand, too. Frank was hanging beside him, still holding tightly on to the front of his coat.

'Hold on!' shouted Detective Bellman. 'Hold on, I'll see if I can find a stepladder or something!'

Sissy called out, 'Frank! Frank! See if you can climb down the wire!'

'Can't let go, Sissy. Sorry.'

'Frank, you have to try! I don't want to lose you again!'

'You never lost me. You never will. Go get Jane.'

'Let go of my coat!' Red Mask roared at him. '*Let go of my coat!*'

'Get Jane!' Frank insisted. Red Mask's lapel started to tear off, and Frank lurched another six inches downward.

Sissy turned around and said, 'Jane – come here, quick!'

Jane Becker came up and stood beside her. 'What do you want me to do?'

'Call him!'

'I can't!'

'Then I will,' said Sissy. 'Red Mask! Can you hear me?'

Red Mask managed to turn his head so that he could see her.

'There's somebody here who has something to say to you, Red Mask!'

Red Mask grunted with effort, but said nothing.

Jane Becker reached into the back pocket of her jeans and pulled out the postcard of Butcher Buck. 'You see this?' she called out, in a shrill, unsteady voice. 'This is you.'

'Tell him!' said Frank. 'For God's sake, just tell him!'

'You were never a real person! You never existed! I invented you!'

As preternaturally strong as he was, Red Mask's hands were

beginning to slide down the elevator cable, leaving a dark smear of blood. '*What the hell are you saying to me?*' he demanded.

'You never existed! When Molly asked me who had stabbed me, I described this statue! It's a wooden statue, in Iowa!'

Red Mask stared at her over his shoulder. She held the postcard at arm's length, so that he could see it more clearly.

'You were never a man, ever. You never lived. You were only made out of wood.'

Red Mask said nothing. But right in front of their eyes, he began to fade. First of all, Sissy could see the elevator cable, right through his hands, as his flesh became transparent. Then his scarlet face began to turn pale pink, as pale as paint water.

Frank looked up at her, still clinging to the last shadowy vestiges of Red Mask's coat. Only a painting like Frank could have clung on so long. He had no more substance, in reality, than Red Mask.

'Sissy!' he called.

Sissy said, 'Frank! We'll bring you back! I promise you, Frank! We'll bring you back tonight!'

But it was then that Red Mask vanished altogether, and Frank fell. He disappeared down the darkened elevator shaft without a sound.

Sissy waited, and listened, but she didn't hear him hit the basement. It was just as though *he* had vanished, too.

Molly came up and put her arm around Sissy's shoulders, and hugged her. 'Oh, Sissy.'

Sissy smeared the tears from her eyes with her fingertips. 'I told him we'd bring him back again. I told him we'd bring him back tonight.'

'We could, Sissy. We could. Do you want me to?'

Sissy turned away from the elevator shaft. Trevor was holding Victoria tight. Detective Bellman was hunkered down next to Deputy, dabbing at his wounds with his handkerchief. Jane Becker was stroking Deputy's head.

Sissy said, 'No. He looked at me, Frank, just before he fell, and he shook his head.'

'You're sure?'

Sissy nodded. 'Frank knew that he had lived his life. He had his memories, and they were enough. His memories made him what he was. That's why Red Mask knew that he was a painting, right from the beginning, while Frank didn't. Red Mask had no memories.'

She smiled and then she said, 'It's time for me to go home, I think. I need to lay some flowers on Frank's grave.'

'Momma?' said Trevor.

'I'm all right,' said Sissy. 'Let's get out of here, shall we? I could really use a cigarette.'

The Painted Man

Two days later, they shared a last breakfast together, eggs over easy and waffles with blueberry preserve. Sissy's bag was already packed and waiting in the hall.

Victoria said, 'I'm going to send you an email every single-bingle day, Grandma.'

Sissy smiled. 'I shall look forward to it. Don't forget to send me some pictures of your play. I'm dying to see you in your Tin Man costume.'

Molly handed Sissy a small blue velvet bag. 'Souvenir,' she said.

Sissy opened the drawstring and looked inside. It held van Gogh's ring.

'Make sure that you never give it to an artist,' said Molly.

Trevor came in from the backyard, and saw it. 'Maybe you should melt it down. We don't want the same thing to happen to anybody else.'

'No . . .' said Sissy. 'Wherever it originally came from, whatever its power is, I don't think it's mine to destroy it, do you?'

'I don't know. The next person it brings to life could be a whole lot worse than Red Mask.'

'Well, that's fate for you. If there's one thing the DeVane cards have always shown me, it's that our lives are made up of choices and accidents. Good choices and bad choices, nasty accidents and happy accidents. This ring brought Red Mask to life, but it also allowed me to see Frank again.'

She stood up and took her coffee cup to the window. Out in the yard, Mr Boots and Deputy were playing together, chasing cicadas. Deputy was still limping a little, but otherwise he looked fit.

'By the way,' said Molly, 'Freddie Bellman called me this morning. I asked him about Jane Becker . . . whether he was going to arrest her for killing George Woods.'

'And?'

'He said that whatever Jane might have admitted to, he's forgotten. So, officially, the CPD is still looking for a man who answers the description of Red Mask.'

Molly put her arm around Sissy and the two of them stood looking out of the window – at the sun shining through the vine trellis and the Shasta daisies nodding in the breeze.

'How about planting some roses?' said Sissy.

Molly laughed. 'Roses? I don't think so. But – look – I have something else for you. Another souvenir.'

She went through to her studio and came back with a sheet of art board. She lifted the tracing paper cover to reveal a watercolor painting of Frank, standing on the seashore at Hyannis, with the wind in his hair.

'I didn't wear my necklace when I was painting it, so don't worry.'

'It's wonderful,' said Sissy. She held it up to the light to admire it. It was so lifelike that he could almost hear Frank talking to her.

'You want a quick smoke before we leave?' asked Trevor.

Sissy shook her head. 'No – no thanks. I don't think your father would approve.' And then, much more quietly, 'Would you, Frank, my darling?'